# TWO MINUTES

ARIEL BISHOP

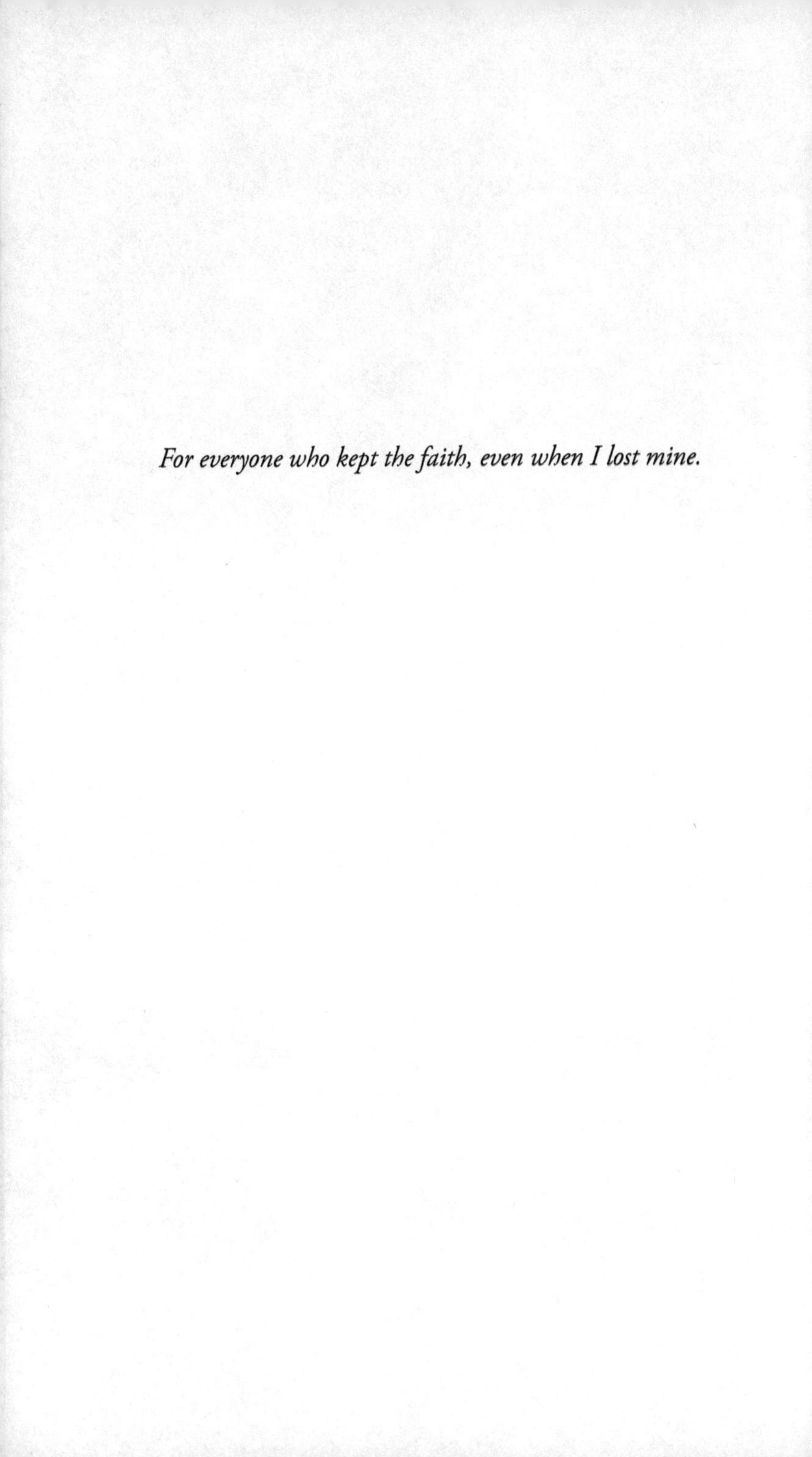

*For everyone who kept the faith, even when I lost mine.*

# CONTENT WARNINGS

This story contains content that may be difficult for some readers to consume. That content includes:

- Alcohol consumption
- Penetrative cis male/cis male sexual intercourse, oral and anal, as well as analingus
- Dubious consent due to alcohol use
- Bondage
- Mild dominance/submission
- Undernegotiated kink
- Extreme anxiety
- Panic attacks
- Verbal abuse by a parent
- Emotional abuse by a parent
- Descriptions of death by cancer
- Deathbed apologies by an abusive parent
- Minor character death on the page
- Character being under the influence of anesthesia
- Mentions of dental surgery

Some of these warnings may seem unnecessary for some, but please keep in mind that it isn't possible to know what is or is not hurtful for someone to read. This warning is included out of respect for those who are sex-averse and do not enjoy reading sexual content, as well as those who may be triggered by certain sexual acts.

Even if something isn't a trigger for you, please respect that it may be for someone else. If you need to heed these warnings, please take care of yourself first; your mental health is the first priority.

And if I forgot to warn for something that you noticed, please let me know!

# 1

## CISCO

Cisco should have seen it coming.

It's not like he doesn't know what West is like. Everyone knows what West is like. The guy took a five-game suspension when the Jackalopes went to the playoffs last year, for fucks sake, and the Gargoyles' winger almost lost the arm.

Chad S. West is basically everything Cisco hates about the way some d-men play, like anyone not on their team is collateral damage. Which, even ignoring how often people get traded, is a dumb way to be. The league really isn't that big. Just don't be a dick, man.

Still, he's somehow surprised when West makes eye contact and fucking winks at him before lunging directly at Cisco's stick and then falling to the ice like the huge diva he is.

The ref's whistle shouldn't startle Cisco, but apparently this is his day to be slow on the uptake. At least someone saw what West did. Cisco slides to a stop and waits for it. He can't wait to blow a kiss as West goes to the box for embellishment.

"Cross-checking, number 40, two minutes," the ref says.

Wait, what?

Stewie isn't on the ice, of course, because why would anything go right tonight? But Suzie is already skating over to the ref, arguing quietly but firmly, so Cisco stands there, holding his stick, and breathes. Because the alternative is using it on West's asshole face, and that'll get him more than a two-minute minor.

Apparently the ref is a Jackalopes fan, blind, or just an asshole, because he isn't having any of it. None of Suzie's arguments are making a dent, and finally he skates away, mouthing "sorry" at Cisco, his usually smiling face like a thundercloud.

Cisco takes a deep breath, lets it out, and heads for the penalty box. This is fine. It's bullshit, and anyone with eyes is gonna be able to tell that it's bullshit. But it's fine. The Jackalopes' power play unit is shit, nowhere near the Abs' penalty kill. He'll do his time in the sin bin, get back on the ice, and it'll be fine.

Only a small fraction of his attention is on where he's going. Mostly he's watching the line changes happen, the teams facing off for the puck drop. He steps through the open door to the box without really looking at the man in the suit who's holding it for him. Collapsing in an ungraceful heap on the bench, he pulls his gloves and helmet off, shaking his hair back out of his eyes. It's getting long enough that he probably needs to cut it soon if he doesn't want to end up back at his college length.

"You cut your hair," an unexpectedly familiar voice says from his right. "It looks good."

Turning toward the voice is a completely involuntary reflex. Cisco couldn't have stopped himself if his life depended on watching the ice. That voice reaches down into his nervous system, commandeers control, and if he could think right now, he wouldn't care.

He tells himself he'll see a stranger when he turns. Just like any of a thousand, a million times he heard an almost-familiar voice or caught a glimpse out of the corner of his eye, only to discover he was imagining things. There's no way—

But no. There he is, familiar dark hair and solemn eyes, high cheekbones and a mouth that should be smiling. He's watching Cisco warily, like he's not sure what to expect, which makes sense. But he's there. Really there. When Cisco reaches out with a shaking hand, his arm is solid, warm under the fabric of his suit.

"Leo." He breathes the name, his voice barely audible.

The familiar mouth curves up just a little at the corners, like it always did when Cisco said his name. "Cisco."

Oh, that hurts, the familiar sound of Leo's voice shaping the syllables of his name. The slight Boston accent had always surprised assholes who expected him to be audibly Chinese instead of speaking the language of the city where he'd been raised. The warmth in his eyes, like they last saw each other yesterday, instead of—

"It's been—awhile."

*Around one a.m. on draft day, Cisco gave up on sleep and reached for his phone. Pulling it under the sheets and duvet, he turned on his side, using his body to block the light before unlocking the screen. If his mom was able to sleep, he wanted to let her.*

*When he opened Whatsapp, his conversation with Leo was the first thing that pops up, obviously. He was probably asleep, like a normal person, but Cisco still tapped out a quick* **can't sleep u up?** *before switching over to his latest time-wasting game.*

*He wasn't expecting a response, but it still stung a little when he doesn't get one. Like, he got Leo not coming with him. It was harder for goalies, fewer spots at the pro level, tougher to get noticed. If their positions were reversed, he didn't know if he could come with Leo, smile and clap while his boyfriend got the thing that he wants most in life.*

*So he got it, but he still missed Leo, wished he were here now. If he was here, they might have been able to get their own room; even though his mom was kind of old-fashioned in some ways, she knew how serious Cisco was about Leo. She basically treated them like they were engaged already, even if Cisco hadn't quite worked up enough nerve to pop the question yet.*

*But Leo wasn't here. So he forced his mind away from the thoughts of what they could be doing if Leo was here, because like hell was he jerking off with his mom right there in the other bed. Even if she was sound asleep.*

*He played the stupid game until the letters were swimming in front of his eyes, until he couldn't think of even basic three-letter words. He wasn't sure when exactly he fell asleep, just that at some point he woke up with sunlight glowing around the edge of the hotel curtains, his phone lying a few inches away from his hand.*

*When he checked the screen, Leo still hadn't replied.*

CISCO'S PHONE *buzzed in his pocket while they were eating an early dinner. His stomach was roiling, rebelling at the very thought of food, but his mom was right; this was going to be a long night. He needed to eat.*

It was probably just his abuela or one of his cousins texting to wish him luck, he thought, and almost didn't pull the phone out to check. It made him sick, when he thought back later on, thinking about how he almost ignored it. Although sometimes he thought it would have been easier, not to know until later.

But no matter how many times he played out the what-ifs in his head, there was no changing it. He fished his phone out with one hand, using the other to cut off a bite of the tenderest salmon he'd ever eaten.

When he looked down at the lock screen, the fork and the salmon clattered onto the floor unheeded.

"What's wrong, Chico?" His mom looked up from her grilled shrimp, her eyes widening at whatever she saw on his face.

He shook his head, unable to speak. His tongue felt clumsy in his mouth, like forming words is beyond him. He just handed her the phone instead, unlocked now to show the text from Leo's sister Elaine, the three short sentences that turned his world upside down in seconds.

**Leo had a breakdown. In hospital under observation. Dad didn't want me to tell you**

"Oh," his mom said. The sound was more of an exhalation than a word. When she looked back up at him, her expression had firmed into decision, even though he could still see an echo of his own stunned grief reflected her eyes. "Do you want to leave? We can get a flight—"

"No." Cisco forced the word out, even though every beat of his heart was telling him otherwise. "No, I—I want to, but—his dad won't let me see him. I'm not officially—anything. And if I miss the draft, he'll kick my ass himself when he gets out. No."

She nodded slowly, setting the phone down and taking his hands in hers. "Okay. Then eat. You'll need your strength. He'll need you to be strong."

*Cisco nodded back, asked their waitress for a new fork with a smile that felt like it would break his face. Forked up another bite of salmon and forced himself to chew and swallow even though it feels like dust and ashes in his mouth.*

*He needed to be strong for both of them, now.*

✕

*"—THE Alberta Abominables are pleased to select, from the University of Minnesota, Francisco Reyes."*

*Cisco shoved his phone with its too-blank screen hastily back into his pocket and stood, making his way to the stage. His mom held his hand the whole way, strong and solid as always.*

*He shook the manager's hand, and the captain's hand, and the coach's hand—he couldn't remember her name, but that was okay, he'd have time to get it. He put the snapback on his head, pulled the jersey over it without knocking it off. Smiled when he was told, looked into the camera when he was told, whent where he was told.*

*Everything was a blur, every second underlaid with the sick drumbeat of worry and fear quickly souring into anger. None of this mattered. Why couldn't any of these people see that? The only thing that mattered to him was lying in a hospital bed back in Minneapolis, and Cisco was stuck here with this bullshit.*

*He managed, somehow, to make it through without saying something incredibly offensive to his new organization. Thank fuck for his mom, papering over the cracks in his silences with her usual charm. It seemed to take forever, but objectively he knew it was less than an hour before they escaped, before it wouldn't be horribly rude to check his phone.*

*The screen was still blank.*

THEIR APARTMENT FELT EMPTY, *aching with it, when Cisco came through the door. Even if he hadn't been told, he thought he would have known something was wrong, just from the way the air hit his skin.*

*He dropped his bag on the floor, kicking the door closed behind him in the same motion. Pulling his phone out was reflexive, even if there was nothing there. Elaine hadn't sent any other updates, and Leo's father wouldn't talk to him, even if Cisco had his number.*

*There was absolutely zero chance that Leo had his phone, but he sent a text anyway, adding it to the end of all the unanswered texts he's sent since draft day, just because he couldn't—he had to do something. Anything. He wasn't giving up on them without a fight. Even if he didn't know who to fight, how to fight, just yet.*

**Miss you. Love you. Talk to me soon, please.**

*He didn't leave the first voicemail until much later, much drunker.*

*"LEO? Baby, I know you can't get this now, I know you—just call me, please. I love you, I just—I just want to hear your voice. Please"*

*"BABY, it's been a month. Elaine won't talk to me, I don't know if your dad got to her, but—look, if you need time, if you need space—I'll give you whatever you need. Just—please —it doesn't have to be you. I don't—I need to know that you're alive. Please, baby."*

⋋

*"I HAVE to go to training camp. I don't know what to do with your stuff. I boxed it up and left it with Lightning—Seth. I hope—I hope you're okay. That's all I want, you know."*

⋋

*"I—I'M not going to call again, baby. You know me—I've got a hard head, but I can take a hint eventually. Just—I love you. Always."*

⋋

CISCO KNOWS HE'S STARING, but he can't look away. Maybe he's hallucinating, maybe if he takes his eyes off Leo, he'll vanish again, gone for another seven years. Maybe this is just the ghost of Leo, of all the hope and love that he used to feel finally made into physical form.

Although he's never imagined Leo with a dog before.

What does he say? What can he say, that he didn't say in the texts or the voicemails or the emails that he sent off into the void, unacknowledged and unreturned. Like the Flying Dutchman, ghost messages coursing through the darkness.

"Leo." He can't stop repeating it, his voice hoarse. "I—"

Before he can come up with any more words, the buzzer sounds.

"Your two minutes are up." Leo says the words slowly, never looking away from him.

When Cisco tears his eyes away, he sees the PK unit heading back toward the bench. He sees Stewie waving him back out onto the ice.

Every fiber of his being says to stay here, not to let Leo slip through his fingers again. But—

"Your team needs you."

Cisco nods at Leo's words, buckles his helmet back on and shoves his hands into his gloves.

Stepping back out onto the ice isn't the hardest thing he's ever done, but it hurts, just the same.

When he glances back at the box, Leo is watching him go.

**2**

---

**LEO**

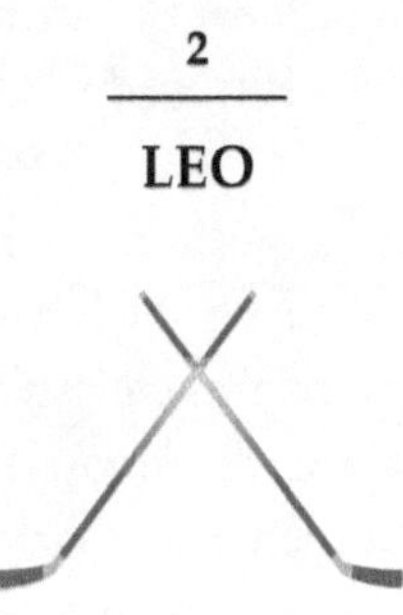

There's no reason for the sinking feeling Leo gets when his boss bursts into his office wild-eyed and panicked. He knows Gen has been waiting for this for months, knows how she's been hovering over her increasingly pregnant wife until Sam began threatening to make her sleep on the couch. This is good news.

"It's time?" He feels stupid as soon as he asks, like he doesn't know the answer.

"Sam's already headed to the birth center," Gen confirms. "I need a favor."

Leo smiles at her, trying to project calm and reassurance. "Name it."

"The Abs are playing tonight—"

*Oh. Oh no.*

"—and I know hockey isn't your thing—"

*Not anymore it isn't, no.*

"—but it's not so bad. Just sit in the box, keep the time for any players who take penalties. Easy. Joelle at the rink can show you everything, and they know about Totoro. I'm sorry, Leo, but—"

"Go." To his surprise, his voice sounds calm. Reliable. Not at all like someone who would very much like to leap to his feet and yell about how this isn't fair, how she should ask anyone else. That he isn't ready. "Go be with your wife. I've got this."

She pulls him into a quick, fierce hug. "You're the best, Leo. And who knows, maybe you'll have fun!"

"Right." He keeps the smile plastered firmly on his face until she disappears out the door. Her footsteps recede down the hall until he's left alone again, with only the reassuring presence of Totoro, his service dog, at his feet, to calm his spinning thoughts.

Possibly he could get someone else to do it. The chance to see an Abs game from right on the ice, to sit in the penalty box? Literally half of Edmonton would jump on that, at a minimum. Hell, he could probably step out on the street right now and auction it off to the highest bidder. He never did figure out how Gen got it in the first place.

The biggest surprise here is that he doesn't want to. Now that the initial panic has subsided, he can't deny the probably masochistic urge to do it. To sit in the box, to smell the ice, to hear the sound of blades carving through it and the clatter of sticks, the roar of the crowd.

He's had enough therapy—shit, has he ever—to admit that he misses it. Hockey was never his first love, not like —like some people. But some of the happiest times of his life happened in or near a hockey rink.

It's not like he isn't happy right now, and there's no reason that thought should feel hollow. He has his work— good, important work that he can leave behind at the end of the day. He has Totoro, a big, adorable mutt who loves to use him as a chair when things are calm and stays by him during his now-infrequent panic attacks. Life is good.

But he can't help wondering

Anyway, he tells himself, it's not like there's much risk of anything happening. Cisco—he can't help flinching a little, just thinking the name, the edges of hurt and love still sharp enough to bruise—Cisco doesn't take penalties. Everyone knows that; he fucking won the Chernowthy trophy for sportsmanship last year.

Speaking of masochism, Leo really needs to stop Googling his ex.

So it's fine. He'll go, he'll see the game. Maybe he'll see others after this, if it goes okay. He'll see Cisco, from a distance, but still. Nothing else will happen.

Whether he wants it to or not.

If there's one thing Leo has learned over the past seven years, it's that wanting isn't enough. Not when you're too much of a coward to do the right thing.

LEO IS JUST STARTING to feel settled when it happens.

Being at the rink again—it's everything he remembered and more. The moment he steps through the doors, it settles over him, like a warm, comforting blanket around his shoulders. He has to shake himself out of it, following the intimidatingly efficient woman who guides him and Totoro across the ice to the penalty box, in front of the seats already half-filled with loyal fans waiting for warmups.

He does his best to ignore the envious looks from the fans as he's ushered into the box, resisting the urge to straighten his already impeccable suit for the thousandth time. It's strange, seeing the ice from the middle instead of the crease, but still so achingly familiar that he has to swallow hard around the lump in his throat. Totoro settles easily at his feet, his warm, solid bulk reassuring against Leo's leg.

After being away for so long, even the warmup, the interminable pregame ceremonies and shows seem interesting. And then the puck drops, and he's lost in the magic, on the edge of his seat like nothing has changed. Like his last game was yesterday, and not almost eight years ago.

It's not all watching the game, of course, but the Abs play pretty clean. His counterpart in the visitors box has a much harder job, a revolving door of Jackalopes players shuttling in and out. Especially West, who is both as good-looking up close as his pictures and just as big of an asshole on the ice as his detractors say.

Through it all, though, some part of him is always aware of Cisco, sitting on the bench, either watching the play intently or joking with his teammates. Even from all the way across the rink, Leo imagines he can feel that familiar smile, the way it used to warm him down to his bones.

And when he's on the ice—

Cisco has always been an exceptional player. Sure, Leo's biased; he fully acknowledges this. But he's not the one who drafted Cisco in the first round. Maybe he wasn't first overall, but the Abs were looking to build their defense and boy, did they.

Watching Cisco play now is as different from watching him in college as a photo of the Mona Lisa is different from seeing it in person. All of the promise he had as a younger player, all the potential, it's all there now, and Leo can't help but watch, following him around the ice.

If he hadn't been watching so closely, he might not have seen it happen. He's not absolutely sure—they're very far away—but he thinks he sees West wink at Cisco. What he definitely sees is West fling himself dramatically at

Cisco's stick, then collapse even more dramatically to the ice.

But when the ref calls the penalty, it's not on West for embellishment, somehow. It's on Cisco, for cross-checking. Which is bullshit, and if Leo had skates, he'd be out there on the ice arguing, just like Cisco's A is. As it is, all he can do is join in the booing of the crowd when the ref shakes his head, in the applause as Cisco skates reluctantly toward the box.

He's so preoccupied by the unfairness of it all that the reality doesn't hit him until Cisco is almost there, close enough to see the warm brown of his eyes under his helmet. Eyes that aren't looking at Leo yet. Heart in his throat, he opens the door, watching as Cisco clumps inside and collapses down to sit on the bench.

He unhooks his helmet and shakes his hair back out of his eyes. It's shorter than Leo remembers, no longer long enough to pull back in a ponytail or bun, but still the familiar rich black. Maybe that's why he says it, his mouth opening without his conscious input.

"You cut your hair." He winces at the inanity, like that's the biggest change since the last time they saw each other, but somehow he's still talking. "It looks good."

This close, he can see the way Cisco's face changes from mild frustration to shock, the way he turns instantly, his whole body moving to face Leo. His eyes widen even more when they meet Leo's, his mouth falling slightly open. Fuck, it shouldn't be what Leo is focusing on, and it's not the only thing, but hell. He looks good.

He always looks good.

His hand shakes slightly when it lands on Leo's arm, squeezes just a little, like he's not sure this is really happening. Leo can relate.

"Leo," he breathes. His lips wrap around the name like

they always did, like there's no word he'd rather be saying. It's soft enough that Leo can barely hear him over the roar of the crowd, but he's seen his name on Cisco's mouth often enough to know what it looks like.

Despite everything, he feels himself smiling, just a little. He could never resist smiling when Cisco said his name.

"Cisco." He savors the taste of the syllables on his tongue, despite—or maybe because of—the way it still hurts, a little. "It's been—awhile."

*"Okay," the coach announced. "We're gonna give our new goalie a workout. Centers and wingers are shooting, junior D is defending. Then we'll do shootout practice. You ready, Carrington?"*

*"Ready." Leo knew what to say, even though he wasn't sure he actually was ready. There was only one right answer, though. He could hear his father's voice in his mind, admonishing him to never let them see him sweat, but he pushed it aside. This was hockey. His father had no place here.*

*One of the d-men positioned himself near the crease, shooting Leo a cocky grin. "Don't worry, rookie. We've got you."*

*Leo got distracted enough by the objectively beautiful mouth shaping those words that all he could do was nod before the whistle blew and he had about twenty hockey players barreling down on him.*

*Lucky for him, it seemed like the hot d-man—Reyes, according to his jersey—was right. He and his partner worked together seamlessly to defend in close. Leo only had to stop about ten pucks, which he somehow managed to do.*

*When the whistle blew again, he was breathing like he'd*

been bag-skated, but the endorphins were sparkling through his system, lighting up every nerve. He felt invincible, like he could do this forever.

Out of the corner of his eye, he saw Reyes take off his helmet, brushing at stray strands of long black hair that had escaped from the thick knot at the back of his head. The rest of him was as pretty as his mouth. Normally Leo would be struck dumb in the face of such attractiveness, but somehow he found the nerve to smile at Reyes and say "Thanks."

"Don't mention it." Reyes smiled back, maybe, just maybe, flirting a little. Leo could dream, okay? "Just doing my job, sir."

"Like you'll be doing your job in this shootout drill?" Leo reached for his water bottle, praying he didn't fumble it.

Reyes winked at him. "Exactly. I promise I'll make any bruises up to you later."

And that—there was no mistaking it. That wink was definitely flirtatious.

Thankfully the coach called Reyes away before Leo had to come up with a response. Maybe, if he could impress Reyes with his hockey, it would overcome the awkwardness that inevitably happens when he opens his mouth.

Probably not, but no harm in wishing.

Capping his water bottle, he pulled his visor back down and settled himself into the crease, eyeing the players lined up before him who are listening intently to the coach's instructions. He did his best not to stare to obviously at Reyes, but when he got another wink, he was pretty sure he lost that battle.

The thing was, he didn't want to look away.

THIS TIME CISCO is the one who can't look away. He's

staring at Leo like he's seen a ghost, like he expects him to disappear. Which, to be fair, is kind of exactly what he did last time, Leo thinks, a familiar pang of guilt curling in his stomach.

"Leo," he says, his voice painfully familiar even through the slight hoarseness. "I—"

The timer goes off, cutting through whatever he was going to say. Leo wants to ignore it, to pretend it didn't happen, but this is Cisco's livelihood, his career, his love. His team needs him, and he's never been the kind of guy to shirk that responsibility.

"Your two minutes are up." He closes his mouth firmly on the other words that try to spill out. Words like *I'm sorry* and *I miss you*. Stupid, empty, useless words, that can't erase what Leo did.

Nothing can.

Cisco glances out at the ice, where even Leo can see that he's getting waved over. But still he hesitates, looking between Leo and the ice like he might actually not go.

Leo's already caused him enough pain for a lifetime. The last thing Cisco needs, the last thing he deserves, is more. "Your team needs you."

That gets him a nod. Cisco buckles his helmet on, shoves his hands into his gloves, his eyes never leaving Leo the entire time. He doesn't look away until he steps through the door Leo holds open for him, gliding across the ice with that so-familiar grace.

Leo watches him go, of course. He could say that there's nothing else to see, but the truth is that, as usual, he can't look away. He doesn't want to look away.

He spends the rest of the game in an agony of suspense, with Totoro glued to him like an extension of his body. Will Cisco get another penalty? Does Leo want him to? He doesn't know.

Despite West's fuckery and the way the ref and the linesemen don't seem to even see what he's doing at least three-quarters of the time, the Abs never let go of their lead. Even one of their fourth-line d-men scores, off what Leo can tell is a lucky bounce from a mile away. But it's still good, and he can't help being savagely pleased on behalf of Cisco's team.

He probably should be more surprised when he swings the penalty box open for another familiar face, but apparently seeing Cisco—speaking to Cisco—used up all his emotional capacity for the night. What isn't surprising is the chilly nod Seth gives him as he settles into the bench. Cisco always did inspire loyalty in his teammates. And he wasn't the only one Leo ghosted after—well. After.

"Long time no see." Seth finally speaks after about thirty seconds of frosty silence.

"Yeah." He's not wrong. "It's good to see you, Seth."

Seth's lips press together for a second. "What did you say to Sunshine?"

"I don't believe that's any of your business." Leo keeps his voice as even as possible, hoping he hid the flinch he couldn't help but feel.

"It's my business if you fuck with my team." Despite the confrontational nature of his words, Seth's eyes dart down to Totoro, and his tone is matter-of-fact.

It's not funny, but Leo smiles anyway. Mostly because he refuses to break down here, so publicly. "We didn't exactly have time for a heart-to-heart in the two minutes he was in here."

"Too bad." Seth puts his gloves back on just as the timer sounds. "Maybe you should have."

The rest of the game is a blur, except for the solid win score on the board. Leo finishes up with the arena staff and leaves as fast as humanly possible, Totoro trotting watchfully at his side. He needs his home and a stiff drink.

Maybe leaving without the chance to talk to Cisco again makes him a coward. Probably it does. He ignores the faint, strident voice in the back of his head and quickens his steps.

Right now, he can't bring himself to care.

3

———

## CISCO

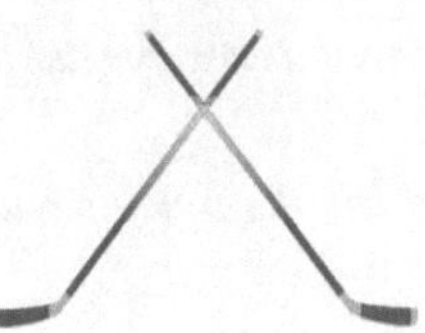

Cisco honestly has no idea how he makes it back to the locker room after the game. Or how he played the rest of the game, when it comes right down to it. He knows he did, he knows they won. But everything seems vague and far away, painted in shades of gray.

He knows the room is filled with jubilation, knows that Guns and Nova are making plans to go out, to celebrate the win, and Tolly's goal. But even though he's been in this room for the past seven years, in good times and bad, he can't help but think back to a different room, a different team. He can almost see Leo grinning at him from across the room, a tease and a promise all in one. Can practically feel the stupid, blind hope that filled him back then, the sense of invincibility.

"Hey." Seth sits down next to him, pitching his voice below the half-dozen conversations already happening. "You okay?"

"Sure." Cisco responds automatically, hoping his face isn't telling a different story. "Why?"

Seth looks at him like he's stupid, which is fair. "Dude, I went to the box, too. I saw him."

"It was good to see him," Cisco says. He regrets the words as soon as they leave his mouth, but what is he going to say?

*He broke my heart and he looks exactly the same.*

*I would have stayed there the whole game just for the chance to talk to him.*

*He's the one who left me but all I want to do is beg him for another shot.*

Thankfully, before Seth can dig any deeper, Guns makes his way to their side of the locker room wearing only a towel. "No more sad faces! We won! Drinks for everybody!"

"Sounds good." Cisco returns to peeling out of the rest of his gear. "But first I'm gonna shower so I don't clear out the place with my stink."

"Good plan." Guns agrees cheerfully, slapping him on the back and returning to his own stall to get dressed.

It's been years since Cisco has needed to fake it until he makes it, but apparently those skills are just like riding a bike.

And if some tears mix with the water in the shower, well. No one else has to know.

Despite his earlier optimistic thoughts, faking it till you make it doesn't really extend to going out with the boys. It's nice to have Mikey out with them again, but he and Tolly are even more wrapped up with each other than before he got injured, somehow. Cisco joins them for the obligatory round of shots, but all it does is make him feel heavier, so weighed down with feelings that he might never surface again.

Seth manages to confine himself to a few disapproving looks before disappearing onto the dance floor with some of the other players. Most of the other players, actually. The only people still left in the little VIP space are Cisco, morosely nursing a beer he's not sure he even wants, and Mikey and Tolly, so caught up in each other and whatever discussion they're having that they might as well be in their own little world.

Except for how they keep looking over at him. Shit.

Before he can panic too much, though, Tolly looks at his beer and then sets it aside, looking up with almost literal hearts in his eyes as Mikey slides out of the booth where they were sitting.

Mikey smiles back down at him, offering him a hand, which Tolly takes without hesitation. They leave without a backward glance, hand in hand.

Despite the way his world has flipped upside down tonight, Cisco can't help smiling as he watches them go. They're cute as hell, and if they didn't remind him so much of the way he and Leo used to be—

He does his best to wrench his mind away from that train of thought, to focus on trying to figure out who won the pool—he might need to actually corner Mikey about when, exactly, they started fucking in order to determine the winner. But he's clearly drunk too much, because he can't stop the flood of memories pouring through him.

CISCO WAITED *until the last of their teammates drifted away, absorbed into the raucous crowd filling the house where half*

*the team lived, before leaning down to speak directly into Leo's ear. "You were amazing tonight."*

*He watched, fascinated, as Leo flushed, the color moving across his cheeks and down his neck, so close to where Cisco's mouth was. It would be so easy to lean in, to press his lips to Leo's skin, to feel the heat of that blush. So easy, but despite Cisco's determined flirting, he still wasn't sure if that was something Leo wanted If it was something he'd ever want.*

*"Thanks," Leo said—yelled, really, turning his head to direct the words to Cisco's ear. Between the loudly thumping bass line and the loud clamor of voices celebrating a win, it was the only way to be heard. It didn't mean anything that he went up on tiptoe to get close to Cisco's ear. That he steadied himself with a hand on Cisco's shoulder. "But it wasn't—I didn't do that much."*

*"You almost held them to a shutout." Cisco couldn't stop himself from arguing, because Leo needed to understand how amazing he was. "Only one goal? Against BU? That's fucking amazing! You deserve a reward for a game that good."*

*Leo pulled back a little, just enough to make eye contact. "Yeah?"*

*Cisco nodded, his stomach full of butterflies. He hadn't intended to escalate their usual flirting this fast, but if Leo was on board, he definitely was. "Whatever you want."*

*He wasn't expecting Leo to close the distance between them, for the hand on his shoulder to pull him down until their lips met, but he sure as hell wasn't complaining. Not when he could finally get his hands on Leo's waist like he'd imagined so many times, backing him into the wall and kissing him like his life depended on it.*

*"Whatever I want?" Leo repeated when they finally broke apart to catch a breath. He already looked a little wrecked, his mouth wet and red from Cisco's, that flush still hot on his cheeks, his chest heaving.*

*"Anything."*

*Since Cisco was already right there, he indulged himself, licking around the shell of Leo's ear and catching the lobe between his teeth. They were still pressed so closely together that he could feel Leo's chest rise with his sharp intake of breath, feel the moan vibrate through his chest when Cisco bit gently at his neck, just below his ear.*

*"Upstairs." Leo dragged him up with a fist in his hair, his sharp eyes catching Cisco's reaction to the tugging sensation. "Now."*

*Cisco stepped reluctantly back, sliding a hand down Leo's arm to grab his hand. He tried not to be too obvious about carving a path through the crowd—the last thing they needed was the rest of the team deciding to surprise them halfway through whatever they were going upstairs for. But almost all of his attention was focused on Leo, the firm grasp of his hand, the tension winding higher between them with every step they took.*

*No one else was fucking in Cisco's room, which was honestly something of a minor miracle, even though he'd locked the door before the party started. It was worth having to fumble for his keys and unlock the door, to be able to close that door between them and the rest of the world. To have Leo push him up against it almost before it's fully closed.*

*It was more than Cisco could have ever imagined, to finally have Leo like this. Leo's hands were everywhere, roaming over his body, impatiently pulling the tie out of his hair until it fell loose around his shoulders.*

*"God, Cisco." Leo groaned, surging up on his toes to kiss him again, hot and hungry and almost desperate. "I want—"*

*Cisco lost the plot a little, finally getting his hands up under Leo's henley to find skin, but it finally occurred to him that Leo never finished the sentence. "What do you want?" He punctuated the question with another kiss, not sure if he wanted to get Leo's shirt off or get a good handful of his ass more. "Whatever you want, Leo. Anything."*

*Leo's eyes slid closed briefly, shuddering. "God, Cisco, you have no idea what I want."*

*"As long as it's me, I'm cool."*

*That got him a smile and another deep, hungry kiss. "It's definitely you."*

*Cisco had no idea how long they made out up against the door like that. At some point Leo got his hands between them, fumbling with the buttons of Cisco's shirt until it was spread open and easy to shrug out of. Cisco took advantage of Leo's distraction to push at his henley until it was bunched up under his arms, finally convincing him to let go long enough to take it off.*

*Making out was even better shirtless, skin against skin, even with the increasingly uncomfortable constriction of his erection where it was trapped in his jeans. But as good as it was, it just made Cisco hungry for more, almost desperate with it.*

*"Bed?" He only had enough air to gasp when he finally forced himself to break the kiss.*

*"Yeah."*

*If Cisco had thought Leo looked wrecked before, it was nothing to how he looked now, his hair messy from Cisco's hands, his muscles flexing under a thin sheen of sweat that made them glisten in the light.*

*"You're so fucking hot."*

*Leo flushed even darker, taking Cisco's hands in his and tugging him toward the bed. But he wouldn't meet Cisco's eyes. "You don't have to say that."*

*"Hey. I mean it."*

*He wasn't sure what he expected, but Leo rolling his eyes and snorting is not it. "Yeah, right, whatever. Can we get back on track here?"*

As much as Cisco's entire body was screaming a resounding affirmative, there was still enough blood in his upstairs brain to have him planting his feet, using his greater mass to pull Leo to a halt. "Leo. How do you not know how hot you are?"

"Are you fucking kidding me?" Leo snorted again. "I'm on a team with guys like you, and Seth, and fucking Chad—yes, he's a dick, but he's hot. Look, I know what I look like. I'm not ugly or anything, but I'm not anything special, either."

Clearly words weren't going to do anything to fix this. But that was okay. Cisco has always been better with actions, anyway.

Lifting Leo's hands to his mouth, he kissed one set of knuckles, then the other, holding eye contact the entire time. "You're wrong."

"Cisco, you don't have to—"

Leo subsided into silence when Cisco let go of his hand to press a gentle finger to his lips. "The first day I saw you at practice, I couldn't stop staring. I don't even remember what I said to you. I just knew I had to talk to you."

"I remember."

"Probably something dumb. It doesn't matter. The point is, I'm going to keep telling you you're hot until you stop arguing with me."

That got him a smile. "So you're saying I should shut up so we can get to the fun?"

"Nah. I'm good either way." Cisco framed Leo's face with his hands, doing his best to like, telepathically transmit how hot he was directly into his brain.

"How about we get back to the part with the kissing for now." Leo's smile widened. He slid his hands around Cisco's waist, pulling him in close.

Cisco went willingly, nudging Leo back toward his bed. "Okay, but I'm going to keep telling you how hot you are."

He really, honestly meant to, but Leo distracted him

quickly with more kissing, with fumbling hands on the button of his jeans, with the little noises he made when Cisco touched him. They probably could have gotten naked faster if they'd stopped kissing, but Cisco couldn't bring himself to care.

"What do you want?" He asked it again once they were completely naked and he managed to reboot his brain from the gorgeousness in front of him.

"I—" Leo hesitated. "Fuck. I don't even know. I just—shit. I'm fucking this up."

Cisco pulled him in for another kiss, did his best to keep it light and soothing even though his cock was making some pretty loud demands. "Hey, no. This is about you, remember. Whatever you want, anything you want. And if you want me to pick, then we can do that, too."

"I want you to fuck me." Leo looked surprised and embarrassed as soon as the words leave his mouth. "But, like, I don't know if I can last that long."

"Me either." Cisco stroked a hand down Leo's back, pulling him closer. "How about we keep that as an option for next time."

Leo blinked at him. "Next time?"

"Well, yeah. I mean, if you want."

"If I want?" Leo grinned like he just played a shutout at the Frozen Four. "Yeah, I definitely want."

Cisco made a note to pursue that incredulous note in Leo's voice another time. "Cool. But right now—is it okay if I try something?"

"Please."

The sound of Leo's voice like that, a little breathy and desperate, was another thing Cisco filed away for later. Because he could. There was going to be a later. At least, there would be if he could make this good for Leo.

"Lie down," he said, punctuating the words with another kiss.

He didn't really want to let go of Leo, and he maybe got distracted watching Leo crawl onto the bed instead of searching for the lube. But eventually he remembered what he was trying to do, when he had Leo spread out on the bed and looking up at him with a mixture of arousal and nerves.

"Hey." He climed onto the bed with the lube, leaning down to kiss Leo again. He was starting to think this might become an addiction, just kissing Leo.

"Hey," Leo said back, his eyes darting between the lube and Cisco's face. "So?"

Cisco grinned and kissed him again, nudging Leo's thighs apart and settling between them. Lucky for them, most of the height difference was in their legs. He broke the kiss with a shuddering moan when his cock brushed against Leo's, the touch lighting up his nerve endings.

Sitting up, reluctant to put more space between them, he squeezed lube into his palm and reached down to line up their cocks. Watching Leo's face when Cisco's hand wrapped around both of them was a revelation. The way his eyes fluttered, his lips parted, the little moan that slipped out—it was so much.

"God, Cisco—"

"Yeah." Cisco braced his free hand on the bed, starting to jerk them both off as slowly as he could stand. He wanted—he needed to come. But he also wanted to stay in this moment forever, with Leo shifting under him, moaning his name. "Fuck, you look so good. You're so hot."

Leo was too far gone to protest this time, just moaned again, running his hands up Cisco's arms and clutching at his shoulders as he fucked up into Cisco's fist.

Between his own arousal and Leo's desperation, it was too much for Cisco to resist. He speeded up his hand, thrusting a little himself. It didn't take very long for them to come, Leo first, then Cisco a couple of strokes after.

Cisco only barely managed not to collapse on top of Leo,

*his head hanging down and his chest heaving like he'd just finished a double shift. He finally recovered enough energy to shift to the side, dropping heavily to the mattress and pressing a clumsy kiss to Leo's shoulder.*

*"Holy shit." Leo spoke without opening his eyes.*

*"Yeah," Cisco said. In the aftermath of his orgasm, the exhaustion of the game and the rest of the day was finally catching up with him. He felt like he could sleep for a week. "I'll get up in a sec, get something to clean up with."*

*Leo leaned down over the edge of the bed and came up with a t-shirt. Which wasn't the ideal clean-up method, but meant that Cisco didn't have to get up.*

*"You're a genius," he mumbled. Accepting the shirt, he wiped the jizz off Leo first, then his own hand and stomach before tossing it back down to the floor. His jaw cracked on a yawn and he flopped back down to the mattress, draping an arm across Leo and trying to work up the energy to get the blanket up over them.*

*Because he was amazing, Leo got that, too, dragging it up with his feet until he could get a hand on it.*

*"The best." Cisco yawned again. "I'm gonna fall asleep. Stay?"*

*"Okay," Leo said.*

*His quiet voice, the warmth of his body, were the last things Cisco remembers before falling asleep.*

"COME IN!" Suzie somehow manages not to drop the baby he's holding while pulling the door open wider. "Merry Christmas!"

"Merry Christmas," Cisco says. "I brought wine."

Suzie grins, bouncing the baby gently when she starts to make noise, lifting her head and looking around to try and see what's going on. "You're a classy guy, Reyes. Come on, we're just waiting on Guns and Nova to show up and then we can eat."

"Maybe we should eat without them. Just so other people get some."

"That's what I said," Angel fistbumps him without looking "But Suzie was all something something not fair something something team cohesion."

Cisco makes the appropriate mocking noises, handing off his bottle of wine to Suzie's husband Chris, and finds a place to sit in the already crowded room.

"Here." Suzie reappears, handing Cisco the miniature person in the red-and-white-striped footie pajamas. "Hold Jocelyn for a sec?"

He disappears before Cisco can protest. Not that he minds. After an initial assessment with her wide, serious brown eyes, Jocelyn seems to accept him as a temporary caregiver, laying her little curly head down on his shoulder and sighing softly.

Cisco rubs her back, humming softly. It's been so long since his niece and nephew were babies that he's a little surprised how easily it comes back to him. But apparently baby-handling is like riding a bicycle, or maybe Jocelyn is just a very agreeable baby. Either way, within a few moments she's snoring soft little baby snores in his ear.

"Okay, listen up." Suzie appears in the doorway, raising his voice to be heard over the babble of conversation. "Food's ready. We're doing buffet style, so line up, get a plate, and help yourself. Kids first, and no, rookies, that doesn't mean you."

Cisco stays seated through the first initial scramble. He's not particularly hungry, and he finds himself unwilling to disturb Jocelyn.

"I can take her," Chris says, appearing in front of him.

"I'm good." Cisco rubs another slow circle over her tiny baby back. "Go get some food. I bet you haven't had a chance to eat with two hands in awhile."

Chris sighs. "God, that sounds like a beautiful dream. Are you sure?"

"Positive. Miss Jocelyn and I are doing just fine. Go eat, maybe have a glass of wine and relax. I can't believe you agreed to host this with a new baby."

"We didn't know we were going to get her as soon as we did," Chris admits. "And then I forgot. Thank fuck Daniel had it catered; if he expected me to cook for this crowd I might have actually murdered him. Seriously, though, thank you."

Cisco smiles. "No problem. My niece and nephew are big kids now and they don't want to snuggle anymore."

Chris takes his leave with one last grateful smile, leaving Cisco to watch the team and their partners and kids swarm around the Christmas buffet.

There's a weird, hollow ache in his chest, watching Angel lift his little girl up so she can point at the kind of stuffing she wants on her plate, seeing Tiger wrap an arm around his new wife's shoulder and press a kiss to her temple. Even the freshly-washed milky baby smell coming from Jocelyn hurts a little.

He's two years older than Chris and Suzie, but here they are, with a family home they can open to the team for the holidays and a new baby. What does he have to show for those years? An expensive condo without even a dog or a cat to keep him company.

Jocelyn stirs, not really fussing, but making little disgruntled noises. He bounces her gently, grateful for the distraction from his thoughts.

They'll be back soon enough.

## 4

# LEO

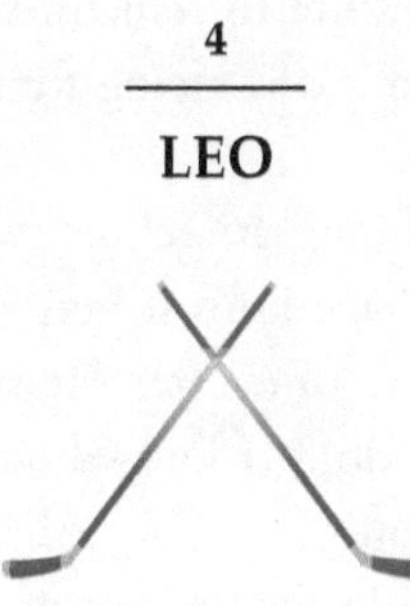

"Hello?" Leo says into the phone, most of his attention on the spreadsheet on his screen. If he can just figure out why this formula has broken down—

"Hi, Leo."

It takes a second for the familiar voice to penetrate his focus. "Gen! How are you? How's Sam? How's the baby?"

"We're good. Tired, but good."

"I've seen the pictures." Leo leans back in his chair, abandoning the spreadsheet for the moment and reaching down to pet Totoro's head. "She's beautiful."

Despite the fatigue obvious in Gen's voice, he can hear that she's smiling. "She looks like Sam, so of course she is."

"Of course," he echoes. "I can't wait to meet her."

"I'll bring her in for a visit sometime in the next few weeks," Gen promises. "But that's actually not why I'm calling."

Leo's mind starts racing, searching for something he might have fucked up badly enough that Gen would have to call him while she's on maternity leave. "Oh yeah?"

"It's just about the attendant thing." She continues quickly, clearly having read the anxiety in his tone.

It takes him a minute to remember what she's talking about, and then his mind is racing for an entirely different reason.

"The attendant thing?" he echoes.

"I really should have known better," Gen says. "But I thought I'd have more time after she was born. And I can find someone else to do it; I know hockey isn't your thing anymore. But someone from the Abs staff was asking if you'd consider filling in for the rest of the season, so I said I'd ask."

Leo forces himself to relax his grip on the phone, his fingers aching from the strain. "Did they say why?"

"No, but I imagine it has something to do with the fact that you're good at everything you do," Gen says. "Look, I don't have to know right now, there's not a game til tomorrow. I just wanted you to think—"

"I'll do it."

He blinks at the soothing blue and green swirls of the abstract painting on his wall, replaying the last few seconds over again. Did he actually just say that?

"Great! I'll call the Abs and they'll set you up with a parking pass and everything," Gen says.

Shit, he said it.

"Great."

He manages to make it through the rest of the conversation without Gen sensing his inner turmoil—she must be distracted by her new baby, or just too tired to notice, for once. Finally, after what seems like a thousand years, the call ends.

Setting the phone down gently on his desk, he turns to look out the window and breathes.

It's going to be fine. Regardless of why Leo said what

he did—which has nothing to do with wanting to see Cisco again—and despite the emotional upheaval of last time, he really did enjoy the game. He's avoided hockey for so long that he'd almost forgotten about the good parts, but being there, on the ice, watching the game, it had all come back.

So why shouldn't he do it? If he enjoys it, and the Abs asked for him, there's no reason to say no.

Anyway, Cisco never takes penalties. Last time was a fluke, a bullshit call and West being his douchiest self. So it's not like they'll run into each other. Really, it's a win-win.

And maybe if Leo keeps repeating that to himself, he'll eventually believe it.

"So," the guy—Jackson, Leo reminds himself—says, blue eyes focused on Leo's face. "What do you do?"

"I'm in human resources." Leo laughs a little, trying to keep his hands still and not pick at the label on his beer bottle. "Not very interesting to talk about. Lots of paperwork, but at least the hours are regular."

Jackson grins, seeming completely at ease somehow despite the fact that they just met in person a few minutes earlier. Especially since he clearly wasn't expecting Totoro. "That's something, for sure. Sometimes I regret getting into personal training, because the hours are all over the place. But I'm never bored. Plus, getting paid to work out is pretty cool."

"Uh, yeah." Leo takes a sip of his beer. "I gotta admit, once I stopped playing in college, I haven't worked out as much."

"You still look to be in pretty good shape." Jackson

gives him a once over that probably should be hot, but leaves him strangely unaffected. "What did you play?"

Leo shrugs. "Hockey. But that was a long time ago."

Jackson perks up. This is the problem with living in Canada; everyone's ridiculously into hockey. "Oh yeah? What position?"

"Goalie." Leo can't figure out why he's so reluctant to open up about this. It's not like he never talks about college or hockey. Forcing himself to take a deep breath, he smiles at Jackson. "It's been awhile, though."

"I played goalie, too," Jackson says. "Lacrosse, not hockey. But still. Small world."

Leo nods. "Sure is. Tell me about lacrosse. How long did you play?"

He only feels a little guilty for the distraction tactic when Jackson takes the bait, launching into stories of his high school and college sports career. He's a good story-teller, expresive and funny and just self-deprecating enough to not be arrogant.

Leo laughs along at the appropriate places, doing his best to act normal, to be normal. Maybe it works—Jackson doesn't seem to notice anything out of the ordinary.

By the end of what was, objectively, a very nice date, Leo is about ready to crawl out of his skin. The urge to escape mingles sourly with the feeling of guilt in his stomach. Jackson is a nice, attractive guy who also played college sports. On paper, they're perfect. What the fuck is wrong with Leo, that he can't muster up the slightest bit of interest?

"Can I text you?" Jackson asks when they're standing outside the restauarant, hovering in that awkward moment where they have to separate but neither of them is quite sure how to start it.

Leo opens his mouth to say yes, but he can't get the word out. "I—"

"That's okay," Jackson says after a moment. He's not mad, his voice kinder than Leo probably deserves. "I had a good time. If you ever want to try again, you know where to find me."

"I'm sorry." Leo fights the urge to explain, to spill out all his sins and the fucked-up inside of his head. He's already turning the guy down; making this an unpaid therapy session would be just rude. "I—I thought I was ready for this."

Jackson smiles at him. "I get it. Like I said, I'm down if you want to give it another shot. Have a good night, Leo. Totoro."

"You too."

All Leo wants in that moment is to be back in his apartment with Totoro sprawled over his lap, but when he closes his car door and reaches for the ignition, he can't bring himself to turn the key. A vision of his future stretches out in front of him, days of work, nights at home eating takeout with his dog at his feet, Tinder dates where he can't bring himself to make a connection because his brain is so fucked.

His phone vibrates in his pocket, interrupting his quiet spiral. He almost ignores it, but finally digs it out to see a text from Gen.

*Pizza u sent just saved my life. Will name nxt baby after u. Xcept no more babies. 2 hard*

Glancing at the gift bag in his passenger seat, Leo texts back. *I have a present for the baby. Is now okay?*

*If u come hold this child for 2 mins so I can pee, I'll double ur pay,* is the instant response.

*You can't do that but I'll be there in 15 anyway,* he

replies, tossing his phone into the cupholder and finally turning the car on.

He kind of zones out on the drive, following the turns his phone directs him through without thinking consciously about it. It's a little alarming, pulling into Gen and Sam's driveway with no clear memory of how he got there. But it's probably fine.

This is the kind of thing that happens to normal people with normal brains all the time.

Grabbing the gift bag, he slides out of the car, lets Totoro out and closes the door behind him, careful to hit the lock button on his key fob before heading for the door of the little bungalow.

Every light is on, glowing against the night, but it still takes long enough for someone to answer the door that he starts to think maybe he should just come back later. But, a few seconds before he's about to turn and head back to his car, the door opens, revealing—

In the nearly four years they've worked together, Leo has never seen Gen look like this. She's always had sort of a comfortable hippie butch aesthetic, but this—Leo recognizes this from when Elaine had her baby last year. The hair that looks like a birds nest, the clothes covered with questionable stains, the wild eyes ringed with dark circles that dart between him and the squirming baby nestled against her chest.

"Here." He doesn't think, just reacts instinctively. "Trade me."

Gen must really be wiped out, because she hands him the baby without question—Gen always has questions.

"Every time I set her down," she says hollowly, taking the gift bag and standing there, swaying slightly on her feet. "Even for a second, she starts crying. I can't—"

When Leo nudges her, she finally steps back, letting him and Totoro inside. "Sam asleep?"

"Yeah, she—yeah. She's probably going to wake up to feed the baby in like—fuck, I don't know. Oh, shit, I shouldn't swear in front of the baby. Did I just fuck her up? Oh, shit, I did it again."

"Hey." Leo shifts the baby until she stops squirming, seemingly satisfied with her position against his shoulder. "She's not going to remember what you said when she was a week old. I promise. Right now, I'm going to hold her, and you're going to go lay down and get some sleep before you collapse."

Gen blinks at him. "But—"

"Go," Leo says firmly. "I can hold the baby until Sam wakes up to feed her."

For once, Gen goes without further argument, weaving slightly as she heads down the short hall to their bedroom.

"We're fine," Leo says to the tiny human in his arms. "Your moms are going to sleep and since you apparently require holding, I'm going to hold you."

He settles gingerly onto the couch under Totoro's intense gaze, but apparently being stationary isn't a deal-breaker for Eloise. He smiles a little, remembering Gen's relief once they settled the nearly-endless wrangling over choosing a name.

Eloise watches him, dark eyes wide against the warm brown skin she inherited from Gen's brother—Leo probably shouldn't know this much about the process of his boss's baby being conceived, but Gen had been so excited when her twin agreed to be a sperm donor, she'd practically floated into the office.

"Yeah." Fishing his phone out of his pocket, he opens his latest coping mechanism game. "We're gonna be just fine."

Eloise regards him solemnly for another long moment, then closes her little eyes with a sigh, her whole body relaxing trustingly against his chest.

Leo does his best to ignore the tiny pang of wistfulness squeezing at his heart. The game helps, eventually, and so does Totoro's familiar presence at his feet. By the time Sam stumbles out of the bedroom, mumbling promises of eternal gratitude, he almost feels back to normal.

But driving home to his empty apartment, even with Totoro alongside him, brings the loneliness rushing back again.

⤬

*"Hey," Cisco said.*

*Leo looked up from his homework, surprised to see Cisco standing in his doorway. "What's up?"*

*"Get your coat." Cisco bounced a little on his toes like he always did when he was excited. "It's a surprise."*

*"I have to study for this Organic Chem test," Leo protested, looking at the mess of notes and flash cards and text-books scattered across his desk.*

*Cisco shook his head. "You've been studying for three fucking hours, Leo. Give your brain a break. Besides, you've gotta eat. You know Coach doesn't want you losing any more weight."*

*Leo checked his phone screen and yeah, sure enough, he's been at this for hours. As if on cue, his stomach growled. "Okay. Where are we going?"*

*"It's a surprise," Cisco repeated, still grinning. "Come on!"*

*Bemused, Leo followed him down the stairs. Shoving his feet into boots, he turned to see Cisco holding his coat, a faint pink flush across his cheekbones.*

*They hadn't really talked about what happened after the*

*party last night, about waking up together in Cisco's bed and the lazy making out that turned to mutual hand jobs and showering together. Leo had bitten his tongue all day long, not because he didn't want to know the answer, but because he was afraid of asking the question.*

*But now Cisco was holding his coat like—like this was a—*

*Leo pushed his arms into the coat sleeves, cutting off that train of thought before he could even think the word. "Okay," he said. Zipping the coat and grabbing his scarf only took a moment. "Now what?"*

*"Your chariot awaits." Cisco opened the door, gesturing Leo out in front of him.*

*His chariot was, apparently, Cisco's ancient sedan, too old to even have a CD player. But the heat worked, which was the most important thing in a Minnesota winter. Leo got in, buckled his seat belt, and did his best not to ask the questions that wanted to spill out.*

*He watched avidly, of course, as Cisco pulled out of the driveway and started to drive. "You're really not going to tell me?"*

*"Surprise." Cisco reminded him, smiling at him for a moment before looking back out at the road. It was probably ridiculous for that look to make Leo feel as warm as the air blowing out of the vents, but if he couldn't be a little ridiculous in his own head, where could he?*

*They didn't drive very far, barely making it off campus before Cisco pulled them into a parking lot. And—it was dumb to feel disappointed that Cisco brought him to the pub-style restaurant where the team always went, but, well, apparently Leo had gone stupid with this little crush.*

*Except while he did his best to swallow his disappointment, to put on his team face, Cisco circled the car, opening* his door and offering him a hand, like he just stepped out of freaking *Pride and Prejudice* or something.

"I wanted to take you someplace nice." His voice is almost too quiet for Leo to hear, his face even redder than before. "But—"

He stopped there, and Leo suddenly felt like the world's biggest dick. He knew that Cisco's family didn't have a lot of money, that he was here on scholarship, that he worked a part-time job as best he could fit it in around practices and classes and studying. But he hadn't stopped to think about the practicalities of that in regards to dating.

"But you said you liked the mac & cheese here when it was cold." Cisco still wouldn't quite meet his eyes as Leo allowed himself to be pulled out of the car. "And—"

Leo cut him off with fingers across his lips, slightly in awe at his own daring. But the fact that Cisco remembered a throwaway comment Leo made months ago—that he wanted to go someplace nice—

"This is great." He spoke firmly, letting his hand linger for a minute before sliding it down to link their fingers together. "Let's go."

"Okay." Cisco breathed. His eyes were bright, and he kept sneaking little sideways looks at Leo, like he couldn't stop himself. Like he didn't want to look anywhere else.

It was the best date Leo has ever had, and it was only just getting started.

LEO STRAIGHTENS his suit jacket as he settles in on the bench in the penalty box. He probably didn't need to come this early, but he has to admit, if only to himself, how eager he is to watch warmups. To watch Cisco.

If he's weak and there's no one around to call him on it, does it really matter?

The time before puck drop passes more quickly than he'd expected. Totoro seems almost bored, clearly having filed the arena and the box as known places. Before Leo knows it the arena is mostly filled, the lights start flashing, and the Abs take the ice against the Manticores.

Three minutes in, he watches, shocked and appalled, as Cisco swings his stick in the direction of the Manticores' first-line center. Right in front of a ref. Sure enough, the penalty is called almost immediately

"What the fuck are you doing?" He hisses the words under his breath, closing the door behind Cisco.

Cisco offers him a lopsided smile, the one that always used to make Leo melt. "I just wanted to talk," he says. Taking off his helmet and sinking down onto the bench, he grabs the towel sitting there.

Leo stands in the corner, doing his best not to get distracted when Cisco runs the towel over his hair. It's not fair, dammit. He always loved Cisco's hair. "You could call like a normal person," he says, tearing his eyes away.

"I don't have your number," Cisco points out.

"If—" Leo jabs a finger into his chest protector, because this is ridiculous. "If I give you my number, will you stop pulling this stupid shit?"

Fuck, he'd forgotten about that smile. The way it lights up Cisco's face, glows in his eyes—there's no mistaking the real reason he got his nickname.

"Cross my heart," he says solemnly, drawing an x over his chest.

"After the game." Leo glances at the timer. "Right now, you have a game to win."

Cisco puts his helmet and gloves back on, shoving his hand into the second glove just as the timer goes off. "After the game," he repeats, grinning again as he moves toward the door.

Leo collapses back down onto the bench, only then noticing the curious looks of the fans seated around the box. It takes all of his self-control not to swear. Probably no one heard what they were saying, but they were obviously having an intense conversation. The speculation is going to be all over the blogs, probably. He'll be lucky if no one gifs this. Even Totoro seems to be judging him, although that's probably his imagination.

Shit.

At this moment, he wants nothing more than to leave as soon as the game is over. Or well, maybe not nothing more.

He made a promise.

# 5

## CISCO

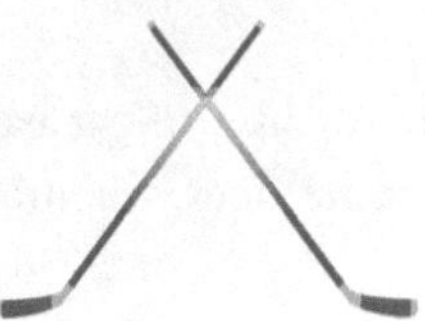

Cisco stares down at his phone screen, ignoring the chirping around him as the rest of the team settles into their seats on the plane. It just figures that almost literally as soon he gets Leo's number, they have to leave for a roadie.

Which is totally the reason he's not texting yet.

Has nothing to do with their history or the years apart.

Nope.

Just as he's about to type a message, the flight attendant announces over the PA that it's time to put phones in airplane mode. Cisco definitely doesn't sigh in relief as he hits the little button and tucks the phone away.

He didn't used to lie to himself this much, either.

Tucking the phone back in his pocket, he gets his iPad out instead, queuing up the next episode of Elementary before taking out his latest crochet project.

"What're you making this time?" Angel asks, looking up from his sudoku book.

"Supposed to be an octopus." Cisco shows him the

pattern he'd printed out for reference. "I thought I'd give it to Suzie for Jocelyn."

Angel shakes his head. "She'll fucking destroy it. You know how kids are."

"That's fine," Cisco says. "Keeps my house from turning into an episode of Hoarders. That's why I give 'em away when they're done."

It takes a minute for him to get back into the swing of the pattern, but once he does, his mind is, unfortunately, free to wander.

What would he even say to Leo? How do you start to talk to someone who used to be so much a part of your life, and then was just—gone. No explanations, no contact, just like he dropped off the face of the planet.

*I missed you.*

*I think I still love you.*

*I thought about trying to find you, but I had too much pride to chase you when you didn't want anything to do with me. Would you have listened if I did?*

"You okay?" Angel asks.

"Fine," Cisco says. "Why?"

Angel fixes him with a serious look. "Because that tentacle is twice as long as the other two."

Shit. He's right. Cisco sighs, pulls his hook free, and starts unraveling the soft pink yarn. "I just got distracted."

"Uh-huh. And that's why you look like someone ran over your dog."

"I don't have a dog."

This time Angel sighs. "Okay, look. Something's off, has been since the Jackalopes game and that bullshit penalty. I don't know what it is, but you've been playing differently, and that makes it my business."

Shit shit shit.

"It's personal." Even as he says it, he doesn't have much hope that it will fend Angel off.

"Nope." Angel's face is sympathetic, but after three years playing together, Cisco knows he's digging in his heels here. "Like I said, it affects your game, that's my business."

Fuck, Cisco isn't sure he can talk about this without crying. Half the team is asleep, but half of them aren't. The only thing he wants less than to talk about this with Angel is to have the whole team around for it.

"The—" he stops, clears his throat, takes a breath. "The attendant that night, in the box? Was someone I knew. I— we were close. But he cut me out, right before the draft. I hadn't seen him in seven years. It was—a shock."

"Wow." Angel is quiet for a minute, digesting that and, hopefully, using his d-man telepathy to figure out what Cisco isn't saying. "Okay, I can see how that would throw you off. How are you handling it?"

Like shit, Cisco thinks, but doesn't say. "I'm working on it. Seth—Lightning, he played with both of us. He knows some of it. You can—tell him I said you can ask, if you have questions."

Thank fuck, Angel seems to pick up on his silent pleading and doesn't push any further. "Okay. But I'm here, you know. If you want to talk. Or if you need to, even if you don't want to."

Cisco bumps their shoulders together by way of thanks, turning his attention back to the his yarn and crochet hook. He makes it through the rest of the flight by determinedly only thinking about the pattern, the job in front of him.

At least there's one thing he can do right.

THEY CHECK into their rooms late enough that Cisco should be ready to sleep. And he's definitely tired, but he can already tell that sleep is nowhere near happening, jittery energy vibrating through him in a way that makes his exhausted muscles feel twice as tired.

Pulling out his phone, he taps the Grindr icon without thinking, then pauses as his screen fills up with pictures, sick guilt twisting in the pit of his stomach.

He's being ridiculous. He knows that, objectively. He and Leo haven't been together for the majority of a decade, for fuck's sake. It's not cheating if he hooks up with a guy, or two, or hell, a whole hockey team's worth. He's as free as a bird, able to fuck whoever he wants, whenever he wants.

Except apparently his emotions haven't gotten any of those memos.

Locking his phone with a groan, he flings it onto the duvet and starts stripping out of his clothes. Thank fuck he gets a single on the road so he doesn't have to explain to anybody what's going on. And he can take as long jerking off in the shower as he wants.

Maybe then he'll be able to sleep.

*THE COOLER AIR washed in around the edges of the shower curtain, even more obvious than the quiet click of the bathroom door closing again.*

*"That better be you, Leo." Cisco said. Turning his back to the spray, he closed his eyes, rinsing conditioner out of his hair.*

*"Who the hell else would it be?" Leo laughed. "Can I come in?"*

*Cisco grabbed the towel he hung over the bar, wiping*

*water out of his eyes. "Sure, come on. We should save water, right?"*

*"The environment is important." Leo stepped into the tub, pulling the curtain closed behind him. "We all have to do our part."*

*He was still smiling when Cisco kissed him, his mouth curved sweetly. Cisco never got tired of this, the feeling of warm skin on skin, the compact muscle of Leo in his arms, the way his lips parted and he seemed to breathe into the kisses.*

*"I should probably let you get cleaned up then," Cisco said when he finally lifted his head.*

*Leo smirked, pushing back into Cisco's hands on his ass. "Oh? Am I dirty?"*

*Cisco couldn't help but laugh, pulling Leo in. "I didn't used to think so."*

*He wasn't interested in having to explain a shower sex injury to the coaches, but they didn't need anything fancy. Cisco slicked his hand with the hotel conditioner and circled it around Leo's cock, hot and hard to the touch. "Like that?"*

*"Fuck." Leo bit his lip. "A little tighter."*

*Cisco followed instructions, diving in to kiss the teeth marks away, leaving a line of kisses up Leo's jawline. "You look so good like this," he breathed. Moving his hand a little faster, he ran his free hand down Leo's back to grab his ass again. "Naked and wet, so hard for me. I could watch you like this forever."*

*Leo sucked in a breath, his hips moving forward to fuck into Cisco's fist, then back, pressing into the hand on his ass.*

*"You—you can—if you want—"*

*"Oh, I want," Cisco said. It was hard to speak, hard to think when all the blood in his body was pooling in his cock, but he did his best. "But not here, baby. Want you spread out on a bed for me, so I can take my time. Want that?"*

"Fuck—" Leo gasped, coming all over Cisco's hand and stomach.

Cisco held him up, savoring the limp, trusting weight as Leo sagged against him.

"Oh God," Leo eventually lifted his head off Cisco's shoulder. "I didn't—let me—"

"I'm good," Cisco said. Despite Leo trying to pull back, he refused to let go. "You don't have to—"

Leo blinked at him, water droplets shining on his eyelashes. "I know. I want to."

It was enough of a surprise, or maybe it was reduced blood flow to the brain, but Cisco couldn't do anything but stare as Leo folded gracefully to his knees, reaching for Cisco's cock.

"Oh fuck."

"It's been a little while since I did this," Leo said. He didn't meet Cisco's eyes, just stroked his fist slowly over the shaft, squeezed gently around the head. "I might not be any good at it."

Cisco laughed shakily. "Baby, anything with your mouth and my cock is going to be good."

That earned him a shy smile. Then Leo's tongue flicked out over the head of Cisco's cock and he lost the last semblance of coherent thought.

Everything was sensation, hot and wet and soft and rough where his cock presses against the roof of Leo's mouth. "Oh, fuck," he choked out. "Baby, I—fuck."

He probably should have been embarrassed by how quickly he was on edge, but he couldn't bring himself to care. "I'm—gonna—"

Leo pulled back, replacing his mouth with his hand. But he didn't move, stayed right there, on his knees, where the first spurt from Cisco's cock landed squarely on his face.

Cisco didn't think he would ever forget that mental image, not if he lived to be a thousand years old. Leo, on his knees in *the shower, water and semen mingling on his face, looking simultaneously smug and shy as his tongue flicked out to capture the fluid coating his lips.*

*"Fuck," Cisco breathed, sagging back against the shower wall. "I think you killed me, baby."*

*"Can't have that," Leo said. He rose to his feet, leaning in for a kiss. "Come on, a little nap and you'll feel good as new."*

*Cisco shifted aside, letting Leo step under the spray to clean up. "Nap with me?"*

*Leo shot a pleased smile over his shoulder. "Thought you'd never ask."*

THE APARTMENT DOOR closes behind Cisco with a click that shouldn't feel final or ominous. As usual, he's being overly dramatic. But he's home. There's no reason not to text Leo. No airplane warning or game to distract him.

Before he can talk himself out of it—again—he pulls his phone out, standing right there by the door, his bags everywhere, and opens Whatsapp. Leo's name is there, of course, from all the times he swore that this time he was gonna do it.

*Hi*, he taps out, hitting send before he second-guesses himself.

He wouldn't blame Leo for making him wait, but the reply is almost instant. *Hi. Back home safe?*

*Yeah.* He hesitates over it for almost a full minute. What else can he say? How can he keep Leo talking? **Coming to the game tomorrow night?**

**You know where to find me. But I'd better not see you in there.**

Cisco takes what feels like his first full breath since the plane took off yesterday. **I know, I know.**

*I'd much rather watch you hand the Selkies their ass*

He's already typed, ***so you still like to watch huh?*** when he realizes how he's headed directly into flirting. And that—that's not what they're doing here. *As you wish* is also out, given what Leo will assume he means by it, even if— well. Best not to go there right now.

He finally settles on a simple, ***Do my best.*** It feels stilted and awkward, but he can a smile still stretches his cheeks, because they're talking. He's talking to Leo. After years of not being able to imagine it ever happening again, he has Leo on the other side of an app, talking to him. In the same city.

It's a gift he never expected. Wanting more would be greedy.

***What are you doing these days?*** he sends. It might be greedy, but he's not willing to let go of the connection, not yet. Hopefully the question of careers isn't as loaded as it used to be. ***When you're not managing a sin bin?***

***Human resources. Super sexy and exciting.***

Cisco smiles wider. Abandoning the bags, he steps out of his shoes and crosses to the couch, doing his best to type at the same time. ***You saying your dates don't ask you to talk pensions to them?***

He's fishing, and he knows it. But somehow he's not disappointed when Leo deflects it.

***Don't really do pensions, but I can talk 401ks all day***

While Cisco is still trying to figure out his next question, the next thing to keep Leo talking, another message comes in. ***My dog is jealous. I'm paying too much attention to my phone.***

***That was your dog in the box? Do you have a pic?***

A pause, long enough for Cisco to loosen his tie, unbutton the top button of his shirt. Long enough for him to get jittery. Then a photo comes through, loading almost instantly.

The dog is a big, floppy-looking mutt, clearly sprawled over Leo's lap and feet. Parts of him are blurry, like he's moving too fast for the camera to capture.

***Sorry***, is the next message. ***Totoro hates being still almost as much as he loves having his picture taken. It's a struggle.***

***He looks awesome,*** Cisco sends back. ***How long have you had him?***

He ignores his abandoned bags, the grumbling in his stomach. They can wait.

This is important.

## 6

## LEO

***W**hy don't you show me—*

Leo rapidly deletes the message, doing his best to pretend that he never even thought it.

Texting with Cisco is good. Easier than talking face to face. He can think about what he's going to say before saying it. When he's not sure what to say, he can send an emoji. It's good. Helpful.

But.

But it's so easy to forget that they're adults now, with adult lives. That it's been seven years and some months—okay, six months and three days, he shouldn't count, but he does—since Leo woke up beside Cisco, since he got to kiss him, touch him.

Since he fucked everything up.

Honestly, he's lucky Cisco is even speaking to him. He doesn't need to fuck that up with pushing boundaries. No matter how much a part of him wants to know how Cisco would react to a suggestive text.

***Gotta take care of some work stuff. I'll see you***

***tomorrow night.*** He feels guilty for the lie as soon as he sends it, but does his best to force the feeling back. Self-preservation is allowed.

***Looking forward to it,*** Cisco texts back.

Leo takes a breath and locks his phone, putting it resolutely down on the end table.

Totoro looks up and whines, snuggling closer as he senses Leo's distress.

Petting the dog is a better use for his hands, he reasons. Soothing for both of them. Much better than text-flirting with the ex he ghosted for the better part of a decade. The ex who has every reason to hate him, but somehow seems not to.

"Bed, Totoro," he says out loud, pushing himself up off the couch.

After only a moment's hesitation, he leaves his phone where it is.

That's enough temptation for one night.

*S*OMEONE MATCHED *with you on Tinder!*

The email subject line is obnoxiously cheerful for this time of the morning. Or maybe that's just Leo's sleep-deprived crankiness talking. It's very possible that he spent most of the night in sleep that was fitful at best, turning over possible responses to Cisco's texts. Possible scenarios for how the game is going to go tonight.

Dragging his mind away from the fact that apparently he's even better at catastrophizing than ever, Leo forces himself to tap the Tinder icon and look at his matches.

He can't remember why he swiped right on these guys in the first place. There's nothing wrong with any of them, of course. Nice, normal guys, nobody who's sent an unso-licited dick pic, nobody who hates dogs or is allergic to them.

Leo opens a message to one, starts to type, then closes it again. Because it's not fair, but compared to the memory of Cisco in the box, sweaty and sincere as he says, "I just wanted to see you," to every other memory of Cisco—

It's not their fault, but none of these guys can compare.

And if his disastrous date with Jackson taught him anything, it's that it's not fair to them, to chat and make plans and go out, like Leo has a chance of actually starting something with them. Like he's ready. Like half his heart isn't somewhere else in the city, going through his game-day routine.

Totoro whuffs, clattering his food bowl against the tiles and jerking Leo out of his reverie. Leaving the phone behind, he gets to his feet and heads over to feed the dog.

Despite everything, Leo can't help but smile at the way Totoro dives joyously into his food bowl. "At least I can still do this, huh, buddy?"

Totoro whuffs again, like he knows what Leo asked. More, like he knows what Leo is thinking and wants to have words with him about it.

For a moment, Leo almost reconsiders the "no more dates" policy he just decided on. If he's assigning meaning to his dog's barks, he probably needs to get out more.

Of course, he will be getting out tonight. And quite a bit more, until the hockey season is over. Not that those outings are likely to help—

The clock display on the stove catches his eye and he nearly jumps out of his skin. "Shit. We're gonna be late, Totoro. Good thing my boss likes me."

In the end, he manages to shove his feet into boots,

pour his coffee into a travel mug, grab his coat and Totoro's harness, and make it out the door in near-record time. And he rolls into the office just in time to hold the door open for Erica, the new temp. So he's not the last one there. At least he's got that going for him.

He buries himself in work, the mundanity of paperwork and bureaucracy, and does his best not to think about the game that night more often than, oh, every five minutes or so.

Results are mixed.

*"Leo?" Cisco's voice was barely audible, even though there was basically no space between them in the hotel bed. If Leo had been asleep, he wouldn't have registered it. "You awake?"*

*"Yeah." He turned on his side, straining his eyes to make out Cisco in the dim light filtering in around the curtains. "What's up?*

*The covers rustled as Cisco turns, too. "Star Trek or Star Wars?"*

*"You seriously woke me up at—" Leo squinted at the alarm clock on the bedside table "—12:37 to ask me that? Really?"*

*"You said you were awake!" Cisco protested. "Besides, it's important. For compatibility."*

*Leo sighed for effect, since it was too dark for Cisco to see him roll his eyes. Probably. "You first."*

*"Star Trek." Cisco responded instantly, without pausing to think about it.*

*"Really?"*

*More rustling; Cisco's hands flashed as he gestured in the dark. "Like, I love me some Star Wars. But Star Trek is like, a* post-scarcity society! People can choose to spend their whole lives doing art, or exploring the galaxy, or figuring out science shit! You can't tell me that's not cool!"

"It's pretty cool," Leo agreed. "I just always figured you'd be more of a Star Wars guy. You know, the good-looking scoundrel who's actually a secret softie with a heart of gold?"

"Han is a favorite," Cisco conceded. "And you can't tell me he and Lando aren't exes. I can love both franchises, and I do. But if I had to pick one? Star Trek, no question."

They lay in silence for a moment, the rhythm of their breathing starting to sync up.

"Hey, you never answered," Cisco said.

"I was wondering when you'd notice." Leo didn't bother to hide his smile. "I get what you're saying about Star Trek. I do. And if I had to pick one to live in, the Star Trek world would be cool as hell. But—"

Cisco waited patiently for him to gather his thoughts and put them into words. Which was good, because Leo had never thought deeply enough about this to figure out the whys, not like the logic Cisco just laid out.

"I think Star Wars just reminds me more of how the world is, you know? And I get why you'd want to live in a different world. But—" He had to stop and arrange his thoughts again. "I guess I like knowing that, even when it's a galaxy's worth of bad shit, there are still people fighting, you know? It's hopeful. I have trouble believing we can ever get to Star Trek's world, even with hundreds of thousands of years to go. But I can believe in people fighting for what's right."

"Wow," Cisco said after a beat. "That's actually a completely valid answer. I still pick Trek, obviously—"

"Obviously."

"—but I can see your point. I guess we can keep being boyfriends."

*Leo had to take a breath, hold it for a count of three, then release it. He almost let it go but, lying there in the dark, Cisco's foot warm where it brushes his, he found courage he didn't know he had.*

*"Are we? Boyfriends?"*

*It was Cisco's turn to pause. "I thought we were. If you don't want—"*

*"I want," Leo interrupted. "Fuck yes, I want. I just—I've never done this before. Not really. Dating or whatever."*

*"Me either," Cisco said. His hand slipped into Leo's. "It's hard, with hockey. But I want to try. With you."*

*Leo's heart was going to explode out of his chest. It ached, but in a good way, like pushing his body to the limit. Like leaving it all on the ice. Like he could lean in, pressing his mouth softly to Cisco's. Just because.*

*"Me too."*

*They fell asleep like that, hands intertwined, breathing each other's air. When Leo woke up, his arm was asleep, contorted at a ridiculous angle to keep holding Cisco's hand.*

*He didn't care.*

SITTING IN THE PENALTY BOX, Leo watches the second period, the puck moving up and down the ice. The Krakens are fighting hard, answering the Abs' single goal with one of their own. At least it's a clean game, as clean as hockey ever is. Sure, there are penalties, accidents happen, but there's no one on the Krakens like West.

He's not disappointed that Cisco is playing sharp and clean, as usual. Of course he's not. That would be ridiculous, when he had extracted a promise from Cisco to stop taking stupid penalties.

Besides, he's always loved watching Cisco play like this.

The way he skates—sometimes Leo thinks he could recognize Cisco from a thousand yards away, just the way he moves.

The idea is ridiculous, of course. Cisco moves like dozens, hundreds of other players. But there's no denying that Leo's eyes are drawn to him whenever he's on the ice, like he's mesmerized. Even if he's pretty sure Totoro is asleep next to him.

"Your boy's looking good," Seth says from the bench next to him.

Leo does his best not to jump guiltily. It's not very successful. "He's not my boy."

Seth raises his eyebrows. "Isn't he?"

"Last time you were in here, you were telling me not to fuck with your team," When Totoro lifts his head, Leo forces himself to moderate his tone. "Which is it, Seth?"

"Oh, I stand by that," Seth says. That mildly unflappable air of his was always annoying as fuck. "But if you're gonna be around, you could at least give the guy some closure. You owe him that much."

And of course Seth times it perfectly so he stops talking bare seconds before his penalty ends. He's on the ice again almost before Leo can open the door for him, let alone react.

But his words linger, repeating over and over until they're all he can think about, until he can almost see them hanging in the air.

He'd originally planned to see Cisco after the game, but by the time the final buzzer sounds, he can't get out of there fast enough. It takes everything he has to walk, not to run like he's being chased.

He knows better than to think he could outrun the words.

By the time he makes it back to his apartment, he has a missed call and three—no, four texts from Cisco. He can't bring himself to open them, to see what they say. Not now.

Totoro woofs softly, low and concerned. Leo goes through the motions of taking him out, grateful when Totoro does his business quickly and efficiently, returning to Leo as soon as possible.

They're barely back inside when the shaking starts. Leo lets Totoro herd him gently over to the couch, bring him the Ativan and a bottle of water, and sprawl over him, a warm, living blanket. He gets his hands in the thick black fur and just...stops.

Of course, he can't stop his brain. At least, not without more permanent measures than—no. He's got just enough willpower to pull himself away from that train of thought. But that means there's nothing to protect him from the storm of words howling inside his head.

Seth. "You owe him that much."

His father. "You can't even pull yourself together enough to try."

His therapist. "You won't be able to put this behind you until you've faced it."

But most of all, always and forever, Cisco.

"I want to try. With you."

"Whatever you want."

"Call me, please, baby,"

"I hope you're okay. That's all I want, you know."

"I love you. Always."

He can remember, bitterly, how happy he had been to hear some of those words. How good they'd felt. In this moment, he hates the version of himself in the past, innocent and unaware of how quickly those soft words could turn into knives.

How much they could make him bleed.

Pressing his face into Totoro's fur, he forces himself to breathe, waiting for the fog to descend.

7

**CISCO**

Cisco isn't panicking.

He's not.

There's no real reason to panic. He and Leo hadn't made definite plans to meet after the game. Leo is his own person. He can leave without seeing Cisco and that's fine.

But it doesn't feel fine.

It feels like draft day, the echoing absence and the pit of uncertainty in his stomach. Like the weeks, the months after, like the texts and voicemails that were never answered.

Like losing Leo all over again.

He should just go home; he's not good company for anyone like this. But the thought of being alone in his apartment, the place where he's already spent so much time missing Leo, is too much to take. So out he goes with the rest of the team, finding a small table in the corner.

What he wants is to slam back shot after shot until he blacks out, until everything is numb and he can't feel. But he's on the downhill slide to thirty, and the thought of the hangover is enough, barely, to have him ordering a single beer. He nurses it slowly, watching his team move around him, but not interacting.

Not, at least, until Mikey sits his ass down with a look on his face that says he's not going anywhere. He rests his cast on the table, like he's daring Cisco to make him move. "¿Que paso?"

Cisco shrugs. He's not getting into this. Not with Mikey, who's still got the new-relationship stars in his eyes. He feels old and bitter enough as it is. No point in actually ruining life for the kids. "Nothing."

"Bullshit," Tolly sits down next to Mikey, leaning into his space way too far for plausible deniability or whatever the fuck they're doing. "You've been weird since that game against the Jackalopes. What gives?"

The silence stretches, echoing even though it's filled with the background chatter of the bar.

"That's okay," Mikey says. "I'll just go ask Lightning. He went to college with you, right? I figure he'll have some ideas."

"Shit." Cisco drains the last of his beer. "Fucking fine. You want to know?"

Most of his anger drains away when he looks at Mikey, open and caring and so, so young. "It was a long time ago," he says, trying to figure out where to begin.

For once, neither of them takes the chance to chirp him about his advanced age. They just sit there, waiting.

"When I played in college, we had this goalie. Leo Carrington. He was good. Starting as a freshman, good. If he'd played a different position, he'd have gone in the first round. If he entered the draft."

"You dated." Mikey makes it a statement rather than a question.

Cisco nods, swallowing around the lump in his throat,

relieved that he doesn't have to spell it out for them. He can't even care about how obvious he's being. "Yeah. It—fuck. It was good. We knew it'd be hard—I always wanted to go pro. But it was worth it. He was worth it."

"Did he want to go pro?" Tolly passes his untouched beer across the table.

"I—" Cisco has to actually stop and think about that one. "I don't know, actually. We talked about it, some. But I don't think it was real to him? And his family—there was a lot of pressure on him. His family were doctors, always. He was pre-med. I honestly don't know how he managed the classes and the games, but he did. He did it all. And then—"

He has to drink down half of Tolly's beer, and his throat still feels like the Arizona desert after.

"I was at the draft, and I tried to contact him, but I couldn't. I got a text from his sister at breakfast. Just said he'd had a breakdown, he was in the hospital."

Mikey inhales, quick and sharp, only letting out the breath when Tolly takes his hand under the table.

"I wanted to go, to be with him but—his dad didn't like me. Wanted someone better, someone ready to be a doctor's spouse. Wouldn't have let me see him, if I'd gone. But I got home, and he was gone. And he didn't answer my texts, or my calls. For weeks. Months. Eventually—I can take a hint, you know."

Tolly's smile looks brittle around the edges. Like he gets it. "So this was, what, thirty years ago?"

"Fuck you." Cisco finishes his beer for that. "It's been awhile, yeah."

"Well, fuck that guy." Mikey looks like an indignant puppy, despite the fact that he's over six feet tall. "You don't deserve to be treated like shit."

Cisco shrugs, just one shoulder up and down. "I mean,

like I said, a lot of pressure. He was adopted, and his dad was always on him. Never mind that pre-med classes are super hard even without playing an NCAA sport. If he got less than a 98 on anything, he'd get a phone call—" He shudders. "He always looked, shit, I don't know how to describe how bad he looked after those."

"Still," Tolly says. "Ghosting you is some seriously rude shit."

"You're not wrong." Cisco wracks his brain, trying to figure out a way to make them understand.

It's not that he wants to defend Leo. Or, well, he does, because that's just his default state, apparently. Protect Leo, defend Leo, lov—care about Leo.

But also, he doesn't know if there's any way that someone who wasn't there could understand. The way Leo would fold in on himself, like he was trying to make himself as small as possible, trying to protect his most vulnerable parts. The way his whole body would shake, but just a little, so you couldn't tell unless you were touching him. Holding him. The way he went somewhere else, in his head, and how scared Cisco was, every time, that maybe this time he wouldn't come back.

Apparently some of that comes out of his mouth, or shows on his face, because Mikey and Tolly are looking at him with identical confused-yet-worried expressions.

"Did his dad beat him or something?" Mikey asks.

"I think—shit, I think beating would have been easier to deal with," Cisco says. "Or maybe he did, but with words. Hell, I don't know. I just know it was bad. And it got worse every time. I was afraid one day it would go too far. I guess it did. And I wasn't there to help."

Tolly reaches across the table, squeezing his shoulder. "It doesn't sound like there was anything you could do."

Cisco shrugs, suddenly exhausted. "We'll never know."

"Wait," Mikey says. "What does this have to do with the Jackalopes game?"

"Leo—he was the attendant. In the sin bin. Has been for all the home games since."

Tolly gets it first, his eyes going wide. "You mean —shit."

"Yeah." Cisco swallows hard, around the lump in his throat. "That was the first time I'd seen him in seven years."

CISCO DOES *his best not to eavesdrop, honestly. Not that there's much to eavesdrop on. Leo's end of the conversation had subsided into one-word answers fifteen minutes ago. Now it was nothing but "yes, sir" and "no, sir" at widely spaced intervals.*

*But he didn't have to be listening to see the effect Leo's father's words were having on him. To see him flinching every so often, in the way that he never did on the ice. Cisco thought, a little wildly, that he could almost see the words flying at him, see them impact.*

*Finally, after an endless forever that only actually took— Cisco checked his phone—twenty minutes, the call ended. Leo set the phone down gently, like he was afraid of what he might do with it, and collapsed back onto Cisco's bed, folding in on himself.*

*Cisco hesitated for a moment. They haven't been boyfriends—he still wanted to smile every time he thought it, even now—for very long. He wasn't sure if he was welcome here, or if his presence would just make things worse.*

*But he couldn't see Leo like this and not try to help. If that was a problem—hell, he didn't want to think about the possible consequences if it was a problem. But better to find out now. When they could deal with it.*

*He didn't realize until he sat down on the bed, but Leo was shaking, tiny shudders running through his body. Reacting instinctively, Cisco put a hand carefully on his back.*

*Leo's breath was coming in fast, frantic pants, his heart beating so hard that Cisco could feel it against his palm. That couldn't be good for him.*

*"Is this okay?" Cisco asked quietly.*

*He got a jerky nod, so small he would have missed it if he wasn't watching, but no other response. Keeping his hand where it was, he pulled out his phone with the other one and searched "helping someone having a panic attack."*

*Of course, the results are a mixed bag. Cisco was terrified to make things worse, but like hell was he leaving Leo alone when he was like this. He had to try something.*

*"Can you come here?" He did his best to keep his voice low and soothing. It took a few seconds, but he finally got another nod.*

*Working together, they managed to get Leo onto Cisco's lap. He burrowed in once he was there, his hands clutching at Cisco's shirt, body still shaking.*

*"Can you try and breathe with me?" Cisco asked. He took as deep a breath as he could, held it for a second, then let it out. It felt dumb, but after a few repeats, he felt Leo try to follow him.*

*He had no idea how long it took, but eventually Leo was limp in his arms, his breathing slow and regular. Maybe he was asleep? Cisco kind of hoped he was asleep.*

*"I'm sorry," Leo said. The words interrupt Cisco trying to figure out the best way to get them horizontal so Leo could sleep.*

*"Hey, no." Cisco stroked a hand down his back. "You've got nothing to be sorry for."*

*Leo snorted, air puffing hot against Cisco's chest. "I can't even handle a phone call with my dad without completely collapsing like a baby. I think that deserves at least a little apology."*

*Cisco kissed his hair. "You don't owe me anything, baby. Is there anything I can do for you?"*

*"I—" Leo sighed. "I don't think so. I just want to sleep forever. Can we do that?"*

*"Practice in the morning, but I think we can manage a solid ten hours between now and then."*

*Leo made a half-hearted attempt to get free. "I was joking, Cisco. I'm fine. Really."*

*"Maybe I want a nap." Cisco rolled them over, barely managing to keep hold of Leo despite his greater height. "Maybe I want to cuddle with my boyfriend. Can we?"*

*"Yeah, okay," Leo muttered.*

*It was a lot easier to get them under the covers when Leo wasn't fighting him. But it took Cisco a long time to fall asleep. And when he woke up from a fitful, restless nap filled with dreams of shadowy figures chasing Leo—well, it didn't take a therapist to figure out what that's about.*

*But Leo was there, safe in his arms, his face finally back to something like it's usual calm, breathing slow and even in his sleep.*

*When he woke, too, he gave Cisco a sleepy smile, but he didn't talk about it. Cisco kept waiting, wanting to let him bring it up at his own pace. But minutes turned into hours turned into days, and they still didn't talk about it.*

*The next time Leo's dad called, it happened again.*

*They didn't talk about it.*

⅄

"Hey."

Cisco looks up at Seth's nudge. "What?"

Seth nods across the ice. "Your boy's back."

Cisco follows his gaze to the penalty box where Leo is settling in and has to lock his knees temporarily against the rush of relief.

By the time he's gotten himself together enough to realize what Seth had said, he's already all the way at the other side of the rink, doing lazy passing drills with Tolly. Too far away for Cisco to protest, even if he was willing to dredge up that can of worms in front of Tolly, to risk re-opening the conversation from the other night.

Even if he meant the protest. If he could look Seth in the eye and say "Not my boy anymore" and mean it...

Well.

He makes it through the rest of warmups and the pre-game show with one eye on the box, like Leo might disappear again if he stops looking. It feels true, possible, sick and heavy in his gut. Like Leo is some kind of Fae creature. Like he has to hold onto him at all costs.

But that didn't work the last time he tried it.

When he goes over the boards for his first shift against the Centaurs, he does his best to put it aside, to focus. Or he thinks he does. He honestly can't tell if his stick getting tangled up in Dendridge's skates is an accident, if he was just a bit too slow to pull it back in time, or if he did it on purpose. Either way the result is the same, though. Another two-minute minor that he can't regret entirely. Not when it gives him this chance.

"What the hell was that?" Leo asks before he's even all the way in the box. Next to him, Totoro looks almost amused.

"Nice to see you too." Cisco barely manages to stop the endearment that tries to attach itself to the end of that sentence. But he doesn't get to do that, not anymore. "And it was an accident. You've heard of them?"

Leo eyes him narrowly. "The refs didn't seem to think so."

Cisco shrugs.

"You've got to stop this, Cisco. " Despite his scolding, Leo is already handing him a towel.

"Hey, I can't control what the refs do."

Leo rolls his eyes, a gesture so familiar that Cisco can't even begin to stop the wave of remembered affection warming his chest. "I know that, idiot. But we've talked about this. You don't have to take bullshit penalties just to talk to me."

"Have dinner with me. After the game." Cisco regrets the words as soon as they're out, but he can't take them back, so he forges on. "To talk. Since I don't have to take bullshit penalties for that."

"If," Leo brandishes a finger at him "you can go the rest of the game without a bullshit penalty—"

Cisco frowns. "Who decides what's a bullshit penalty?"

"I do." Leo says. The firmness of his tone absolutely doesn't send a shiver of remembrance down Cisco's spine. "If you can make it the rest of the game without one, I'll go to dinner with you."

"And if I can't?"

Leo grins at him. For a second, it's like no time at all has passed, like they're standing in the 3M center, their whole lives ahead of them. Together.

But the moment passes, as they all do.

"If you can't." Leo leans in close, as if they could be overheard above the noise of the game and the crowd. "Then you can text me."

Cisco's two minutes end before he can formulate a reply to that. But he finds himself smiling as he skates away, anyway.

The rest of the first period seems to drag by. It feels

strange to be so hyperaware of his play, even though he knows intellectually that not taking penalties used to be normal for him. He misses an easy pass from Angel, finds himself slammed into the boards by Merkowitz, who steals the puck and goes on a breakaway with it. CC stops it cold, thank fuck, but it's still a sobering moment.

"Reyes! Get your head in the game!" Coach Jackson barks as he comes back to the bench, her face like a thundercloud.

"Yes, ma'am."

When he blinks the sweat out of his eyes, he can see Leo's raised eyebrows from all the way across the ice. He makes his answering shrug as broad and obvious as possible, and then does his best to put Leo out of his head for the rest of the game.

It's a mixed bag, but he at least manages to pull it together enough not to get singled out for another dressing down. As soon as the final buzzer sounds, cementing the Abs' 3-1 win, he's on his feet and heading for the tunnel.

He doesn't even bother to take off his skates before getting his phone out, pulling up his text conversation with Leo. ***Dinner? Just tell me where.***

The smart choice here would be to put the phone away and get cleaned up before checking again. He's about to do that, his thumb reaching for the lock button, when the reply pops up on his screen. ***not sure how far you want to go from the arena***

His first impulse is to say that it doesn't matter, but then he thinks about how terrible it would be if they were constantly interrupted by fans wanting a picture, an autograph. He doesn't get that shit as much as the forwards, but it still happens. Especially on a game night. ***further is probably better, unless you want a lot of interruptions***

The little dots dance on the screen as he waits for Leo's response, ignoring the clamor around him.

***not really,*** is the answer he finally gets. ***how do you feel about a diner***

***sounds good***, he sends back, only because common sense tells him that "I don't care as long as you're there" is too much. Too soon.

Also not true, because he does need to eat. But Leo knows that as well as he does.

***text me the address***, he sends, then resolutely puts his phone away to start stripping out of his gear.

All through shedding his gear, he tells himself it's just dinner, it doesn't mean anything. But he can't seem to get rid of the bubble of hope in his chest, can't seem to stop himself from scrubbing down extra thoroughly in the shower.

He takes the time to do more than just run his fingers through his hair afterward, re-dresses in his game day suit instead of a t-shirt and sweats before allowing himself to check his phone.

Leo has sent him an address, one that will only take about twenty minutes to get to, according to his phone.

"Everything okay?" Tolly asks quietly.

Cisco's head snaps up. The locker room has mostly cleared out—he has a vague memory of brushing off the players who were planning to go out with some kind of bullshit excuse. "Yeah." He tries, but he can't quite contain his tiny smile as he puts his phone away. "Everything's good."

Tolly studies him for a minute longer, then nods. "Well, if it ever isn't, you know where to find us."

"Yeah, yeah." Cisco ruffles Tolly's still-wet hair. "Get out of here, quit keeping your boy waiting."

If he needed any confirmation of what was going on

between Tolly and Mikey, the flush on Tolly's cheeks would have been enough. But that's not exactly a problem, and anyway, Cisco has other things on his mind right now.

He gathers his things, sends Leo a confirming text, and heads for his car with a smile he can't quite shake.

8

───

## LEO

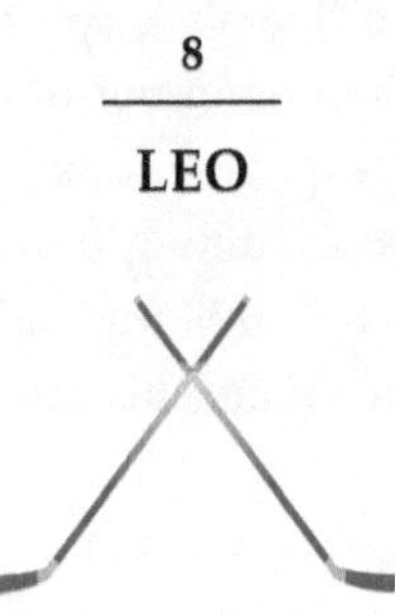

I t doesn't take long for Leo to realize this was a mistake. The bitch of it is, he doesn't really care.

He really had tried, though. He'd picked the diner in part because it was the least potentially romantic situation of the available restaurants. Bright lighting instead of low candlelight or dim shaded fixtures, vinyl booths instead of small, intimate tables. And they were less likely, in his experience, to make a stink about Totoro than fancier places. Besides, he remembers how much they had to eat in college, and Cisco's in the CHL now. He needs a place where he can order as much food as possible, not some trendy miniature portions place.

Leo settles into the booth to wait, Totoro tucked out of the way under the table, confident in his choice. But not confident enough to keep the butterflies from settling into the pit of his stomach. Once he's exhausted the distraction possibilities in the menu—he isn't playing hockey any longer, so one entree will be enough—he pulls his phone out, opening up a mindless game for distraction.

He still jumps every time the little bell over the door jingles, though.

Thankfully, Cisco doesn't keep him waiting long. The third jingle is him, coming in out of the Alberta winter all red-cheeked in his expensive-looking leather coat, eyes scanning the half-empty dining room. His face lights up when he spots Leo, his smile just as sweet as when they were in college, even though his face has changed, leaner and sharper.

He gives a dorky little wave, his face flushing darker as he starts toward the booth. The diner isn't nearly big enough to let Leo brace himself as Cisco crosses the space between them—let's be real, probably the entire continent of North America wouldn't be big enough for that.

All too soon, Cisco is sliding into the other side of the booth, their knees bumping under the table in a way that shouldn't be familiar but is. "Hey. I'm not supposed to pet Totoro while he's working, right?"

Leo doesn't know why he's surprised by that. "Right. Maybe when we leave."

"Okay. This place looks great." He's unwinding his scarf, giving Leo a little respite from having to make eye contact, taking off his coat and suit jacket. "Like that one by campus, remember?"

"Jack's, yeah." Leo clears his throat even though he doesn't need to, pushes his menu across the table to give him something to do with his hands. "I guess? It doesn't look like it."

"Nah, but there's more than looks," Cisco says. "It feels like Jack's, a little. I hope the food is good; I'm starving. Do you know what you're getting?"

"I was going to try the mac and cheese."

Cisco's eyes go soft and warm. "You had that on our first date. Remember?"

"Yeah." Leo has to reach for his glass of water and take a drink, swallowing hard around the lump in his throat. "Yeah, I remember."

"I was so embarrassed," Cisco admits. "Taking you to to Bridgeview like we hadn't eaten there a thousand times. But I didn't want to wait to ask you out until I got paid."

Even though Cisco's face has lost that last little bit of softness it used to have, Leo can't handle the feeling of deja vu that washes over him. It's not that he doubted this was, well, not "his" Cisco anymore, but the same one. But like this, with their legs brushing together under the table, with Cisco smiling across at him, achingly earnest and open, it's almost like no time has passed.

Thankfully the waitress comes to take their orders before he does something stupid. Well. Stupider than agreeing to this dinner. Which, in the grand scheme of self-preservation, is far from the smartest choice he's ever made.

Ordering is only a brief respite, though. All too soon the waitress is whisking their menus away, leaving them alone in a silence that practically screams from the weight on it.

"What are we doing here?" Leo's mouth moves without his conscious input. The words are out there, impossible to take back, so he forges ahead. "Are we—are we just catching up?"

"Is that what you want?"

He drops his eyes away from Cisco's face, down to where his hands are shredding the straw wrapper into tiny pieces of confetti. When he finally finds his voice, the words come out in a whisper "I don't know. I don't know why you even want to see me, after the way I treated you."

At least Cisco doesn't pretend not to know what he's talking about. "We don't have to do this. If you—we can make small talk and eat our food and then go home. If that's what you want. I'm not trying to pressure you into something. I just—"

The silence that falls then is even heavier than before, so thick Leo thinks he can feel it in his lungs, choking him. He can't bring himself to look up at Cisco, even though it stretches on and on, endless seconds between his heartbeats.

"I just miss you." Cisco's words are more breath than sound, barely audible above the background murmur of conversations around them.

Leo nods. He can look at Cisco's hands, the cuffs of his dress shirt over his surprisingly delicate-looking wrists. He can follow the line of his arms up to his chest, to his throat under the loosened collar of his shirt. He can see his Adam's apple bob in his throat, the stubble shadowing his jaw, the plush curve of his mouth under the strong line of his nose.

"I miss you, too," he admits.

Cisco reaches for his hand. Slowly, telegraphing his movements, giving Leo time to pull away. Like he'd want to. "I'm here now. Tell me about human resources."

That startles a laugh out of Leo, tricks him into actually meeting Cisco's eyes. "Really? You want me to tell you about hiring procedures and pensions and 401ks?"

"If it means you're talking to me." Cisco's eyes are steady on his. "Tell me about taking your dog for walks, or your grocery list. I don't care. Just talk to me. Please."

Maybe it's the echo of Cisco's increasingly desperate messages, the ones Leo listened to over and over when he should have deleted them, trying to work up the nerve to call. Maybe it's a masochistic desire to drive him away. Or maybe it's just that these words have been building up for seven years, waiting for an outlet. Whatever the reason,

Leo grounds himself with Totoro's solid presence, looking at their joined hands and saying, "I didn't try to kill myself. Back then."

Cisco lets out a quiet, shaky breath. "Okay. Good. That's—good."

"I figured you probably thought I did." Leo peeks at Cisco's face, but he can't interpret the mixture of expressions there. Some part of him mourns it, missing the way he used to be able to read Cisco like a book, but most of him is busy pushing forward, trying to get the words out before they dry up. "It was bad, but—it wasn't that. I—I started seeing things. Hearing things. I thought I was handling it, but it got so bad—I couldn't sleep. I finally checked myself into the hospital."

The movement of Cisco's free hand, reaching for him and getting halfway across the table before pulling back, is achingly familiar and foreign at the same time. "I'm so sorry."

And that's so unexpected that Leo finds himself blinking, trying to process the words in any way that makes sense. "What do you have to be sorry about?"

"So much." Cisco squeezes his eyes closed. His face is doing something that makes Leo's heart ache in his chest. "I didn't know. I knew you had anxiety, I knew it got bad sometimes, but I thought it was just your dad. I never should have left you."

"Yes you fucking should have." Leo forces himself to lower his voice again, hoping no one noticed the little spike in volume, setting a reassuring hand on Totoro's head where he'd lifted it. "It was the draft, Cisco. You couldn't miss that."

Cisco's jaw sets, a familiar, stubborn line. "I could have. I would have."

"I'm glad you didn't." Leo lifts a hand when Cisco

opens his mouth again. "I—look, I know it's a dick move to drop this on you and then cut it off, but I just really need to not have this argument right now. I'm just sorry for ghosting you, after. By the time I was ready to talk, it had been so long, I just—I was scared."

"Scared of what?" Cisco asks after a moment.

Leo lets out his breath. "That you wouldn't want to talk to me. Or that you would. I was—it was hard. Right now, I'm probably the closest to the Leo you knew that I've been since then. But I'm not the same."

"I'm not either," Cisco says. His hand stays exactly where it is, warm and comforting, wrapped around Leo's. "I'm pretty sure no one is the same person they were seven years ago."

"Yeah. I just—I don't know if I'm a person you want to know anymore. I was too scared to find out, before."

Cisco takes a minute, doesn't rush into platitudes or instant protests Leo won't believe. It used to be one of his favorite things, he remembers. The way Cisco always considered, never took what he said at face value.

"Maybe you aren't," he says finally. "But there's only one way to find out."

"Yeah." Leo feels shaky all over, like his blood sugar dropped too low and he mainlined four shots of espresso, like he just worked out on an empty stomach. But the hope blooming in his chest can't be denied He wants this. Maybe he's never stopped wanting it, wanting Cisco. "Okay."

"So," Cisco says. He reaches for his water, his other hand still holding Leo's. "Tell me about your dog."

The laughter that bursts out of Leo's chest might be just slightly hysterical, but it feels good. Like Cisco's hand on his, like Cisco's answering smile.

He feels good

*"How are you feeling today, Leo?"*

*Leo lifted one shoulder and let it fall, the least possible movement that could count as a response.*

*Dr. Liu made some kind of note on the paper in front of her. "Are you still experiencing the hallucinations?"*

*He shook his head. That was the only good thing about this experience. The voices, the things on the edge of his vision, they'd disappeared with the medication.*

*"Excellent. That's a good first step. Have the physical symptoms disappeared as well?"*

*That—was trickier to answer. He let another shrug suffice.*

*"Leo." He could hear the unvoiced sigh in her voice, the one she wouldn't let out because it wasn't professional. Little did she know Leo was an expert at telling when he'd disappointed someone. "You don't have to talk to me. But the medication is only treating the symptoms. It's not going to get to the root of your anxiety. I'd like to help you, so you have a start on getting your life back."*

*That startled a bitter laugh out of him. "Going to patch me up and send me back to Daddy?"*

*"You're an adult, Leo," she said. "Your father isn't in charge here."*

*"He's paying." Leo turned his eyes back out the window. It was cloudy today, thin, wispy gray things that dimmed the sky to a dreary blur. "Pretty sure that puts him in charge. How long did he give you to 'get me back on track'?"*

*"You believe your father doesn't care about you unless you're 'on track?'"*

*Another laugh. This one felt like it ripped its way out of his throat, left him bleeding. "He adopted me from China because he thought he could shape me into the son he wanted.*

*A grateful orphan to carry on the Carrington legacy, another Dr. Carrington to bring glory to the name."*

*He regretted the outburst instantly when her head tilted slightly to the side. Damn her and her leading questions, making him expose his vulnerabilities.*

*"Your sister was also adopted, was she not?"*

*"Hedging his bets," Leo said. Why the fuck not? He'd already started talking. Maybe if she understood how massively fucked up he was she'd finally back off and stop trying to fix him. "Why settle for one exceptional child when you can have the matched set?"*

*Dr. Bao made a humming noise under her breath, her pen scratching across the paper. "What about you, Leo? What do you want?"*

*He meant to make a flippant answer, something about a hot bath and a glass of wine. But when he opened his mouth, somehow the truth came tumbling out. "Rest. I'm going to break, I can feel it. I keep stretching and stretching, and eventually I'm not going to stretch any further."*

*He closed his mouth with a snap and refused to speak for the rest of the session, terrified that his last secret would shine through his eyes, would fall off his tongue. No matter what she said, some of this was going to get back to his father. Maybe not from her, but Carrington money could do whatever his father willed it to. He'd lost count of the ways it had shaped his life, seeping into every corner until everything was stained with it.*

*Everything except Cisco.*

⤬

*"*—AND THEN—OH, SHIT."

Leo follows Cisco's gaze to where their waitress is

pointedly wiping down the table next to them. "What time is it?"

He pulls his phone out to check it, reluctantly letting go of Cisco's hand as he does the same. The digital display reads seven minutes after midnight, the closing time posted on the diner door.

"Wow, I did not realize it was that late," Cisco says. Tucking his phone back in his pocket, he pulls out his wallet, leaving two twenties on the table.

"Are you seriously tipping more than our whole dinner cost?" Leo shrugs into his coat, trying not to drag it out. Guilt over keeping the diner staff here wars with his reluctance to leave, to step out of this moment and back into reality. He's still not entirely sure this isn't a dream. Part of him expects to wake up in his bed with Totoro taking up most of the space as usual.

Cisco slips out of the booth before putting his coat back on and looping the scarf around his neck, all while following Leo out the door. "It's not like I can't afford it. Besides, it's the least I can do after tying up the table for hours. And they were super cool about Totoro."

Leo pauses outside the door, trying to figure out how to handle the inevitable awkwardness of parting, and also if Totoro can wait to take care of his business until they get home.

"Walk you to your car?" Cisco asks.

"Uh, sure. It's over here?"

They fall into step easily, naturally, as they make their way toward Leo's boring gray sedan. He shoves down the feeling of embarrassment. The sedan is a practical, responsible choice for someone with his salary and lifestyle. It's in good shape, even if it isn't the most expensive option on the market. There's nothing to be embarrassed about.

It just seems so boring, compared to whatever ridiculous sports car Cisco probably drives.

"What are you thinking?" Cisco asks.

Leo stops next to his car door, debating how much of the truth to tell. "Wondering what kind of car you drive."

"Some kind of SUV? I don't know. I just wanted something that wouldn't get stuck in the snow."

The answer is so Cisco that Leo can't help but laugh. "Of course you did."

"Hey, we can't all be from Boston." Cisco bumps their shoulders together gently, grinning. "Some of us didn't grow up with the gross white stuff."

"You say that like I don't remember you dragging me out into the first snow every winter." Leo turns to face him and oh, this was a mistake. Standing close enough to feel the warm cloud of Cisco's breath against his skin, to remember the way their height difference disappeared when they both leaned in—

The moment seems to last forever, like time slows down just for them. Leo has plenty of time to think about what a bad idea this is, how he shouldn't be doing this. But Cisco is right there, looking even better than his most rose-tinted dreams, and Leo *wants*.

He's not sure which of them moves first. It was probably him, but it seems like they both come together seamlessly, as in-sync as they ever were. They lean in, lips meeting, Leo's hands landing on Cisco's shoulders while Cisco pulls him in closer with a gentle grip on his waist.

And then he can't think rationally in words and sentences anymore. It's familiar, but not. It's warm and soft and echoes with a hundred, a thousand memories, rising up so fast he thinks he might drown in them.

He wants more. He needs more.

Licking into Cisco's mouth is more of the familiar-strange, and so is pulling Cisco in close, until there's no space between their bodies. It feels good, right, in a way Leo hasn't felt in a long time. Maybe years.

It's a near thing, but he manages to control his whimper when Cisco breaks the kiss. All he can think is *more*. More of this, more of Cisco, more of them.

He'd forgotten what it was like to be a them.

He's opening his mouth to say something, anything, to invite Cisco back with him—

—and Cisco steps back, cold air rushing in where he'd been warm against Leo's body.

"Thanks for dinner," he says. His voice is soft, but something in it dries up the words in Leo's throat. "I'd like to do it again sometime. If you want."

All Leo can do is nod dumbly. That's the least of what he wants, but it's more than he ever thought he'd get.

And then Cisco is gone, and there's nothing left to do but drive home, pretending he isn't carrying a Cisco-shaped empty space with him.

## 9

## CISCO

"What's got you smiling like that?"

Cisco does his best not to jump as Angel steps up onto the treadmill next to him. Based on Angel's smirk, he didn't do a very good job. "Nothing. Just looking at dog videos."

Angel shakes his head and starts hitting buttons on the treadmill. "No, I don't think so, Sunshine. That's not a dog video smile."

"How the fuck do you know?" Cisco locks his phone and sets it on the little shelf on top of the treadmill, starting up his own program. "Have you been watching my smiles? Do I need to apologize to Breanna for stealing her man?"

"I think Bree would be cool with you joining in, if you're finally acknowledging our irresistible chemistry." Angel bats his eyelashes obnoxiously.

Clearly the only choice is to smack him with the sweaty towel hanging over the treadmill railing.

"Gross," Angel sputters, batting it away. "I take it back,

buddy. No threesomes for you. But seriously. Who are you talking to?"

Cisco bites his lip. A part of him, a big part, wants to talk to Angel about it. But he's kept Leo secret for so long, safely inside where no one can see, that he's not quite sure how to start.

Thankfully Angel can read him as well here as on the ice. Or maybe Cisco is just that obvious. Whatever it is, the way Angel says "Is this about that guy? The one from college?" gives him the opening he needs.

"Yeah. We've been texting. Probably too much. And we had dinner the other night, after the game."

"So that's where you disappeared to." Angel breaks into a jog as the treadmill speeds up, not even breathing hard yet, smiling because he's one of those assholes who actually likes cardio. "That's good. Right?"

Cisco shrugs, starting his own jog. "I think? I don't know, man. It's not weird, and that's weird, you know?"

"You don't make any sense," Angel says. "But yeah, I know. What makes you say you're texting too much?"

"He has a real job." Cisco forces himself to breathe evenly, to pace himself. "He probably doesn't have time to be texting me like this. I should probably stop."

Angel snorts. "He's a grown-ass man. If he doesn't want to talk to you, he can tell you so. Or he can ignore your texts."

"I don't know. I'm trying to give him space. Not to rush."

"You've been waiting on him for seven years, you said." Angel shakes his head. "That's not exactly rushing, bro."

Cisco blows out a huge breath, thankful he can blame it on the treadmill. "Yeah, but I don't know how much of his problem before was me pressuring him. I kept talking like we'd play hockey together forever. I'm just like his asshole dad."

Somehow, Angel finds the coordination to smack him, hard, while continuing to run. "That's bullshit, and you know it. Like I said, he's a grown-ass man. I don't know the whole story of what happened, and it's not my business. But if you think he's worth it, if he's gonna be worth it for you, he needs to be able to tell you when it's too much."

"Fuck." Cisco devotes his breath to running for a few minutes. "This shit is hard."

"Amen." Angel looks disgustingly put-together, like he's taking a nice stroll along a country road. "Good thing I've got Bree to keep me straight. Is your boy gonna do that for you?"

Cisco laughs so hard he snorts, even though he doesn't really have the air for it. "No, I think that ship has sailed, bro."

Angel rolls his eyes. "Whatever. You know what I mean. Don't dodge the question. Is he good for you?"

The question stuns Cisco into silence for a few minutes. He knows what he wants to say, but— "I don't know. He used to be."

"Well, then. You should find out."

Cisco blows a raspberry. "You're not my real dad."

"Yeah, yeah. Search your feelings, young padawan. You know it to be true." Angel picks up the pace, humming something that it takes Cisco a minute to recognize.

When he does, he strongly considers retrieving his towel just so he can throw it at his asshole d-partner again. "Stop it."

"Lets," Angel croons. "Let's stay together. Lovin' you whetherrrrr—"

"Oh my God I hate you." Cisco jams his earbuds in

and turns up the music on his phone, doing his best to ignore Angel in the background.

He is definitely not smiling as he finishes his run.

CISCO WASN'T PLANNING on taking any penalties. Okay, so no one is ever technically planning on taking penalties, per se. Unless you're that douchebag from the Jackalopes—yes, he knows the guy's name, no, he's not going to use it, even in his head. It's a personal choice. But anyway, he wasn't planning on it.

But some idiot rookie decided that being the smallest guy on the team—which still doesn't mean small, exactly—meant Suzie was a good target. And maybe they're not teaching rookies how to make clean hits anymore, or maybe the guy slipped. Cisco doesn't much care about the reason. He cares that Suzie had to go through concussion protocol in the first five minutes of the fucking game. And that the kid only got a two-minute minor for what was obviously a bad hit.

So yes, maybe he boards the rookie a little harder than strictly necessary. Sue him.

It doesn't occur to him that this might have unexpected consequences until he enters the penalty box to be met with Leo's disapproving face. Even Totoro looks disappointed.

"You promised!"

"I promised no more stupid penalties," Cisco protests. "That wasn't stupid, it was necessary. Did you see how he hit Suzie?"

Leo sighs. "That was pretty bullshit."

"Exactly." Cisco rubs the towel over his hair. "You can't

let rookies think they're getting away with that shit. Builds bad habits."

"You're not his dad," Leo says.

Cisco laughs. "No, thank fuck. Maybe if his dad had taught him some manners he wouldn't be shaping up like the second coming of that douchebag from the Jackalopes. Also, you look nice today."

Leo stops with his mouth open, forgetting whatever he'd been about to say. "I—what?"

"I mean, you always look nice," Cisco corrects himself. "But that's a nice sweater. It looks soft."

"It is." Leo looks down at it, then back up at Cisco. "Warm, too."

Cisco nods. "Good. You're not working up a sweat, you need something to keep you warm."

Whatever else Leo might have said was cut off by the buzzer.

"Back to work." Cisco buckles his helmet back on. "I'll see you later?"

"Yeah." Leo still sounds a little off-balance, but there's no hesitation in his answer.

Cisco barely resists the urge to blow him a kiss as he skates away.

*"ARE YOU FUCKING BLIND?" Cisco yelled at the linesman.*

*"Watch it, unless you want to sit the game out," the man replied, skating away.*

*Still fuming, Cisco skated over to where Leo is brushing himself off. "You okay?" Biting off the endearment was hard, but they'd both agreed; keeping their relationship off the ice was the right call. Besides, he didn't want to let BU know they could get to him through Leo, or vice versa. Probably. No, definitely. Leo was pretty calm, but Cisco wouldn't bet against him in a fight.*

*The mental image of Leo throwing a punch in his goalie gear helped dissipate the last of his anger. Well, that and the smile Leo gave him.*

*"Yeah, I'm fine. I get worse during shootout practice."*

*"That was classic goalie interference," Cisco grumbled. "The refs are fucking blind."*

*Leo hip-checked him. "Then you'll have to work extra hard so we can beat them, won't you?"*

*Cisco had never wanted to kiss anyone this much in his life.*

*He settled for a hip-check in return, skating off to take his position. He was determined to focus on the game--*

*Until one of BU's d-men came in behind Leo, plowing into him like they were playing football, not hockey. The hit swept him out of the crease, opening the way for the BU winger to score on the suddenly empty net.*

*The refs had to call that one, thank fuck, but Cisco was seeing red. It didn't matter that Coach Davis pulled his line back to the bench. This anger was cold, slow-burning.*

*He could wait.*

*He finally got his chance near the end of the second. The d-man who'd hit Leo was, poetically, just as blindsided when Cisco ran him into the boards.*

*"Hands off the fucking goalie," he muttered before backing off.*

*Every minute of the penalty was worth it. Especially when Seth managed to score a short-handed goal right before Cisco got out of the box.*

CISCO PULLS into the parking space Leo indicates and

puts the car in park. His hand is halfway to the ignition button—still so weird, having a button and not a key—before he second-guesses himself, stopping with his hand in mid-air. Is it presumptuous to turn off the car? Should he just smile and say good night? Are they good enough that he can ask for a hug, or should he just lean in for one?

Still lost in all of these questions, he turns to Leo, still not sure what he's going to say, and finds their faces only inches apart. Even with that much warning, even after the other night at the diner, the kiss takes him by surprise.

Thankfully his instincts take over, responding for him until his brain has time to catch up with what's happening. Not that it's much good for anything other than the brain equivalent of running in circles repeating *Leo!* and *kissing!* in varying tones.

But kissing Leo is muscle memory, even after so long not doing it, like skating or hockey drills or brushing his teeth. His body can do it without his conscious input, hands coming up to gently cradle Leo's head, letting Leo's lips coax his apart, savoring the familiar-but-strange taste of Leo's tongue in his mouth.

They need to talk about this, he knows they do. But when Leo breaks the kiss and murmurs "Come inside?"

There's no possible universe where Cisco would say no to that.

"Yeah." He can't resist leaning in for another kiss, another taste. Just to be sure he isn't dreaming, isn't making this up.

Part of him would be happy to stay here forever, just kissing Leo, sharing each other's breath. But with the car turned off, the cold outside is creeping in through the windows, enough that he's starting to feel it even through his coat. He pulls back reluctantly, savoring the chance to look at Leo like this. Like he'd never expected to see him again, soft and flushed and just-kissed.

"Still want to go inside?"

Leo nods, biting at his lower lip where it's wet and red from Cisco's mouth. "Yeah. If you—"

Cisco takes his hand. "I want."

He kind of hates that they have to separate to leave the car, but as soon as he's locked the doors, Leo is taking his hand again, holding Totoro's leash in the other. Cisco follows willingly, up a flight of stairs, still holding Leo's hand as he uses his other to unlock the door.

The door closes behind them and Leo reaches for him —only to be interrupted by a pointed whuffing noise from Totoro.

"He's probably hungry. Just give me a sec. Totoro, release." Leo takes his coat off and heads into the kitchen area.

The change in demeanor is instant. Instead of the alert, reserved dog Cisco's gotten used to seeing as Leo's shadow, Totoro all but prances in Cisco's direction, tongue lolling out, looking even larger than usual compared to the relatively small scale of Leo's apartment.

"He's huge." After removing his own coat, Cisco holds his hand out to be sniffed. "How did you get the apartment to let you have him?"

"These are the most dog-friendly apartments I could find." Leo says. "And I had several letters from my therapist."

Totoro licks Cisco's hand after a few inquiring sniffs, then, at the first sound of food rattling into a bowl, bounds toward the kitchen.

"Where were we?" Leo strokes a hand over Totoro's head and walks back toward Cisco, his eyes hot and intent on his face.

Cisco swallows hard, cursing himself for the words that are about to come out of his mouth. "Are you—are you sure?"

"I'm sure." Leo takes another step toward him. "I've been sure, Cisco. This isn't like some one-night stand with someone I met at a bar. I know you. You know me."

"Okay," Cisco says. Part of him, the petty, still-hurting part, wants to argue, wants to say that maybe they did know each other. Wants to point out all the years when they didn't. But even as he thinks the words, he knows they aren't true.

And anyway, he's not about to be stupid enough to talk himself out of this, out of the thing he's wanted and imagined for years. Out of Leo leading him through a doorway and into a bedroom, pushing him against the door and kissing him breathless.

The echo of their first time together makes him ache, so he shoves the memory to the back of his mind and focuses on the now. On Leo's mouth, hot and hungry as it devours his, nibbling at his lower lip, kissing down his jaw when they have to part for breath. Leo's hands, shoving his coat off and tugging impatiently at the knot of his tie, warm through the fabric of his shirt. Leo's body against his, familiar and yet not all at once.

Once Cisco shakes himself free from the paralysis of memory, he tries to reach for Leo, but Leo bats his hands away, pushing them back down to his sides.

"Let me." He unbuttons Cisco's top button, then another, his fingertips brushing skin every time. "Just—let me, okay?"

"Okay," Cisco murmurs. He presses his palms against the door behind him, grateful for the support. He's almost dizzy with want, with longing and something that used to be love.

If he reaches for Leo again, his hands will shake. So he stands there while Leo undoes one button at a time, pulling his shirttails free of his slacks, then running his hands up under the sides of his shirt, spreading the fabric wide and touching seemingly every inch of Cisco's chest and stomach.

Cisco does his best to remember how to breathe when Leo unbuttons his cuffs and pushes his shirt off his shoulders and down his arms, letting it fall to the ground. He doesn't want to push Leo, or make him uncomfortable, but this is all so dream-like—he wants to know it's real. So he reaches out, lets his hands fall on Leo's waist, on the sweater that is just as soft as it looks. "Can I?"

He waits for Leo's nod before sliding his hands up under the fabric to find skin. Part of him wants to draw it out, to make Leo wait and shiver and want like he does. But the rest of him, most of him, is suddenly desperate for the feeling of skin on skin, of their bodies pressed together.

So he doesn't linger over it, but he does allow himself to touch, to flatten his palms against Leo's stomach and slide them upward, to brush over Leo's nipples just to see if they're as sensitive as he remembers. Smiling at the shiver that runs through Leo's body, he gets the sweater up over his head and tosses it aside, pulling Leo back in almost in the same motion.

Kissing Leo always took his breath away, and this is no exception. Cisco loses himself in it, the perfect heat of Leo's skin against his, mouth on mouth, their hands moving slowly at first, then gaining confidence.

He's hard, but that's just a dim thing in the corner of his awareness. Every sense is filled with Leo. The familiar sound he makes when Cisco's hands slide up his back, the taste of his lips, his tongue, his skin, the scent of aftershave and sweat and sex radiating off of him.

Cisco is embarrassingly certain he could come like this, making out against the door like a couple of teenagers. But as much as certain parts of his body are willing, he isn't a teenager any longer. A fact that is made annoyingly obvious by the way his shoulder decides to complain just as things are getting good.

He forces himself to pull back enough to speak. Which doesn't have to be that far, when you come right down to it. "Bed?" His lips brush against Leo's skin when he speaks, eliciting a gratifying noise.

"Yeah." Leo shivers a little under his hands. "Yeah, we should—c'mon."

Getting to the bed is an interesting challenge, seeing as neither of them are interested in letting go, but somehow they make it without injury. Leo reaches for Cisco's belt as they stand at the side of his bed, still more interested in getting him naked than the reverse. At least this time he lets Cisco return the favor without protest.

A small part of Cisco wants to take his time, to catalog the differences between Leo-then and Leo-now, to find every one of them with his hands and his mouth. But then Leo pushes him down on the bed and climbs on top of him, and in the throes of a full-body kiss, that seems like something that can wait.

"Wanna fuck you," Leo breathes. "Can I?"

Cisco blinks, marshaling his few active brain cells to parse that sentence. When he finally manages it, the last bits of blood in his brain head directly for his cock, so all he can do is nod silently.

Thankfully something in his face, or maybe the way he's gripping Leo's hips, conveys his absolute sincerity, because Leo doesn't waste any time checking in, leaning over to open the bedside table drawer. He tosses a package of lube onto the mattress, then hesitates for a minute. "Condom?"

"Uh..." Cisco feels the blush spread over his entire body, and not in a good way. This is awkward. "Probably. I've been tested, but—you should be safe."

Leo just nods, like he was expecting it, and pulls out a condom, too. Probably he was. It would've been stupid for Cisco to stay celibate for seven years, on the off chance Leo would come back. Even if, right now, that feels like exactly what he should have done. He does his best not to think about the fact that Leo probably hasn't been sleeping alone for every one of those nights, either.

Then Leo opens the lube, drizzling it over his fingers, and Cisco loses every thought except anticipation. Leo doesn't draw it out or tease him, just settles between his legs and starts working a finger inside him.

Cisco has never been so grateful for his toy collection as he is in this moment. He'll never forgive himself if he comes before Leo even gets inside him, but if the prep takes too long, he's absolutely certain it will happen. As it is, looking up at Leo, feeling his fingers moving inside—it's a lot. It's so much.

He has to close his eyes and take deep breaths when Leo adds a second finger, not from the intensity of the stretch, but from the emotions flooding his body. It's fanciful thinking, but it almost seems like his body opens more easily for Leo than for one of his toys. Like it's been waiting for Leo, all this time.

"I'm ready," he breathes. Possibly he's stretching the truth a little, but probably not. Anyway, he needs Leo to get on with things before he embarrasses himself.

"Are you sure?" Leo pointedly scissors his fingers apart, but Cisco's body just lets him, relaxes for him.

He nods. "Please, b—Leo. I'm sure."

Leo doesn't visibly react to his slip, just pulls his fingers free and reaches for the condom. His head is ducked as he rips open the package and rolls the latex over his cock. "Still good?"

Cisco reaches for him, pulls him in. "Please, fuck me. C'mon."

Without further ado, Leo lines himself up and starts pushing inside. Cisco forces himself to relax, to bear down and open.

It doesn't take much effort; he's surprised by how right he was when he'd said he was ready.

Leo works his way inside in short, shallow thrusts that steal Cisco's breath away, leaving him gasping out his approval. "So good."

"I need a minute." Leo comes to a stop once he's as deep as he can go, his eyes closed and forehead furrowed. "It's—it's been awhile."

"For me too," Cisco agrees. He hesitates for a moment, then runs a hand down Leo's arm, tracing the lines of muscle there. As his body adjusts to the intrusion, he lifts a leg, wraps it around Leo's waist, lets out a little whimper at the way that changes the angle.

Finally Leo opens his eyes again. "Oh, yeah?"

It's Cisco's turn to close his eyes, not willing to admit that he hasn't bottomed since they were together. The moment feels fragile, like he could break it if he breathes the wrong way. And he's never been especially good with words. "Yeah. Please."

Leo takes him at his word, fucking him slowly at first, then faster as he grows more confident. Cisco holds onto his arms and meets his rhythm, following along as Leo picks up the pace. Every nerve ending in his body lights up, like fireworks in the dark. He needs to come, but he never wants it to end.

Then Leo leans forward and braces his hands on the bed, changing the angle, and there it is. Biting his lip to keep from yelling, Cisco holds on for dear life as Leo fucks him, nailing his prostate with every thrust.

"Can you still—come like this?" Leo's breath is coming harder and faster, his chest and face the same splotchy red they always turn after exertion. "Can you—do it —for me?"

Cisco has no idea, but he wants it, more than he wants anything in the world right now. So he nods, closing his eyes, fingertips digging into Leo's biceps as he balances on a knife-edge, pleasure so sharp it might cut him to ribbons.

"You can." Fuck his entire life, fuck everything, he'd forgotten what it was like to hear that note of command in Leo's voice. "You're going to come for me, just like this. Come untouched, all over yourself, just from me fucking you, because I told you—"

The rest of the words are lost as Cisco comes, everything that isn't his orgasm blotted from his perception with the force of it. When he comes back to awareness of his body, his eyes are wet, but he doesn't care, floating in the post-orgasm bliss, the moment when all the questions and thoughts disappear and he can simply be. Can savor the way Leo goes still above him, eyes closed in his own orgasm.

It's the first chance he's really gotten to study Leo like this, since his unexpected re-entrance into Cisco's life. To catalogue the little differences, the minute changes that happened over the years of separation. There aren't any fine lines visible, not yet, but Leo's face is slimmer, more defined than it was. More mature. The shy boy Cisco first met behind a goalie mask is now a man, fully formed.

He gives into impulse and tugs Leo down on top of him. The solid weight is so good, so right; he closes his eyes and drifts in it.

"I should get up," Leo says.

Cisco startles at the unexpected sound. He has no idea how much time has passed, although judging from the tacky feeling between their bodies, it's been a few minutes at least. "Probably. If we don't want to end up glued together. Again."

He doesn't let go, though, even when Leo laughs so hard he shakes with it.

## 10

## LEO

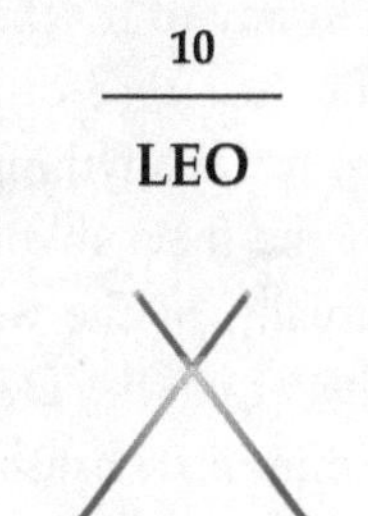

It's not like Leo planned this, okay?

Although if he's honest with himself, he'd definitely hoped it would end up here. But he didn't expect it to be so soon. He'd figured on at least two more not-quite-dates—okay, fine, he knows damn well they were dates. Or at least, he wanted them to be dates.

Whatever.

The point is, he hadn't even planned on the kiss. But Cisco had stopped the car, and he was right there, the security lighting outside the apartments casting his features in sharp relief. He looked like something carved from stone, some statue created by a master of the art, not a flesh-and-blood man. Leo hadn't even realized he was getting closer until he was, until they were close enough that he could feel Cisco's breath, warm and real on his face.

The kiss, well. He's never been much good at escaping Cisco's gravitational pull.

And yes, okay, he'd issued the invitation to come inside, but by that point he suspects most of the blood in his brain had vacated the premises for other locations. So really, he can't be held responsible for his actions.

He doesn't regret it, any of it. The kiss, the invitation, the mind-blowingly hot sex that came after. He doesn't think he knows how to regret anything that has to do with Cisco being here. Not the inevitable laughter as they peel themselves apart eventually, or the way dried jizz pulls at the trail of hair on his stomach. Definitely not the way Cisco keeps touching him, little brushes of fingers like this is all as dreamlike as it seems to Leo.

"Can I borrow your shower?" Cisco throws down the washcloth he was using, clearly giving up on getting clean that way.

Something about the situation, about actually having Cisco here with him, makes Leo bold enough to say, "Only if I get to join you."

Cisco's grin softens into something warmer. "Whatever you want."

The apartment shower isn't really big enough for both of them, even though Leo hasn't maintained much, if any, of his hockey muscle. But he can't bring himself to care about that. If they were back in college, he would absolutely have been hard again and ready to go. As it is, he just —feels really, really good. By the end of it he's a little drunk on the feeling of Cisco's skin against his, or maybe on the afterglow of really good sex.

Whatever the reason, he finds himself asking, "Stay?"

Cisco pauses, still gloriously naked, his boxers in hand. "If you want?"

"I want." Leo swallows hard, trying to force down the torrent of words trying to rise up like vomit. Having really good sex one time isn't enough to erase the years, everything between the people they used to be and who they are now. He knows that. "I mean, if you need to go—"

"Leo." Cisco drops the boxers and crosses to the bed, taking his hands instead. "There's nowhere else I'd rather be."

Squeezing back, Leo lets go long enough to open the bedroom door. Totoro trots in quietly, giving them a look that probably isn't as judgmental as Leo imagines, and curls up quietly on his bed in the corner, tucking his nose under his tail.

They slip into the bed together again, to sleep this time. Leo is probably the most physically comfortable he's been in years, despite being slightly overheated. Everything about this is so familiar, Cisco's body next to his, the way Cisco curls into his side, the texture of Cisco's hair under his fingers. But there are enough differences that he finds it hard to sleep. Cisco's hair is shorter, no longer the flowing mane he remembers, and the CHL life has added a good twenty pounds of muscle, minimum, to his body.

But if he's honest with himself, that's not the real reason he's staring into the dark, still wide awake despite the late hour. He can't escape the superstitious fear that if he lets go, if he surrenders to unconsciousness, that Cisco will be gone when he wakes up.

Not that he thinks Cisco would run out on him, take a walk of shame while he's still sleeping to avoid any awkward conversations. No, the fear that keeps making his breath catch in his throat is the idea that he might wake up back in the hospital, or in his first apartment after being discharged. Alone in his self-imposed isolation, wanting to ask for forgiveness but not knowing how.

They skipped that step, somewhere between him telling Cisco what happened and ending up here. He owes Cisco a thousand apologies for what happened—no. For what he did. For cutting him out and never stepping through the door Cisco had left open for him, not until fate threw them together again.

But the middle of the night is not the time for that conversation. It's not the time for any conversation. He needs to be asleep right now. They both do.

Cisco's voice is barely louder than a whisper, slow with sleep, just like a hundred other nights. "If you could have any superpower in the world, what would it be?"

Leo finds himself blinking back tears, grateful for the darkness that hides them. "Flying."

"Boring. Everyone says that." The kiss Cisco presses to his shoulder is in stark contrast to the dismissive tone of his voice. "I want to be invincible."

The familiarity of the argument that ensues is enough to quiet Leo's mind, to let him slip into sleep with Cisco still wrapped securely around him.

WHEN HE WAKES up in the morning. much too early, the rush of relief at finding Cisco still there leaves him weak, certain he'd wobble if he stood. Thankfully, Cisco is still curled around him like the world's cuddliest octopus, keeping him firmly in place.

His phone is in it's usual place on the bedside table—good job, last night Leo, for fishing it out of your pants—and he manages to get a hand free to grab it. It's not quite late enough for his alarm to go off, but it's close enough not to be worth going back to sleep.

He needs coffee. Coffee will fix the fog in his head from an inadequate amount of sleep—not that he regrets the sex, or the conversation that followed. But he's getting too old to stay up half the night and then bounce out of bed the next morning. That's what coffee is for.

Except when he starts to wriggle his way free, Cisco holds on tighter, arms and legs clamping down with the strength of a professional athlete. "Too early," he mumbles. It sounds like Totoro's protesting whine when he has to go out in the snow to do his business.

Despite his predicament, Leo can't help smiling, or stroking a hand across Cisco's hair. "I forgot how much you hate mornings."

"The worst." Cisco does his best to burrow his face into Leo's shoulder. "G' back t' sleep."

"I have to get up for work soon. If you let me up, I can make coffee."

Cisco actually lifts his head for that. "Coffee."

"Fresh and hot," Leo wheedles. "But you have to let me get out of bed."

"Hmmm." Cisco's eyes slowly sharpen, his expression turning into something very familiar. "I can think of a better way to wake up."

The kiss starts off soft and sleepy, but it doesn't stay that way. Leo has a fleeting thought about morning breath, but Cisco doesn't seem to mind, exploring every corner of his mouth with single-minded intensity. By the time they break apart for air, Leo's morning wood has turned into something hot and urgent, demanding his attention.

Cisco finds the sensitive spot on his neck and starts to nip and suck at it, his stubble rasping against Leo's collarbone. "What do you think? Better than coffee?"

Leo threads his fingers through Cisco's hair, tugging gently, the way he used to like. "Convince me."

"Yes, sir."

The flash of teeth and Cisco's familiar smirk are the only other response he gets before Cisco starts moving down his body, blazing a trail with hands and lips and teeth and tongue. Before Leo loses all sense of rational thought and becomes a creature of pure sensation, lost to everything outside of this moment, this feeling.

Before Cisco's mouth engulfs his cock in soft, wet heat.

The next several minutes fragment into flashes of sensation. The slick-softness of Cisco's hair under his hands. The vibration of Cisco's moan around his cock when Leo's fingers tug, seemingly of their own volition. The helpless hitching of his hips, despite his best efforts to keep them down on the bed. The movement that has him opening his eyes, confirming that yes, Cisco is jerking off right now, without noticeably destroying his focus on the task at hand.

Leo is fairly sure he comes in an embarrassingly short amount of time. He just feels too good to care. Especially when Cisco collapses bonelessly, head pillowed on his thigh, in the way that says he managed to find his own orgasm, too.

"You could have waited for me," Leo says. Not right away. After he's caught his breath. He's not really upset about it; he's not sure he can be upset about anything right now. But some small voice whispers that maybe, just maybe, his chances to make Cisco come are limited. And maybe he just lost one.

"Next time," Cisco promises. His voice is still fuzzy with sleep, or maybe that's the rasp he gets after a blow job. Leo's inclined to believe it's the former, though, since his eyes are closed, his whole body limp and relaxed. He makes a soft, contented sound when Leo's hand strokes through his hair.

Leo thinks vaguely that, back when his therapist had asked him to describe a peaceful moment, she was probably thinking of something like this.

Of course, this is exactly when his alarm goes off.

It's not the jarring, strident sound he'd used to force

himself out of bed during college; he'd invested in an app that played a soft, soothing playlist, slowly increasing in volume. But no matter the actual sounds, the meaning is still unmistakable. Even in his half-asleep state, Cisco gets it, groaning and nuzzling his face further into his leg.

"You pro athletes may be able to stay in bed all day, but some of us have real work to do." Leo attempts to roll out of bed, but finds himself held in place. "Cisco."

Cisco lets go with a yelp as Totoro crosses to the bed, shoving his cold nose into Cisco's side. "Fine, call off your dog, I'm up. Shower together?"

For a moment, a single, selfish moment, Leo lets himself shove his worries and anxieties back. Lets himself believe it can be this easy. "Only if you wash my back."

He knows what Cisco will say even before he says it, but that doesn't erase the thrill he feels at the soft words.

"Whatever you want."

*"I CAN'T BELIEVE we have this whole place to ourselves." Leo dropped his bag just inside the door, throwing himself on the king-sized bed like a kid jumping into a pool.*

*Cisco shoved the door closed behind him. "I know it's not much—"*

*"It's a whole room, and a whole huge bed, to ourselves. For three days." Leo sat up, taking his shirt off in the same motion. "No teammates banging on the wall if we get a little loud. Just you, me, the bed, and that nice big Jacuzzi in the corner."*

*Cisco grinned, crossing the room to join him. "Yeah. You know you're fucking me in that later, right?"*

*"Who said you get to bottom?" Leo mock-pouted at him,*

barely able to keep from laughing. "What happened to 'whatever you want, baby'?"

"We have three days," Cisco said. He barely paused to take his own shirt off before crawling up the bed, eyes hot and intent on Leo in the way that always made him shivery. "We can do whatever we want."

Leo smiled, pulling Cisco down on top of him. "Whatever we want, huh? So what you're saying is we're both getting fucked in the Jacuzzi?"

"If we try hard and believe in ourselves, I think we just might pull it off."

"I hope you brought enough condoms." Leo joked.

Cisco's face did something unexpected at that. "I did," he said slowly. "And we can totally use them. But you know we talked about—not."

Leo swallowed hard. "Yeah. I haven't slept with anybody else since we got tested at the beginning of the semester."

"Me either." Cisco rolled to the side, lacing their fingers together. "I don't want to pressure you. If you want to use condoms, I'll use them for the rest of our lives. But if you don't —I thought we could try. While we have...this."

"I'd like that." Leo pushed the part of his brain that latched on to "the rest of our lives" back down where it belonged. Now was not the time. "But there's just one really important question."

Cisco smiled, a little of the tension leaving his face. "Oh yeah? What's that, baby?"

Leo maked his face as solemn as he could, fighting back the bubble of laughter threatening to emerge. "How do we decide which of us gets to bottom first?"

It only took a few seconds before Cisco burst out laughing, his amusement drawing out Leo's, like it always did. "God, I love you."

And even though Leo should probably be panicking—even

*though he knew he probably would be panicking very soon, in that moment, the words just felt like a warm blanket, settling over his shoulders.*

"So." Cisco hesitates by the door, somehow managing to look even hotter in his rumpled clothes from last night. "We have a roadie starting tomorrow."

"Yeah," Leo says. He'd been happy about that, before. A break from the way being around Cisco makes him feel, makes him want. But somewhere along the way Cisco became a part of his life again.

He keeps waiting for the panic to set in, but it just feels—good. Right. Warm and comforting, like all those years ago when he'd been a stupid boy who didn't know how to handle a declaration of love.

"I have practice but, could we do something tonight?" Cisco scratches absently at Totoro's head, his eyes never leaving Leo's. "It doesn't have to be anything fancy. I just —I'd like to see you again before we go."

He looks so uncertain, like Leo was ever going to turn him down. "I'd like that."

The way his whole face lights up, the way he reaches for Leo, their hands sliding together, is like a sunny day after a week of snow and ice. "Can we—you don't have to answer me right now. Just think about it. But--I'd really like it if we could try again. I missed you, baby."

"I—" Leo feels almost dizzy with the possibility, the potential of this moment. Depending on what he says right now, a whole universe of paths open up before him.

But in the end, when he looks at Cisco, there's no way he can say no.

"I'm afraid," he admits. His voice is barely above a

whisper, but he forces himself to maintain eye contact. If they're doing this, he doesn't want to start it with a lie. "I'm afraid I'm going to hurt you again. I'm afraid I'm going to break us again."

"Me too," Cisco says. "But if there's a chance, baby. It's worth it. You're worth it."

He's opening his mouth to say—something, some denial or further plea for validation, but his phone rings, loud and obtrusive in his hand. And the screen says that it's Gen calling.

"I—I have to take this. It's my boss."

Cisco squeezes his hand. "Go ahead. I don't want to make you late. We can talk more tonight. But I mean it. You're worth it."

And then he's gone, before Leo can even say a word to convince him otherwise.

## 11

## CISCO

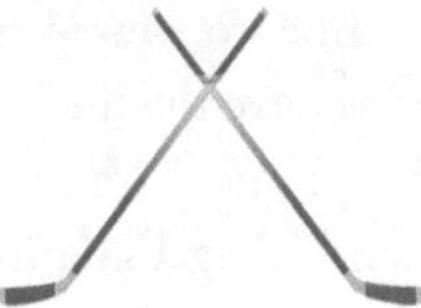

Cisco can't remember the last time he felt like this, happy and terrified all at once. This—having another chance with Leo, he's wanted this more than anything, for so long he can't remember what it was like not to want it.

And now he has it. He just has to not fuck it up.

"What's up?" Angel nudges him out of his reverie, bumping him gently into the side of the plane. "You look like you found a puppy and adopted it and then somebody ran it over."

"Don't you ever get tired of talking about my feelings?"

Angel shakes his head, neatly dodging Cisco's sad attempts at deflection. "Nope. You know I like the drama."

"Then why don't you pick a fight with your fiancee?" Cisco grumbles. Digging around in his crochet bag, he swears, yet again, that he's going to buy a case so all his hooks don't end up at the bottom.

"Are you kidding me, bro? I like my face unbroken and my balls where they are. Besides, you wouldn't really want to have to break in another d-partner, would you?"

Cisco rolls his eyes. "Whatever, man. You don't like drama, you just ran out of new episodes of Real Housewives of Seattle."

"No, seriously." Angel's face takes on an unusually serious expression. "You can talk to me, or I can text your sister."

"Like Paola has time to worry about my bullshit," Cisco scoffs. "The twins have the flu."

Angel pulls out his phone. "Wanna bet?"

"Stewie!" Cisco calls. "Angel's daring me!"

Their captain's sigh is audible even from three rows away. "Angel, you know that's a fine."

"Exception," Angel replies. "It's for his own good. I'm afraid we're headed for a repeat of the 2012 season."

Most of the plane goes silent at that. "Provisionally accepted," Stewie finally says.

Angel turns back to him as conversations slowly resume, shit-eating grin firmly in place like he didn't just give the rest of the team an excuse to be nosy motherfuckers about Cisco's emotional state. "So? What's it gonna be?"

"It's not that bad," Cisco mutters.

"Bro, this is the same dude you were fucked up over back then." Angel shrugs. "I'm hoping it doesn't get that bad, but we need you intact if we're gonna make the playoffs, not breaking your hand on some idiot from the Giants' fourth line. So talk. You can talk to me, or Paola, or your mom, or hell, get drunk and pour out your troubles to some friendly bartender. But you can't just keep everything inside."

After a moment's consideration, Angel emerges as the lesser evil, if only slightly. His mom and Paola will be supportive, but, well. They saw what he was like After Leo, and he does not want to listen to even one lecture about how he's setting himself up to get his heart broken again.

"So we've been texting," he starts.

"Yeah, I already know that."

Cisco rolls his eyes. "Context, motherfucker. Do you want me to talk to you, or do you want to run your mouth?"

Angel mimes zipping his lips.

"Anyway. Texting, and we've had dinner a few times, when we were both free."

"Just dinner?" Angel waggles his eyebrows.

Cisco opens his mouth, then closes it again. He wants to say no, wants to say it's none of Angel's business. Wants to keep that night and morning with Leo close to his chest and precious, where no one else can tarnish or cheapen it. But lying to your best friend and d-partner isn't a good idea, or a good sign for the future of a relationship.

Do he and Leo have a relationship? They have to, right? Cisco asked if they can try again, and Leo said yes. That's a relationship.

"I'm going to take the fish face and the silence to mean 'no, Angel, not just dinner, we made sweet, sweet love—'"

Hitting your d-partner in the face with a bag full of yarn probably isn't a good idea either, but hell, it got him to shut up. At least the yarn and the bag are both soft.

"Fine," Angel says. He shoves the bag back toward Cisco with more force than is strictly necessary. "So you're talking, you've had dinner, and probably more, which you're not talking about. What's the problem?"

"I—" Cisco stumbles to a halt, trying to find the words to explain it. "I fucked it up, last time. I pushed too hard, didn't pay enough attention to the pressure he was under. And he didn't speak to me for seven years. I have to be careful. I can't—I can't do that again."

Angel's face is serious for the first time since they began the conversation. "Do you think he'd do that again? You're both different people than you were back then, you know."

"I know." Cisco rubs a hand over his face. "I'm just—it's good, you know. It feels good. But I keep thinking it's gonna disappear."

"Maybe you should talk to Paola, or somebody else who knows more about your situation," Angel says. "Or like, a therapist? I don't know. You know I'm here for you, but even someone as hot and amazing as I am can't work miracles."

Cisco snorts. "I don't trust Paola or Mami not to read him the riot act for before."

"Would that be so bad?"

"He was in the hospital." Cisco buries his face in the bag again. Where did that crochet hook go? "It wasn't his fault."

It's Angel's turn to roll his eyes. "He was in the hospital for seven years?"

"He's allowed to not want to talk to me." Cisco has had this argument with himself so often that he can do this in his sleep, arguing either side, and that was even before Leo's description of what he'd gone through. "If seeing me, talking to me, would have made it harder for him to get better—it wouldn't have been worth it. I'd go another seven years without talking to him if it's the difference between him happy and healthy or him in a hospital bed."

"Okay," Angel says slowly. "But what do *you* need?"

Cisco is starting to seriously feel like a fish, what with the mouth opening and closing all the time as he tries to come up with an answer. "I—I don't know."

Angel pats his knee gently, pulling out his earbuds. "Maybe that's something you should figure out, huh?"

Humming a noise that could be agreement or could be

not, Cisco returns his attention to the search for the missing crochet hook. He has to pull all of the yarn out of the bag, but he finally uncovers it.

Unfortunately, crocheting is only enough to keep his hands busy, not his mind. After the third time his attention wavers and he has to rip out half-a-dozen stitches, he nudges Angel with his elbow. "Hey. What're you watching?"

Angel hands him an earbud by way of answer. It turns out that he's watching one of those bullshit reality fitness shows, something where people compete against each other to finish weird obstacle courses the fastest. It's loud and flashy and constantly demanding his attention.

It's perfect.

Cisco settles back into his seat, his fingers busy and his eyes on the screen of Angel's iPad, pretending that he's not a roiling ball of worry underneath it all.

OF COURSE, his determination not to talk about Leo with Paola only lasts about five minutes into their next phone conversation.

"Cisco!" The volume of her voice is nearly enough to blow his eardrums out even through the phone. "You have to come get your niece and nephew before I murder them. You don't want your only sister to go to prison for killing her kids, right?"

He kicks his shoes off by the hotel room door, holding the phone a careful distance from his ear. "You do know I'm in Idaho right now?"

"How would I know that? I'm not your wife, it's not my job to keep up with your schedule." Her voice drops to a whiny tone that's all too familiar after a childhood spent in adjacent bedrooms. "For real, though, I don't know how much more of this I can take. They're driving me up the fucking wall."

"They're sick,' he says. "How hard can it be to take care of sick kids?"

She makes an inarticulate growling noise. "I swear to God, Francisco Emanuael, I will drive their asses up to Edmonton the next time they come down with something and leave them on your doorstep if you say that to me again."

"I'm sorry, I'm sorry." He barely manages to hold back the laughter trying to bubble up in his throat. "Your children are a trial and you're a saint among women, a true paragon of a mother."

"Fucking right." She sighs. The distinctive glugging sound of liquid being poured fills the fleeting moment of silence. "Anyway, enough about my boring life. What about you? Met anyone new lately?"

His mind whirrs with unexpected panic. "No," he says. Quickly. Too quickly.

If Paola ever decided she was tired of being a stay-at-home mom, she'd make a hell of an interrogator. Even though he would have sworn his tone was completely level, something makes her pounce. "Oh really?"

"Really. Nobody new. Pinky swear."

The silence draws out, tense with anticipation. "You're telling the truth," she finally says. "But there's something..."

He opens his mouth, then closes it again. Anything he says is just going to give her more ammunition. Better to stay quiet. Maybe she'll give up.

"So not somebody new." Her voice is slow and deliberate, like always when she's thinking out loud. "But the only ex—Francisco Emanuel Andreas Vergara de los Reyes!"

Even though she's not physically here to hit him, he flinches anyway. That reflex is going to be with him his entire life. "What?" His voice sounds weak even to him.

"You didn't."

"Didn't what?"

He's surprised he can't hear her teeth grinding through the phone. "You didn't get back together with that son of a bitch who broke your heart. Tell me you didn't. Tell me you're not that stupid."

"It's not like that, Paola."

She groans. "God save me from idiot men. Seriously, did you learn nothing last time? He doesn't care about you. He used you then, and he's using you now, and when he's tired of you again, he'll drop you like—"

"Stop."

Cisco has no idea which of them is more surprised: Paola at the sharpness of his tone, or him that she actually stops when he asks.

"It's my choice." He softens his tone. "You don't get to make it for me."

"But—"

Cisco sighs. "I'm not discussing it, P. You've made your opinion clear."

Silence echoes in his ear for long, long moments, heavy with the weight of all the words she isn't saying.

"Okay," she says finally.

He lets out his breath. "Okay."

"So." She pauses. "What are you crocheting?"

The concession and the subject change are so sudden that it actually takes him a minute to think about it. "I'm making a little Captain America and Bucky for Tolly's birthday, but it's a surprise, so I can't work on it if he can see."

"Aww." It's a relief to hear the smile back in her voice. "You're a good friend, Cisco."

His face heats. "It's not that big a deal."

"You literally turned your therapy into something where you do nice things for other people. Which is very you, so I shouldn't be surprised. You've been like that our whole lives, ever since you were born. Just—" He can practically hear her biting back the words she wants to say. "Just take care of yourself too, okay?"

"I will," he promises.

Before they can say anything else, a clamor arises in the background. Paola sighs. "The monsters are awake."

"Better go feed the beasts."

"Yeah, yeah. I'm dropping them with you for two weeks this summer, just watch." Her voice softens. "I mean it, asshole. Take care of yourself, okay? At least until you get back home so Mom and I can help."

He smiles. "Whatever you say, bicha."

The call ends with her outraged spluttering echoing in his ears.

*"HEY." Cisco kept his voice quiet, trying not to startle Leo. Also trying not to get kicked out of the library, for that matter.*

*He still got two dirty looks and three despairing ones from the students who'd staked out their territory in this corner, but midterms were like that.*

*Of course, the only person who didn't look up was his boyfriend. Leo kept working through his flash cards, lips moving soundlessly as he went. His hair stood up where he'd been running his fingers through it, there were dark circles* under his eyes, and Cisco was pretty sure he was wearing the same clothes he put on after practice ended twelve hours ago, except now the neck of his t-shirt was ragged and wet where he'd been chewing on it.

Physical contact was tricky when he got like this, but Cisco risked a hand on his shoulder, moving slowly and telegraphing his movements, even if Leo didn't look up at him. For once, luck was on his side. Leo jumped a little at the touch, but didn't yell like he had that one time, loud enough that Seth came bursting in, convinced someone was being murdered.

"Cisco?" He lowered his voice at the dirty looks from literally everyone. "What are you doing here?"

"Your last class lets out at two, right?"

Leo nodded, confused and slightly impatient.

"Well, it's eight-thirty, and you've been in here the whole time." Cisco let his hand drift to the back of Leo's neck, squeezing gently. "I came to see if you were ready for a break."

"I can't." Leo shivered a little under his hand, already turning back to his flash cards. "I have my Organic Chem test tomorrow and I'm not ready, and Micro on Thursday, and—"

Cisco squeezed again, interrupting the increasingly panicked—and increasing in volume—stream of words. "Yeah, I figured you'd say that. So I smuggled you in some supplies."

It took a moment before the words penetrated Leo's study haze, but eventually he blinked and looked back up at Cisco. "Supplies?"

Setting his backpack on the chair, Cisco made a point of looking theatrically around before unzipping it. It's possible that he was being a little too dramatic, but it was fun, the way Leo's eyes widened as he pulled out protein bars, bottled water, Gatorade, and Leo's favorite chocolate.

"I know you don't want to leave to get food." He passed over a protein bar, one of the mint chocolate ones Leo likes.

*"So I brought food to you. Don't want you forgetting a formula or whatever because of low blood sugar."*

*"Cisco." Leo seemed at a loss for words. At least he didn't waste any time opening the bar and biting off a piece. "You didn't have to."*

*He shrugged. "I know. But you need to eat. Coach doesn't want you losing any more weight this early in the season. And it's not like it would hurt me to study."*

*Placing his books on the only free corner of the table that hasn't been taken over by Leo's obsessively-planned arrangement—"I like to know where everything is, okay?"—he opened his own bottle of water. Pretending to be engrossed in whatever the fuck he's supposed to be reading for English class, he watched out of the corner of his eye as Leo inhaled the protein bar and downed half a bottle of water.*

*In the end, Cisco actually did get some studying done, and he managed to coax Leo out of the library and into bed with enough time to sleep before practice the next morning. He even got Leo to sleep instead of staring at the ceiling mouthing chemistry formulas to himself, by dint of a very creative blow job.*

*All in all, he'd call that a win.*

CISCO HESITATES outside the office doors, checking the nameplate and comparing it to the company name in his phone, as if he hadn't memorized it when Leo texted it to him. It's as good an excuse as any to hesitate and pretend his stomach isn't a roiling mass of uncertainty.

Because sure, Leo asked if they could meet here–super last-minute, so sorry–but Cisco can't escape the feeling that being here is going to cross some boundary, put some pressure on Leo, and fuck everything up.

The thing that finally gets him moving is the very real fear that he'll be late and Leo will think he's losing interest, or worse, not coming. Pulling his game-day face on like armor, he pulls the door open and steps inside.

"Hi, welcome to Akiyama and Stevens," the young man behind the desk says. "Can I help you?"

"I'm supposed to meet Leo Carrington?" Cisco means the words to come out strong and confident, but it ends up with a questioning inflection anyway.

The man's professional smile doesn't waver as he reaches for the phone. "Sure, I'll let him know you're here. If you'd like to have a seat?"

Cisco does as directed, telling himself it's dumb to be disappointed. Leo has always been a private person; it wouldn't be like him to be shouting their relationship from the rooftops and telling all his co-workers. Anyway, it's not even like Cisco has told a lot of people. Only his closest friends on the team, and Paola. And he hadn't so much told Paola as caved under her inquisition and uncanny powers of deduction.

His spiraling thoughts are interrupted by the sight of Leo coming down the hall with Totoro, slightly rumpled after a long day of work, but still looking so good Cisco almost doesn't notice the woman following him.

Almost

"—seriously, Leo, what do you—" She stops short when she sees him, her eyes raking assessingly over him before swinging back to Leo. "Do you have a date?"

"Don't sound so surprised," Leo retorts. "I can have dates."

She rolls her eyes. "Nobody's saying you can't have dates, Leo. Hi, I'm Gen."

Cisco shakes the hand extended in his direction, doing his best to maintain eye contact. Gen, who apparently knows Leo well enough to be surprised that he has a date, stands almost as tall as Leo, comfortable in a plaid button-down and jeans. Her black hair, only a few shades darker than the rich brown of her skin, is buzzed close to her skull, letting her striking features stand out, strong wide nose and lips that look like they're usually curved in a smile.

"Cisco," he says.

"I'd like to say I've heard all about you, but–" She shoots Leo a reproving glance. "I'm sure you know how Leo is."

Leo snorts. "What if he's some random hookup I found on Grindr, Gen?"

Gen laughs as Cisco does his best to pretend he doesn't care if Leo picks up guys on Grindr or not. "Please. First of all, you deleted Grindr after a week because, and I quote, dick pics are fine but you're looking for something serious–"

"I could've reinstalled it–"

"And second, even if you had reinstalled it," she continues "you wouldn't give a hookup the office address, because you're not that dumb. Ergo, date."

Leo sighs. "Sure, pull out the Latin."

She pats him on the shoulder, the gold band on her ring finger glinting in the light. Cisco shouldn't find that so reassuring, but hell, he's only human. "You love it. Anyway, Cisco, nice to meet you. I'd love to stay here and torture Leo more, but if I don't get home soon, my wife may murder me or leave me for someone who can hold the baby while she sleeps."

"Nice to meet you, too."

That's all Cisco manages before she sweeps out the door with a backwards wave, leaving them in silence.

"Sorry about Gen," Leo says. His cheeks are stained

pink and he can't quite meet Cisco's eyes. "She's appointed herself my honorary sister, which apparently means embarrassing me whenever she gets the chance."

"She can never meet Paola," Cisco says.

That gets Leo to look at him, and earns him a tiny smile. "I don't know, I think it would be interesting to watch. From a safe distance."

"I don't know if there is a safe distance." Cisco shoves his hands in his pockets. Grabbing Leo and kissing that little, secret smile is not appropriate for the workplace. "Did you need to get anything, or–"

"No, I'm good." Leo hesitates a minute, then reaches out, pulling one of his hands out and lacing their fingers together. "Let's go."

And despite everything, all the questions and doubts and worries, Cisco is smiling, too, as they walk out the door.

## 12

# LEO

"Everything okay?"

Leo looks up from his plate. "Huh? Yeah, why?"

"I don't know." Cisco shakes his head. "You just seemed a little far away. What were you thinking about?"

"Oh, just a work thing." Leo can see the question coming, so he scrambles for a way to deflect it. "You never told me when you started crocheting."

Thankfully, Cisco goes with it. "It was after my concussion a few years ago. Uh, you might not—"

"I know about it." Leo's face heats, but hell, they're dating again. It's okay to admit it. "I read any news story I could find about you, even before I moved to Edmonton. You were out the whole second half of the season, right?"

"Yeah." Cisco's face goes grim for a second with the memory. "At first it was just normal. But after a month, I was still having symptoms. They sent me to specialists, and all they could tell me was to rest. No screens, no bright lights, no loud noises—"

Leo winces. "No hockey."

Cisco nods. "No hockey. So I—I got pretty depressed. They couldn't tell me if I would ever play again, even."

It seems impossible to imagine. Cisco and hockey have been entwined in Leo's head for so long he can't imagine how to separate them. He knows, vaguely, that Cisco will retire at some point. But surely that retirement will involve skating, and hockey. He'll coach a peewee league, or maybe a college team. Something.

"That sounds rough."

"It was." Cisco pushes the last remnants of his risotto around on his plate, his eyes far away. "They sent me to a therapist. She's the one who started me on crocheting. It was something I could do. Maybe I couldn't skate, maybe I couldn't work out or watch a game or go for a run. But I could make the world's ugliest hat, or a scarf, or a blanket. Eventually I got bored with those, but I got a book from the library with these little animals in it. The twins loved them."

Leo swallows a pang, remembering what it had been like to be folded into Cisco's family, imagining what they think of him now. Even Totoro's reassuring presence can't erase that sting. "And you kept going."

"It's—" Cisco actually looks at him while searching for the word. "It's soothing. But also it feels good, just like when I started. If I have a bad night, if I can't find the puck, if I can't keep them away from the net, I can do this thing. I can make something that's real."

"Sounds awesome."

Cisco nods. "Yeah. It is."

They finish their meals in comfortable silence. Leo hates his brain a little—okay, a lot. He hates it a lot. Because things are good with them. Easy, right. And the sex is even better than he remembered, somehow.

So of course he can't stop picking at it. Can't stop

imagining that there's something off with Cisco. That maybe he's not as committed as before. Which, to be fair, would make sense, given the way Leo treated him before—

"Hey, earth to Leo."

"Sorry. What were you saying?"

Cisco looks at him for a second like he's going to ask, and for a second Leo thinks about saying it. About laying his cards on the table and finding out, once and for all, if he dares risk his heart, again.

But then Cisco says, "I was just wondering if you wanted dessert." and the moment is gone.

"No, I'm not hungry." Leo says.

"Do you want me to take you home?"

Cisco is a gentleman, Leo tells himself. It doesn't mean he doesn't want this. If he wasn't in, Leo would know. He would.

"We can go to mine, or yours," he says. Forcing himself to be bold, leaving himself open is hard. "As long as it's someplace with a bed."

The way Cisco's eyes darken is all the reward he could ask for. "I think we can manage that."

Leo waits through paying the check, lets Cisco hold his coat and open the door for him, and tells his brain to shut up.

It doesn't listen. It never does.

HE DOESN'T EVEN WAIT for Cisco's door to close behind them before pushing Cisco up against the wall, desperate for something to take him out of his mind. And even more than that, desperate for Cisco. They just ate, but he feels suddenly ravenous. Not for food, but for the taste of

Cisco's mouth, his skin, for the sounds he makes during sex.

Cisco goes with it, takes his weight with barely an exhale, opening up for his kiss so easily. Lets Leo take what he needs, kisses back until the hunger burning in his gut is sated, at least a little.

"What do you want, baby?" he murmurs when Leo finally breaks the kiss.

Leo opens his mouth to say that he doesn't know. But what comes out instead is, "Everything."

"Whatever you want." Cisco looks him steadily in the eyes. He looks mussed, his hair rumpled from Leo's hands, his mouth bitten red and his tie loosened.

Leo wants to *wreck* him.

Before he can say it, though, Cisco's eyes go over his shoulder. "Totoro?"

"Shit." Leo steps back. "Uh—

Cisco ducks his head. "There's a dog bed in the corner. If he wants."

Sure enough, when Leo looks, a brand new extra-large dog bed has pride of place in the corner of Cisco's living area, next to a water bowl and a matching empty one. Swallowing back the swell of emotions, Leo unclips Totoro's leash, releasing him to go investigate his new digs before turning back to Cisco.

"Bed." He breathes the word more than says it.

Cisco swallows, like he can sense the promise in that single word. Maybe he can. "Down the hall."

Reluctantly, Leo eases back, gives him room to move. "Let's go."

He lets Cisco lead the way down the hall—might as well enjoy that view—and into a bedroom with a wall of windows looking out over the city. Right now, though,

Leo's focus is on the massive king-sized bed that takes pride of place.

Stripping Cisco out of his layers is always a pleasure. Leo loves all of it; the contrast between the crisp cotton and smooth wool of his suits and the living warmth of his skin. The little shivers and sighs when he lets his fingers brush over the curve of Cisco's neck, the line of his collarbone, the tight nub of his nipple.

He takes his time over it, slowing down even further when he gets to the belt. There are so many good chances here to tease, to let the backs of his fingers brush against Cisco's stomach as he slowly works the leather tail free of its loop, as he tugs it slightly tighter to let the prong free.

Pulling the belt completely out of the loops is another way to prolong things. Cisco doesn't protest, but by the time the belt hits the floor, he's breathing hard, his cock tenting his slacks even more than when Leo started. He hisses out a breath when Leo touches it, the barest brush of his fingertips, but still he stands there. Waiting.

Leo reaches for the button on his slacks, slowly slips it through the buttonhole. The zipper is almost silent, he pulls it down so slowly. And then it seems only natural to push the slacks down Cisco's legs, following them until he's kneeling on the floor, Cisco's cock straining against the fabric of his boxers, bare inches from Leo's face.

He eases those down to the floor too, licking his lips when Cisco's cock bobs free. Tearing his attention away, he looks up to find Cisco looking back, his eyes wide and dark, hands fisted at his sides. "Anything I want?"

"Anything." Cisco answers without hesitation.

Leo barely manages to control the shudder that races through his body, his mind whirring with the possibilities. "On the bed," he orders. "Hands and knees."

Cisco obeys without question, turning and crawling up

onto the bed, settling on his hands and knees in the middle.

There's no rush, despite the steady drumbeat of blood in his cock, so Leo takes a moment and lets himself enjoy this view, too. He hasn't really gotten the opportunity before to appreciate Cisco's body as it deserves. Sure, he's seen the locker room videos—everyone has seen the locker room videos; there are at least three fan blogs dedicated entirely to screencaps of Cisco from various sources—and the charity calendar which always sticks with the winning theme of "Abs with Abs" and routinely sells out three or four printings.

But this—this is different. This isn't Cisco after a game, flushed with victory or slumped in defeat. This isn't Cisco at a photoshoot, his body oiled to bring out the muscle definition as he looks coyly away from the camera.

This Cisco is just for him. He pushes away the question of how many other men have seen Cisco like this—he would have  noticed Cisco's flinch at the mention of Grindr, even if he hadn't seen the familiar icon on his phone screen, back when all this first started. None of that matters right now.

What matters is Cisco on his hands and knees, shivering occasionally like he's overcome by the picture his imagination paints, the anticipation of what they'll do. And Leo hasn't even touched him yet. Not really.

"Are you cold?" he asks. It's half a real question, half part of this thing they're doing, the roles they're slipping back into like they never left them. Like they've been doing this for the past seven years. "You're shaking a little."

Cisco laughs. "I don't think I could be cold if I tried."

"Good." Leo peels out of his own clothes as fast as he can, knowing he won't want to take the time later, and climbs up on the bed as well, stroking a hand down Cisco's back. "Although that does ruin my chance to say something cheesy like 'I'll warm you up, baby.'"

That gets him another laugh. Leo lets his hands roam, relearning Cisco's body by touch as well as by sight. His hands know the way better than his mind does, instinctively searching out all the sensitive spots he should have forgotten years ago.

"What am I going to do with you?" he muses. It's not a question that needs an answer, and Cisco doesn't bother. It's possible he can't, that he's already slipped into that headspace where he struggles to find words.

Just to be sure, Leo shifts around until he can see his face. Cisco's eyes are half-closed, his face dreamy and more relaxed than Leo has seen it since the moment he said Cisco's name in the penalty box.

"You good, baby?"

Cisco slowly lifts his hand and gives a thumbs-up.

"Good." Their old signal, Cisco naked and waiting for his touch—everything is bringing Leo back to this place, these feelings and he's not even upset. There's no room for that, for anything other than Cisco. "And how do you let me know if you need to stop?"

After a second of hesitation, Cisco's hand taps the bed twice.

"That's so good." Leo tangles a hand in Cisco's hair, pulling it up for a kiss. Cisco opens to him even more easily than before. Like this is the only thing he'll ever want, ever need. Like Leo is the only thing he needs.

It's a heady feeling. Leo throws himself into the single-minded intensity of it, planning his route like a general coordinating a campaign, grateful that they'd sorted out the issue of testing weeks ago.

There's no reason not to indulge himself, so he does, starting at the nape of Cisco's neck and leaving a trail of nips and kisses and licks down his spine and across his shoulders.

By the time he reaches the dimples at the base of Cisco's spine, Cisco is soft and pliant under his hands and mouth. Leo doesn't waste any time, just spreads him wide with one hand on each cheek and licks a broad, wet stripe over his hole.

Moaning wordlessly, Cisco pushes his hips back toward Leo, silently asking for more. Leo barely has a moment to think how perfect this is, how he can leave his thoughts behind and sink into pure physicality.

He has no idea how long he spends slowly licking Cisco open, savoring every taste, every sound, every movement. However long it takes, it's enough. Enough time for Cisco to go soft and pliant under him, opening for one finger, then two. Enough to make Cisco cry out in surprise when Leo scissors his fingers apart, making room for his tongue between them.

Enough time for Cisco to come untouched, his body shaking and shivering through it, beautiful and uninhibited.

Without the distraction of drawing out Cisco's reactions, Leo's own arousal is suddenly, brutally insistent. Straightening up, he stretches his back absently, gently patting Cisco's hip.

"Roll over for me, please, baby. I want to see your face."

It's a few seconds before he gets a reaction, but soon Cisco obeys, rolling onto his back and blinking wide, dark eyes up at him. His cock is still half-hard against his stomach, his body utterly relaxed.

Leo has never been able to look at him like this and not think "mine."

His hand is on his cock before he even realizes. The

first stroke is a relief and a torment, too much and not enough all at once. He's too desperate to come to go slow, to draw it out. It feels like no time at all before he's tipping over the edge, making a mess of Cisco's abs and softening cock.

When he curls into Cisco's side, holding him, it's a long, blissful time before the doubts come back.

*LEO HAD no idea why most of their deepest conversations seemed to happen at night, when they should both be sleeping. All he knew was that after a few months of roadies and whispered discussions, he knew Cisco better than he's ever known another person.*

*But he still thought twice—okay, fine, more like twelve times—before he said, "Do you want kids? You know, someday?"*

*Cisco made the little humming noise that meant he was thinking about it. Leo didnt even think he knew he was doing it. "Maybe? I don't know. I want to go pro, and that schedule would be hard. I'd be gone so much. I'd feel bad leaving them."*

*"You'd have enough money to pay someone to take care of them," Leo pointed out, even though he's pretty sure he knew what Cisco's reaction would be.*

*"It's not the same." Enough light filtered in around the blackout curtains that he could see Cisco bite his lip as he searched for words. "My mom had a hard time raising us after Dad died. But she made sure—we always knew she loved us, how important we were to her. If I'm not sure I can do that for a kid, I don't know if I should have one."*

*Leo resisted the urge to rub at his chest. The ache he felt wasn't physical. Touch wouldn't make it go away.*

*"What about you?" Cisco asked after a second. "You're good enough to go pro too, you know?"*

*Swallowing was hard when it felt like something was clutching at his heart. "It's harder for goalies," Leo managed. "And you know I'm pre-med."*

*"You always say that like you've been sentenced to life in jail." Cisco slowed down, his voice becoming cautious. "You know you get to make the decisions, right? Not your dad."*

*Leo shrugged. "He's paying for this."*

*Cisco opened his mouth, then closed it again. The wash of relief that went through Leo was almost shocking in its strength. The last place he wanted to think about his dad, to talk about the expectations that came with the Carrington name—the name he'd never asked for—was here. This space was for them, for Leo and Cisco.*

*When they were alone like this, just the two of them, he could pretend it would last forever.*

"YOU KNOW Mikey and Tolly don't care what you wear, right?" Cisco asks.

Leo huffs, discarding the fourth shirt that just doesn't look right. "Easy for you to say. Not all of us have millions to spend on custom tailoring."

"Okay, first of all, they're both rookies," Cisco says. "So they're maybe making one million a year."

"Oh no." Leo feigns a gasp, doing his best to channel the snotty ladies from half-remembered society functions. "A single million? The poor dears. They're practically destitute."

Cisco rolls his eyes. "Yeah, yeah. But babe, I guarantee they're going to show up in jeans. Mikey will probably be wearing some sweatshirt with a zillion holes in it. The boy does not know how to dress if he's not in a suit or a jersey."

Remembering some of Cisco's college-era clothing choices, Leo raises judgmental eyebrows at him. "Hello, pot."

"Hey, I don't do that shit now," he protests.

Shaking his head, Leo turns back to his closet. "Did you have to tell them what happened back then? They probably hate me." *And I don't blame them.*

"Babe." Cisco comes up behind him, wraps his arms around Leo's waist as Totoro sandwiches him in from the front. "They don't hate you. They both understand pressure and how it gets to you. I promise. It's gonna be fun."

For just a second, Leo lets himself relax back against Cisco's chest. "Fine, but if it's not, you owe me a blow job."

Cisco's lips curve into a smile as he presses a kiss to his cheek. "Hey, I'll do that for free. But if we're bartering sexual favors—"

Leo waits, but nothing else seems to be forthcoming. It probably shouldn't be endearing that Cisco still has to be coaxed to talk about what he wants in bed if it's even remotely kinky, but Leo loves these little hints of the boy he used to know. The way it makes this thing they're doing seem familiar, right. "Did you want something?"

"I—" Cisco's chest expands against his back as he takes a breath. "Do you still remember your knots?"

"I do," Leo says. He can't hold back the smile. "Or you could go look in the second drawer of my nightstand and tell me what ou think."

He shouldn't have spend so much money on them, but he hadn't been able to resist, imagining Cisco's reaction. Cisco doesn't disappoint, lifting the leather cuffs out of their box with careful, reverent hands. "How long have you had these?"

"I bought them last week," Leo admits. He can't tear his eyes away from Cisco's fingers, stroking over the soft inner surface of the cuffs. "I saw them, and I knew they'd look amazing on you."

With a shuddering breath, Cisco sets them gently back in their box and closes the drawer. "Well, now you have longer to pick a shirt, since I'm not showing up to dinner pitching a tent in my pants."

"I'd say sorry—"

"You really aren't." Cisco flashes him a grin. "I'm not either. So when Mikey and Tolly love you, and you have a fun time, you're gonna use those on me tonight, right?"

"Actually, when it's weird and awkward because they hate me for breaking your heart, you're gonna blow me." Leo pulls out his purple button-down, closing the closet door decisively. "Wearing the cuffs."

"So you're saying even when I lose, I win." Cisco's grin widens. "This is the kind of game I can get behind."

And even though Leo is depressingly sure this is going to be a miserable evening, he'd do just about anything to see Cisco smile at him like that.

"Be right back." Cisco squeezes Leo's hand as he slides toward the edge of the booth. "Gotta piss."

Tolly rolls his eyes. "Such flowery language. No wonder all the fans are all over you, Sunshine."

Cisco doesn't bother responding except with a raised middle finger as he leaves the table.

Leo laughs along with Mikey and Tolly, but the laughter can't ease the dread roiling in the pit of his stomach. They've both been very nice all evening, but it's awkward. There's no way for it to not be awkward. Everyone except Leo is on the same team, spending most of their days and a lot of evenings together. Leo might have played hockey in the past, but he's outside that close-knit circle.

And that's not even considering the elephant in the room.

"So." He forces his tone to be cheerful, reaching down to ground himself with a hand on Totoro's head. "Mikey, are you tired of everyone asking how you're feeling?"

It's Mikey's turn to roll his eyes, sighing dramatically. "So tired, Jesus. But it's great having the cast off."

"You say that like you don't still try to trick me into doing shit for you," Tolly says.

"Awww, but babe. That's how we got together! It's romantic!"

Tolly sighs, his eyes fond. "Whatever you say."

It hurts a little to see them, the ease between them, the love radiating from them even when they're pretending to be annoyed with each other. Not that Leo isn't happy for them. He is, because they're Cisco's friends, and Cisco says they're good guys. And more than that, because everyone deserves to feel like that at least once in their life, to feel free and easy and purely happy in love.

Like Leo had felt, before he threw it away.

And of course, this moment, when he's feeling the full weight of his guilt, is the one where they turn to him, faces suddenly serious.

"Leo," Tolly starts. "You and Cisco—"

It's rude, but Leo lifts a hand to cut him off. At least it's not as rude as bursting into tears or running from the table, which are the other two options. "You're worried about him. I get it. You wouldn't be good friends if you weren't worried about him. I'm sure everyone who knows is. His sister is probably especially thrilled."

Their winces are just confirmation of what he already knows. It shouldn't hurt this much, but remembering how nice Paola had been when she'd met him, imagining how cold she'd be if they met again—Leo shoves the thoughts aside. They aren't useful, and he can't change things that have already happened.

"I can't change the past," he says. "I wish—you have no idea how much I wish I could. If Cisco never talked to me again, it'd be more than I deserve. But all we can do is move forward. So that's what I'm trying to do. Hopefully I can make it up to him, even a little bit."

Neither of them looks any less worried—Mikey might actually look more worried. But they don't have time to say anything else before Cisco is back, sliding into the booth and slinging an arm around Leo's shoulders.

"What'd I miss?"

"Leo was just asking when I get to come back," Mikey says. Which is almost true. Sort of.

The blinding smile Cisco gives him, so utterly happy that Leo is getting along with his friends, is almost enough to wipe away Leo's lingering guilt.

Almost.

## 13

## CISCO

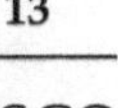

"**S**o."

Cisco knows he sounds impatient, but he honestly doesn't care. The only reason he waited until they were inside Leo's apartment to bring up the topic was because there were other people around as they walked back in from the garage, more in the elevator.

Once, he would have whispered in Leo's ear anyway, getting them both so worked up that they could barely make it in the door before tearing each other's clothes off. But now—he's not sure if that's okay. Past Cisco was a lot more willing to push boundaries, more confident that Leo would follow wherever he went.

Cisco pushes the thought aside. That was then, this is now. And right now, he has Leo.

"So?" Leo returns the word, raising his eyebrows like he doesn't know exactly what Cisco is talking about. Like he isn't already half-hard, enough for there to be a significant bulge in his slacks, like he wasn't even before he took a minute to get Totoro settled.

Cisco feels almost giddy with it, the familiar steps of

this dance, the promise of sinking into that headspace where he doesn't have to think or worry. "So, Tolly and Mikey don't hate you."

Leo purses his lips, then concedes the point with a nod. "They don't."

"And it wasn't weird and awkward." Part of Cisco is screaming at him to stop, remembering the butter-soft leather against his skin. But he's a professional athlete. Competitiveness is kind of part of the job description.

"Not nearly as much as I thought it was going to be," Leo agrees. "Did you have a point?"

Cisco licks his lips slowly, never breaking eye contact. "I think that means I win."

His heartbeat picks up, thudding in his chest, as he sees the familiar competitive flash in Leo's eyes. As Leo stalks toward him, backing him slowly down the hall. "You do, huh?"

"Yeah." Cisco has to clear his throat before continuing. "Because I said it wouldn't be. So I win."

For a second, it looks like Leo is going to argue, but then the moment passes. "What happens when you win?" Leo asks.

Thank fuck Leo's apartment isn't very big, because Cisco's legs are getting weak just from the way Leo is looking at him. It feels like a touch, like—like Leo owns him, and he knows it, and wants everyone else to know it, too.

Cisco has no idea how he lived without this for so long.

He stops when the backs of his legs hit the bed, holding his ground as Leo keeps coming, moving in until there's only the barest whisper of space between their bodies. "I win, so I get to blow you."

"You do?" Leo's hands rest on his hips, sliding slowly

under his sweater and pushing it upward. "Is that what you want?"

Cisco can't think of anything he wants more. Except—

This is the hard part, the part he hates and loves at the same time. The way Leo makes him ask for it, the way his whole body goes hot with embarrassment. It's worth it, it's always worth it. Saying the words gets him almost as worked up as the actual sex, just imagining it, picturing it. And watching the effect on Leo—

He realizes suddenly that he's been quiet for long enough that Leo's peeled his sweater off, lost in thought. "Yeah, that's what I want. But—"

Leo starts stroking his hands over Cisco's chest, down his arms and back up again, lighting up his skin like the Fourth of July, every nerve ending on high alert. "Ask me, Cisco. Say the words."

"The cuffs," Cisco chokes out. "Can I—I want the cuffs. Please?"

For a second, he thinks Leo is going to turn him down. Or worse—better—make him beg. But then Leo's hands fall away, and he takes a step back.

"Bring them here."

Cisco thinks for a minute his legs are going to give out, but he manages to pull it together enough to take the few steps to the bedside table. The cuffs are still there, in the second drawer, nestled safely in their box.

He takes them out with shaking hands, remembering the mixture of arousal and jealousy he'd felt picking them up earlier. Imagining Leo using them with someone else. The rush of pure joy and relief he'd felt when Leo admitted to having just bought them, to buying them just for him, had been so intense Cisco was amazed he hadn't collapsed on the spot.

When he turns back, Leo is sitting on the side of the

bed, his shirtsleeves rolled up to expose his muscled fore-arms. His cock is hard, tenting his slacks, and his eyes are hot on Cisco.

Cisco has no idea how he crosses the space between them. One second he's standing by the table, cuffs in hand, and the next thing he knows, he's standing between Leo's spread knees, holding them. Waiting.

"Turn around," Leo orders.

Sucking in a breath, Cisco obeys, putting his hands behind him as he goes.

Leo's breath is warm against the small of his back, as warm as the brush of his fingertips when he takes the cuffs. "Good, Cisco. So good for me."

Cisco has to lock his knees at that. The rush of blood to his cock is almost painful, sudden and dizzying.

And then the first cuff wraps around his wrist, and he doesn't have to think, doesn't have to try. All he has to do is stand, waiting, as Leo buckles the leather around each wrist in turn, running his finger along the edge of the cuff afterward to make sure they aren't too tight.

"How's that? Are your shoulders okay?"

Cisco knows that Leo wants him to respond, but it still takes a major effort of will to think about it. Does he have shoulders? Who cares? "It's fine. Good."

Leo's hands pet up his arms again, soft and possessive. "Good. Turn around, baby."

Biting back a protest—Leo's hands on his skin feel so good—Cisco does as he's told, turning back to face Leo. Thankfully, he doesn't have to keep standing for long.

"On your knees," Leo says. He makes a surprised noise when Cisco folds obediently to his knees, but when Cisco sneaks a look at his face, he looks pleased, his mouth curving up slightly at the corners. "Good, baby, that's so good."

Cisco wants to complain, to say that it's not fair for Leo to remember what hearing that does to him, to use it against him. But words seem difficult and far away right now. Not nearly as important as Leo's knees bracketing him, Leo's cock hard in his slacks, Leo's hands stroking up over his shoulders and curling around his neck.

"You with me, baby?" Leo asks.

Words aren't happening, but Cisco manages a nod. That earns him Leo's hands in his hair, pulling him closer to where he wants to be.

"Good." That word again, lighting him up like Leo is touching him everywhere, all over. "Unzip me."

It takes Cisco a minute to regain enough focus for that, to problem-solve. He's actually out of it enough that he starts to reach for the zipper with his hands, before the cuffs bring him up short.

This is the best and worst form of torture. He can't believe he'd forgotten what this felt like, clenching his abs to keep from collapsing as he leans in. The urge to bury his face in Leo's crotch, to lick and suck him through the fabric, is almost unbearable. But Leo's hand in his hair, tugging lightly, reminds him of the rewards for obedience.

After a couple of tries, he manages to get the zipper tab between his teeth, pulling it down enough to let Leo's cock spring free. Only the thin fabric of Leo's boxers stands between him and his goal now. This close, Cisco can smell him, the familiar musky scent he's never been able to forget. He leans forward, his mouth watering, only to come up short as Leo's hand tightens in his hair.

"Pull them down." Leo's voice brooks no disagreement. "Then you can have what you want."

Biting back a whimper, Cisco leans in again, catching the elastic waistband in his teeth. His nose drags over soft skin as he pulls the fabric down, Leo's cock rubbing against his cheek as he finally bares it.

This isn't the first time he's blown Leo—hell, it's not the first time he's blown Leo today—but Cisco is suddenly desperate for it, his mouth watering, his own cock almost unbearably hard in his jeans. "Please." He gasps the word out, straining against Leo's grip. "Please—"

"You're so pretty when you beg." Leo's voice is elaborately casual, his free hand wrapping around the base of his cock. "Do you think you can do this without choking yourself? Without your hands?"

"Yes, please, Leo," Cisco begs. "Please—"

And then Leo's hand in his hair isn't restraining any longer, but guiding him forward, toward where his cock is straining, hard and flushed, like it's trying to get to Cisco, too.

Cisco opens his mouth and loses himself in it. He doesn't even have to focus on moving. Leo moves him where he wants him, and then holds him still to fuck his mouth. Cisco doesn't have to worry, or guess, or think.

He can just be.

"So good, Cisco," Leo pants. His thrusts are going just the tiniest bit erratic, but his hands are steady on Cisco's head. Comforting. Safe. "So good for me, you're always so good, baby. Wish I could keep you like this forever—"

He cuts off, shuddering all over as he comes, hot and wet and salty down Cisco's throat.

Cisco just barely has the presence of mind to close his mouth around the head, to suck like Leo likes him to. He keeps up the gentle suction until Leo pulls him away, dragging him up for a deep, filthy kiss.

"That was perfect, baby." Leo's hands are everywhere, stroking over his skin like he's trying to cover every inch of it with his touch. "Do you want the cuffs off now?"

"No, please—"

Cisco can't find any more words, but those are enough.

"Shhh, baby, don't worry. I've got you. C'mere."

Leo peels him out of his jeans and underwear, unclips the cuffs from each other and then connects them in front of his body. "Hands and knees, baby," he says.

Once Cisco is arranged to his liking, Leo takes an eternity working him open. Every time Cisco gets close to the edge, thinks he can come just from the pressure of Leo's fingers fucking him open, Leo slows down, pulls back.

Finally, finally, Leo says "gonna fuck you now," his voice low and hoarse.

"Please." Cisco isn't entirely sure he doesn't sob the word, but he doesn't care. he can't care. All he wants, all he needs, is for Leo to let him come. To make him come. "Please."

He doesn't even have the presence of mind to be surprised that Leo's hard again, only grateful when Leo fills him in one deep thrust, hot and hard and perfect.

"No, you're perfect." Leo's breath is coming hard and fast, in time with his movements. He fucks Cisco with long, deep strokes, nailing his prostate each time. "Perfect for me, my Cisco. Always so good, so perfect. You look so good in my cuffs, baby, so good on your knees, so good in my bed. You do whatever I ask. I lo—I wish I could fuck you forever, just always—"

Cisco comes so hard he's not entirely sure he doesn't pass out. The orgasm feels like it lasts an eternity, Leo fucking him through it until he's wrung out, oversensitive and overstimulated, everything but Leo gone from his awareness.

He whimpers a protest when Leo pulls out and moves off the bed, but doesn't move, using all of his reserves not to collapse in the puddle of his own sweat and jizz.

"Shh, baby, it's okay." Leo strokes a hand over his back. "I'm just getting a washcloth, but first I'm gonna take the cuffs off."

"No!" Cisco jerks his hands in to his chest without thinking, barely rolling to the side enough not to end up in the wet spot. "I—can I keep them?"

He's not sure what expression is on Leo's face, but his voice is soft when he says, "Sure you can, baby. Just let me unclip them, okay?"

True to his word, Leo unclips them so Cisco can move his hands freely, his fingers brushing over the cuffs to check for any irritation. Cisco lies there, drifting, until Leo comes back with a warm cloth to clean him up.

Cuddling requires one of them moving into the wet spot, but Cisco decides that's a sacrifice he's willing to make. Well, not decides, as such. "Decides" is too formal a word for his thought processes. But there are cuddles, so he can think about it tomorrow.

The last thing he hears as he drifts off to sleep is Leo murmuring "Perfect" into his hair.

Cisco stares at his phone.

He's been putting off this call for far too long. His mom's texts have gone from casual to obviously worried. But after what Paola said, he hasn't been able to bring himself to call his mom, to hear it from her, too.

On the other hand, if she doesn't actually hear his voice soon, he wouldn't put it past her to do something extreme. So he opens his contacts, takes a deep breath, and touches her picture.

Unsurprisingly, he doesn't even hear a ring before she picks up. "Chico?"

"Hola, mami," he says.

"It's been almost a month since the last time you called," she says. Her voice is gently chiding, just like in the half-dozen voicemails he hasn't responded to, but he can hear the real worry underneath the rapid-fire Spanish. "You forgot how to use a phone?"

He can't help smiling. "No, I've just been—busy."

"Too busy for your mother." She clicks her tongue at him. "Does 'busy' have a name?"

Cisco takes another breath, considers lying for about half a second, and rips off the bandaid. "It's Leo."

He'd braced himself for her to misunderstand, but judging by her sharp inhale, she gets it immediately. "Your Leo?"

"Yeah." He can hear the softness, the love in his voice. Maybe it makes him an idiot, or a sap, or any of the things Paola accused him of. But he doesn't care.

His mother must hear it too, because she doesn't berate him like Paola had. "Are you sure this is a good idea, mijo?"

"I know what I'm doing, mami." He's trying for firm, but it just comes out tired.

"I just don't want you to get hurt again," she says. "You remember—"

Oh, he remembers. "That's not going to happen again. We're different people now, both of us."

She sighs. "Maybe so, Chico. But different person or not, you've still got that big soft heart. I just don't want to see it broken again."

"I don't either," he admits. "But I love him, mami."

In the moment of silence that follows, he can almost see her face. It's an expression he's seen many times before. When he told her he'd gotten the hockey scholarship—to Minnesota. When he said "The coaches think I'll be drafted." When they'd Skyped after his first hockey fight.

So he can almost taste the mingled pride and worry when she says, "And I love you, too. And Leo, you know that. But I loved you first, mijo. So let me worry about you a little, hm?"

"Like I could stop you."

He's glad he risked the joke when she laughs, a little watery-sounding, but a laugh all the same. "You know better."

"I do."

After a few seconds, she clears her throat. "So will we still see you for Easter? You could bring Leo."

"Mami, Easter is still—"

"Three months away," she says. "Which is how long it will take me to calm your sister down if you're bringing him, so you should let me know."

Cisco opens his mouth to reply, then stops, frowning. "Did Paola tell you?"

"You think your sister tells me anything?" His mother sounds amused. "No, but I know she's been upset about something. I don't like to pry—"

Snorting out loud is absolutely a stupid idea, but Cisco can't quite muffle it.

"Francisco Emanuel Andreas Vergara de los Reyes!"

"Sorry, mami."

She sniffs. "As I was saying, I don't like to pry, but once you told me, it all made sense. So yes. You should bring him to Easter."

"I'm not sure if we're—there yet," Cisco admits.

"Chico." He's not sure if her voice is more chiding or pitying. "You love him. Bring him. I'm sure that family of his isn't doing anything worth going to."

He probably should argue with her about that, but

even if Leo was talking to his family right now, she's not wrong. "Okay, mami. I'll ask him."

"Good. And do something nice for his birthday."

"How do you remember when his birthday is?" Cisco asks.

She laughs. "You think I was going to forget? You called me every day for two weeks. One day I think every hour, changing your mind about what you were going to do. I told you it didn't matter, that he'd love whatever you did. And I was right, wasn't I?"

"You're always right, mami."

"And don't you forget it."

He closes his eyes, suddenly filled with a rush of home-sickness. With them closed, he can pretend that she's right there, smiling smugly at him and about to ply him with too much food. The slamming door in the background and the thundering sounds of Paola's twins running through the house, yelling "Abuela! Abuela!" complete the illusion.

"Your niece and nephew are here," his mother says. "So I'll hang up now so you can save your eardrums. Te amo, Chico."

"You too, mami."

He plugs his phone in to charge and heads to the bedroom. It's time for him to nap, and definitely not the time to obsess about the fact that he's going to be on a roadie for Leo's birthday. Not to mention the fact that he has no idea what to do for it.

Nope. Definitely not the time.

*"Happy birthday." Cisco whispered the words as Leo's eyes fluttered open.*

*He was never going to get used to the way Leo smiled at*

*him first thing in the morning, soft and open and so happy it made something clench in Cisco's chest. The way his hair stuck up all over, making him look like an adorable hedgehog, the creases on his face where it had been pressed into the pillow— it was Cisco's favorite part of the day.*

*"Hi." Leo's jaw cracked with a yawn halfway through the word.*

*"I know you have class at nine," Cisco said. "But I wanted to make you breakfast."*

*Leo woke up enough to notice the tray loaded down with slightly burnt bacon, Eggos, and scrambled eggs, plus the sad bouquet of grocery store carnations that was all Cisco could afford. "I—you—"*

*"It's not much." Cisco couldn't bring himself to watch Leo's face any longer. "I just thought—I wanted—never mind."*

*"It's perfect."*

*Leo's voice, those words, were maybe the only thing that could get him to look up. But when he did, it was worth it, because Leo was beaming at him, even brighter than his first-thing-in-the-morning smile. For a fanciful second, Cisco could imagine that Leo was the sun he orbited around, the light that brought him life.*

*"Happy birthday," he said again.*

*Leo's smile got impossibly brighter, like the inane words were some kind of signal.*

*Maybe that's why it happened. Or maybe Cisco just couldn't hold the words inside any longer. Whatever the reason, he heard himself saying "I love you" without making a conscious decision to do so, too late to take them back.*

*Not that he wanted to.*

*Not when Leo nearly upset the tray, flinging himself into Cisco's arms. Not when they were kissing, so deeply Cisco felt like he never needed to come up for air, like he could live just on this, on nothing but Leo.*

*Not when Leo pulled back just far enough to say, "I love you, too."*

*It was Leo's birthday, but Cisco felt like he'd gotten the gift.*

Cisco is distracted.

Thankfully it hasn't affected his play yet, because none of the coaches has yelled at him and even Angel hasn't seemed to notice anything. But he knows it. A tiny part of his attention is always on the penalty box where Leo sits.

And he keeps catching himself almost, almost taking a dumb penalty. It would be so easy. Their penalty kill is good, and the Sasquatches's power play unit is...not great. He could have two whole minutes with Leo.

Even as he's thinking it, he knows he's being dumb. He can talk to Leo any time. They talked this morning, before Leo left for work and Cisco headed out for practice. Just because Cisco has to get on a plane pretty much right after this game is no reason to be all mopey. It's just a two game roadie, Vegas and Albuquerque, and then right back.

He keeps thinking about it, though.

By the end of the second, he knows he has to fix this, somehow. He manages to catch Ashley, one of the equipment managers, without anyone noticing and convince her to get a note to Leo.

That helps, but it doesn't completely get rid of the jittery feeling in his gut, the uncertainty and, yes, the anxiety. Even when Ashley gives him a thumbs-up. Even when they win in OT off of Suzie's shootout goal.

He carries that feeling with him through press, through

possibly the fastest shower and change of his life, through the back halls of the arena and to the conference room Ashley points him to.

When he steps inside and sees Leo waiting, Totoro at his feet, it's like surfacing from under the water and taking his first long breath. He has no idea how he crosses the space between them—one minute he's in the doorway, the next he's pulling Leo into his arms.

For a moment he worries that he's crossed a line, but Leo goes into his arms easily, willingly his body fitting perfectly against Cisco's.

"I don't want to go."

The words are muffled against Leo's hair, but he still hears them. Of course he does.

"It's just two games. You'll be back before you know it."

"I hate missing your birthday." Cisco can't make himself pull back just yet, doesn't want to see the disappointment he's imagining on Leo's face.

Leo sighs. "I don't like that either, but it's just a day, Cisco. We can celebrate when you get home. Promise."

Cisco holds on for another minute before forcing himself to let go. "Yeah. Any requests?"

Leo pulls him in for a quick kiss, soft and gentle. "Surprise me. You know what I like."

The smile pulls at Cisco's face, but he doesn't mind. "Yeah. I—I have to go. But I'll see you when I get back, yeah?"

"Yeah." Leo's hands squeeze his shoulders for a minute before letting go. "Go kick some ass."

Not saying "I love you" before walking out the door is maybe the hardest thing Cisco has ever done.

**14**

---

**LEO**

"**H**appy Birthday!"

Leo nearly jumps out of his chair as Gen bursts through the door with more energy than he's seen her show in weeks. Actually— "What are you doing here? You're not back from leave for another three weeks?"

She shakes her head, grin firmly in place. "I'm not here to work. I'm here to surprise my friend on his birthday and take him out to lunch. Assuming your hot boyfriend isn't coming to sweep you off your feet for a little afternoon delight, that is."

"You're so sleep-deprived you're mixing your metaphors." Leo turns back toward his computer, grateful that the need to save his progress gives him a reason to partially hide his face. "And lucky for you, since you didn't call ahead, Cisco is out of town on a roadie. I'm all yours."

"Then let's go." She props one hip on his desk while he pushes back his chair and shrugs into his coat. "I still owe you big-time for the other night. Sam is convinced you're a saint."

Leo shakes his head. "It wasn't that big of a deal. I held her for like, maybe an hour. It's not like I saved your life."

"I beg to differ." Barely giving him a chance to clip on Totoro's leash, she pulls him out of the office and toward where her Subaru is parked on the street. "But enough about me. I haven't had the chance to grill you about your tall, dark, and handsome d-man. Were you ever planning to tell me you were dating an Ab?"

"Not if I could help it." Leo tries not to pout as he buckles his seatbelt, but he's pretty sure he doesn't succeed. "Anyway, he wasn't an Ab when we started dating."

Gen blinks at him for a moment before remembering to start the car. "Reyes has been on the Abs for—hell—"

"Seven years," Leo supplies. He should have known better than to bring it up, but Gen would've dug it out eventually. Might as well get it all over with. "Right out of the draft, but he did spend a little time playing in Calgary at first before they called him up for good."

"You have not been secretly dating a member of the Alberta Abominables for seven years, Leo."

He shakes his head. "No. No, but remember, I told you, when I was in college—I played. Goalie."

Even with the sleep-deprivation still evident in her face, it doesn't take long for the penny to drop. It never does with Gen. "You played with him? You two were dating back then?"

"Yeah." Leo swallows back the lump in his throat. If there was any justice in the universe, talking about this shit should get easier. Totoro squeezes his head between the bucket seats, nudging up against Leo's arm. "But around the time he got drafted, I—I was having a bad time. I ended up in the hospital."

Gen makes a soft sound, acknowledging the truth she's

pieced together from what Leo's let drop over the years they've worked together. "You broke up?"

"I—I couldn't talk to him." Leo forces himself to relax his hands, to make them lie gently on his thighs instead of gripping together. "At first I couldn't talk at all. And then, once I was better—I didn't know what to say. So I didn't. When I was in the box with him for that game, the night Sam went into labor—that was the first time I'd seen him since then."

"Leo Carrington." Gen parks the car and turns to face him. "Are you telling me that you let me send you into a situation where you were forced to interact with the ex you haven't seen since your extremely traumatic breakdown? And you didn't say anything?"

It's Leo's turn to blink at her. Of all the things for her to take him to task about— "I—Sam was in labor. It wasn't that big of a deal."

"You're still having trouble talking about it in complete sentences," she says. "So clearly it is. Repeat after me. 'No, Gen, sorry, I can't do that.'"

"No, Gen, sorry, I can't do that," he repeats.

She nods, turning off the ignition. "Good. Now come on. We're going to order at least three desserts and I'm going to tease you about your sex life to make up for the fact that mine's AWOL. I already called ahead to let them know about Totoro."

Leo reaches for his door handle, vaguely startled by the fact that they've arrived. He'd been too strongly focused inward to pay attention to the drive. "Only three? Maybe we should call Sam and ask her how many desserts I deserve."

"Come hold the baby again sometime this week so we can both sleep at the same time and I'd go as high as six."

He laughs, holding the door for her. His stomach is

still a little tight, his hands still a little shaky, but that wasn't as bad as he'd thought it would be. Maybe, eventually, he'll get to a point where it's easy. Easier.

"Deal."

"I'm being completely unreasonable," Leo says.

Totoro stares back at him, mouth falling open in a doggy grin. His tail thumps on the floor at the sound of Leo's voice.

"We've only been back together for a few weeks." Talking to the dog is better than talking to himself—marginally. But Leo can't keep these thoughts inside any longer, where they swirl around and around until he's dizzy with them, like— ironically—a dog chasing its tail. "It's completely ridiculous for me to be disappointed. He doesn't have any obligation to be with me. And it's not like he's doing something fun without me instead of spending my birthday here. It's literally his job!"

Whuffing slightly at the rising pitch of his voice, Totoro jumps up onto the couch, resting his head on Leo's lap.

Leo sighs, one hand coming up to scratch automatically at the spots around Totoro's ears. "I know, buddy. I've got to get over this."

His phone buzzes on the end table. He reaches for it a little too eagerly almost knocking Totoro to the floor. But it's not Cisco's name on the lock screen. It's Justin. They'd matched a few months ago, had fun talking, but never managed to make their schedules match up for a date.

*Hey, cutie*, Justin sends. *I finally got that family emergency sorted out. Wanted to see if I can take you out on the town sometime soon.*

*Sorry,* Leo types back. *I'm actually seeing somebody right now.*

Justin immediately sends back a string of sad emojis, including one of the ones with literal streams of tears falling down its little yellow face. *Serves me right for not snapping you up when I had the chance. Hmu if that changes, k?*

*You'll be the first*

Leo feels sick to his stomach as soon as he sends the text. He has no business being even this flirty with Justin, not when he's with Cisco.

But is he, though?

He shoves the thought away as soon as it rises, but it keeps coming back. Of course. Taking a deep breath, he tries to remember what they told him back in the hospital. Face the fear, the question, look at it logically.

Okay. So.

Is he with Cisco?

If he closes his eyes, he can see Cisco standing there, his face open and vulnerable, hear his voice saying "I'd really like it if we could try again."

Even if Leo never actually gave him an answer, even if he just let himself slide into how easy it was to be with Cisco, he's not fooling himself. Cisco's never given less than a hundred plus percent in his life. If he said he wanted to try again, he meant it. He's all in.

So then, is Leo in? Or out?

The last few weeks have been pretty damn idyllic, aside from the occasional burst of crippling self-doubt. Like a second chance, getting to see what his life could have been like if he hadn't fallen apart. He's still just as terrified as he was that first morning, so afraid he's going to fuck up that he can barely breathe with it sometimes.

If he's the reason he loses the best thing in his life not once, but twice—

"MAKE A WISH!" Cisco pushed the cake with its twenty flickering candles closer to Leo.

The echo of out-of-tune singing still rang in his ears, but he took a breath and did as he was told, blowing out all nineteen in one breath, to the general cheers and applause of half the team.

"I still say you should've let us have this party back at the house." Shoresy leaned over as Cisco started cutting the cake. "We could've had the rager of the year."

Leo grinned at him, hoping it hid the nausea in his stomach. It was bad enough being the focus of the team members they could cram into his and Cisco's tiny apartment. The idea of the hockey house, crammed full of strangers, all those eyes on him—he barely suppressed a shudder.

"Cisco wanted to make a cake."

Shoresy shook his head. "Of course he did. Next year, dude! We'll even get mister big shot to come back from whatever team he gets drafted to. Not that we'd have to ask. He'll probably book tickets as soon as he gets the jersey."

Leo swallowed hard, bile rising in his throat. He had to get over this. He had to. How was he ever going to be a doctor, to save lives if he got sick at the slightest hint of pressure? It was still his sophomore year, for fuck's sake.

Cisco was going to be drafted. Everyone knew that, including Leo. He probably could've been drafted instead of coming to college, although now that Leo had met Yesenia Reyes, he understood why that wasn't an option for Cisco, why Cisco was already making plans to finish his degree through distance learning after the draft.

*If he'd been drafted out of Juniors, Cisco would've spent some time in the minors, putting on muscle, refining his play, maybe getting called up, maybe not. But now, after playing first line on a team that had gone to the Frozen Four three times in the past four years?*

*Cisco was getting drafted, and all the predictions said he was going in the first round.*

*And Leo was happy for him. He was. This was Cisco's dream, and he was one of the lucky few where circumstance and skill and talent combined to let him do what he dreamed of doing. Leo was so happy for him it hurt, sharp and clean, down the center of his heart where it was going to break when Cisco left.*

*Because no matter what the coaches said, what Cisco said, getting drafted as a goalie was an incredible long shot. And even if, by some miracle Leo was drafted, he wouldn't be going to the same team. Which was something he could never get Cisco to admit, even though they both knew he was right.*

*Just like they knew Leo would probably turn it down even if a team did offer him a CHL contract.*

*If thinking about Cisco made him nauseated, thinking about telling his father he was going to play professionally made Leo break out in a cold sweat.*

*Edwin Carrington had always been quietly, coldly furious that Leo chose hockey over something more civilized, like golf, or tennis or, if one must play a team sport, lacrosse. But by the time he realized Leo was serious about pursuing hockey, he would have looked bad for withholding it from him.*

*So Leo had the best equipment, the best trainers, because if a Carrington did something, even something as low-brow as hockey, they would be the best. By the time he was preparing for college, his father was almost resigned. After all, Harvard and Yale both had hockey teams.*

*Attending Minnesota, halfway across the continent from*

*his father, had been the biggest rebellion of Leo's life. And he'd paid for it every day since then, taking the verbal lashings of their weekly phone call. He registered as a pre-med major, and his father wrote the checks, and when Leo graduated, he would attend medical school like every Carrington man (and some of the women) before him.*

*He could see the course of his life, laid out in front of him like a game board. And nowhere on that board was a spouse who played professional hockey, who was gone as often as he was home, sometimes more. Who wasn't the sort to smile prettily and make nice at fundraisers and the society round.*

*"Hey." Cisco set a plate with a slice of cake in front of him. "You okay?"*

*The smile Leo gave him wasn't forced at all. "I am now."*

*The rest of the team hooted and groaned when Cisco leaned down to kiss him, but Leo didn't care. He didn't have to be a psychic to know they don't have a future. But he was selfish enough to want every piece of happiness he could get before that.*

LEO NEARLY DROPS his phone when the incoming call notification pops up with Cisco's name. Hitting pause on yet another Queer Eye rewatch, he swipes to answer the call. "Hello?"

"Hey." Cisco sounds a little tired, which makes sense, given what Leo had seen of their game against the Vampires. It had seemed like he'd nearly played the entire game, even after the brutal check he'd taken near the end of the second. "Happy birthday."

Something warm bubbles up in Leo's stomach. He settles back against the couch cushions, stroking Totoro's ears absently. If he closes his eyes, he can almost pretend that Cisco is here with him, that in a minute they'll turn off the TV and go to bed together. "Thanks."

"Did you have a good day?"

Leo smiles; the question is so quintessentially Cisco. "Pretty good. Gen came and took me out to dinner. Apparently since I held her baby for an hour so she could sleep, I can do no wrong. I got three desserts."

"Good. You deserve—" Cisco cut off, breath hissing through his teeth in a noise Leo knows down to his bones.

"That one check?" He'd been out of his seat, shouting at the unhearing television. "Sanderson was trying to take you out."

Cisco makes a noncommittal noise. In the background of the call, Leo can hear sheets rustling, then the intake of breath as he probably applies an ice pack. "It was a clean hit."

"Sure it was." As much as Leo doesn't want to admit it, Cisco is right. Sanderson had clearly enjoyed what he was doing, shit-eating grin clear on his face as Cisco's d-partner came skating over with blood in his eye. But there was nothing dirty about it. "Tell me you at least didn't break a rib?"

"X-rays came back fine." Cisco sighs. "But I don't want to talk about me. I want to talk about you, and your awesome birthday desserts."

Leo rolled his eyes, but complied. "They had these little mini-pies? I got a key lime, and an apple, and a pecan—"

"It's pronounced pe-cahn, heathen."

"Maybe in Oklahoma," Leo retorts. "*Anyway*, they were delicious. I thought Gen was going to have to roll me out of there."

Cisco chuckles. "Sounds awesome. Wish I could've been there."

"Me too." Leo swallows around the lump in his throat. "But you'll be back tomorrow."

"And I have the whole day off." Cisco lowers his voice, the slight rasp sending shivers down his spine. "Tomorrow you're all mine."

If Leo is a little breathless when he says "can't wait," who can blame him?

He manages to get Cisco to hang up after the second jaw-cracking yawn that he can't manage to talk through. It's late enough that he should probably be heading to bed himself, but he sits there for a few moments, staring at the paused screen on the TV.

Taking a few deep breaths, he opens his contacts and scrolls through until he finds the one he's looking for. Composing a text only takes a few seconds and he forces himself to hit send before he can think about it too hard.

Dislodging Totoro, he heads to bed with feelings of anticipation and anxiety chasing themselves around in his stomach. As scary as this step is, though, it's necessary.

If he loses everything again, Leo refuses to be the reason for his own downfall.

## 15

## CISCO

There's no logical reason to feel nervous, but Cisco can't deny the butterflies dancing in his stomach as he knocks on Leo's door promptly at seven-thirty. Maybe he's being paranoid, looking for trouble where there is none, but there had been something in Leo's voice on the phone the night before—

Totoro is much too well-trained to bark at the door, but Cisco can hear his nails clicking on the floor as he walks closer. And then Leo's steps, quiet and sure despite the early hour.

He has just enough time to pull himself together before the door opens.

"Cis—" Leo cuts off mid-word, staring.

Cisco pushes the massive bouquet a little closer to him, peering over the top. "Happy birthday."

After a few seconds, Leo visibly shakes off his surprise, stepping back and shooing Totoro out of the way to let Cisco in. "I think that might actually be bigger than you are."

"Well, I did miss your actual birthday." Honestly, the

bouquet is almost certainly overkill, but Cisco had gone a little crazy at the florist's. There's so much he wants to give Leo, so much he knows Leo won't accept from him right now—maybe not ever, as much as he hates to think it. Plus, well. "Mikey and Tolly might have egged me on. A little bit."

"Just a little, huh?" Leo moves the stack of books from the center of his dining table. "Good thing it came with its own vase."

Cisco hadn't even thought of that, hadn't considered that Leo might not have a vase. But he's not about to complain about dumb luck. He sets the bouquet down on the table and steps back. "It's probably stupid, I just—"

Leo's hand slipping into his cuts off his babbling. "They're beautiful, Cisco."

He ducks his head, face going hot. "I remembered that you liked them."

"I do." Leo kisses him lightly, but the kiss goes deep and hot almost instantly. Cisco has no idea which of them deepened it, only that suddenly they're wrapped up in each other, not an inch of space between their bodies, devouring each other's mouths.

"Missed you." Leo breathes the words across his lips. "So much."

As tempting as it is to let Leo move him as he will, Cisco forces himself to step back. "I missed you, too. But I have plans for your birthday."

Leo lifts a suggestive eyebrow. "Plans?"

"Not those—well. Not just those kind of plans." Cisco's face feels like it's on fire and he can't figure out what to do with his hands. "I wanted—I want to make it special. Especially since I had to miss it."

"You're here now." Leo takes his hand again. "And you've got me for the day. So what are we doing?"

Cisco squeezes back before letting go. "It's a surprise. Get your coat."

Leo shoots him a look, but turns toward the coat closet. Which gives Cisco time to put part two of his plan into effect. He reaches into his pocket and pulls out the large bone, crouching down to Totoro's level. Not that it takes much. "This is for you." He offers the bone, holding his breath a little as Totoro considers it. "We're going to be out for awhile, but I thought you might enjoy it when we get back."

After an endless moment, Totoro takes the bone almost daintily, giving him a last look before carrying it over to his bed.

"Bribing my dog?"

Cisco straightens up, trying not to flush any deeper. "A gift, not a bribe. He works hard taking care of you. He deserves a treat, too."

This time when Leo pulls him in for a kiss, it's soft and sweet. Not a *hello* kiss or a *I want you* kiss. Maybe just a *because we can* kiss.

Not that Cisco cares. He'll take all of Leo's kisses he can get.

"So." Leo pulls back, wrapping a scarf around his neck. "Where are we going?"

"I told you, it's a surprise." Cisco waits for Totoro to be harnessed and leashed, then opens the door and gestures Leo in front of him. "After you."

Leo eyes him narrowly, but exits the apartment, turning to lock the door behind them. "All right. I'm trusting you."

Cisco is suddenly, deeply grateful that Leo's back is to him. It gives him time to blink back the tears that well up at the sincerity in Leo's voice. It's about something stupid, but he still means it. He trusts Cisco.

It's so much more than he ever thought he'd have again.

When Leo turns back in his direction, he's ready to offer his hand. This is something he gets to do, holding hands with Leo and leading him to where his Range Rover is parked.

"How are you feeling?" Leo waits until they're moving through the streets, Totoro settled in the back seat, to rest a hand on Cisco's knee, his other hand holding the coffee Cisco had picked up for him. "Is your side still hurting?"

"Probably will be for awhile." Cisco barely resists the masochistic urge to press on the bruise over his ribs; it had gone a spectacular purple by the time he got up this morning. "But it could be worse."

Leo hums his acknowledgment; they both know it's true. But then his hand starts moving up Cisco's thigh, slowly, so slowly. "Are you sure I can't convince you to tell me where we're going?"

Cisco can't help but smile as he turns onto Jasper Avenue. "Not a chance."

His hand keeps moving, fingers drawing patterns over Cisco's pants as it goes. "No?"

"No." Cisco reaches down, taking the wandering hand in his. "Anyway, you'll find out in like fifteen minutes if you can be patient."

Leo's pout shouldn't be adorable, but Cisco is just that far gone. "Fine."

Cisco probably shouldn't be enjoying this so much, but he hasn't gotten to do anything like this in years. He didn't realize how much he'd missed having someone to spoil until now. Of course he brings piles of presents whenever he goes home for a visit, but it's not the same.

So he takes the circuitous route he'd previously planned, hoping Leo is unfamiliar enough with this part of the city that it doesn't give away the surprise. They pull into the parking garage with a few minutes to spare before eight, but someone swings open the service door when they approach.

"Right this way, Mr. Reyes." The woman—her name tag says *Nadie*—is far too cheerful for this time of the morning, but then again, Cisco is too, right now. She's also far too professional to betray any curiosity about Leo or to try and interact with Totoro, which he appreciates. "Did you want to make any changes to the itinerary?"

"No, thank you."

She smiles back over her shoulder, leading them deeper into the service corridors. "Okay. Marc is ready for you, and he'll let me know when you're ready to move on."

Cisco returns her smile. "Perfect, thank you."

"Where are we?" Leo hisses under his breath.

"You'll see in a minute." Cisco squeezes his hand, barely restraining the urge to bounce on his toes. "Just hold on a little longer."

Sure enough, after a couple more minutes of walking, Nadie pushes open a door and holds it for them. "Here we are. You have my number; please text if there's anything else you need."

Cisco leads Leo out into the mall proper, watching him take it in. The shops, silent and still with their gratings pulled down, the banner that says "Welcome to Marine Life," the giant fish mouth encompassing the staircase leading down.

When Leo turns to look at him, his eyes shine with unshed tears. But he's smiling, even if it's wobbly. "You remembered."

"*THIS IS what I miss most about Boston.*" *Leo's voice was hushed as they walked through the five-hundred-foot tunnel, surrounded on all sides by water and sea life.*

*It was kind of terrifying, if Cisco thought about it too hard, so he didn't. He had better things to think about, like the rapt, almost reverent look on Leo's face.*

*When Leo had shyly asked if they could go on a date, he wasn't sure what he'd expected, but it hadn't been the Mall of America. Or the aquarium—he hadn't even known that there was an aquarium anywhere near here. But Leo had made a beeline for the entrance, paying for their tickets and regaling Cisco with facts about each new species of marine life they came across.*

*"When I was little, I wanted to be a marine biologist."*

*Cisco almost, almost asked why Leo wasn't majoring in marine biology, when he was clearly still fascinated and entranced by everything around them. He just barely managed to swallow the question back when he realized how dumb it was. He knew the answer. It was the same answer to everything that wasn't quite right in Leo's life. It all went back to his father.*

*Most days, Cisco was incredibly grateful for the thousand-plus miles between Minneapolis and Boston. He knew intellectually that punching Leo's useless adoptive father in the face wouldn't make anything better. He knew it would just make things worse.*

*But it would be so satisfying.*

*Here and now, though, he had better things to do with his time. Like watching Leo's face as he followed the path of a stately sea turtle, or turned his head to keep a school of small silver fish in view as they darted through the water. Like holding Leo's hand, warm and secure in his.*

*"You would've been a good one," he said.*

*Leo looked confused at first, but then his smile turned brilliant and just a little shy. "You think so?"*

*"You're good at everything you do, so I don't see how this would be different."*

*The smile lighting up Leo's face warmed Cisco down to his toes. This? This was what mattered.*

"That was amazing." Leo almost looks like a teenager again as they climb the stairs out of the aquarium, his face shining like the sun. Even Totoro reflects his happiness, tail like a flag behind him as he trots at their side.

Cisco never really understood why the team called him Sunshine—not literally, he gets the associations that lead to hockey nicknames and Reyes to rays of sun to sunshine is pretty obvious—but anyone who looked at Leo like this should be able to see how much better it fits him.

He settles for squeezing Leo's hand gently. "It's not over yet. There's a reason I kind of rushed you through the end there."

"Yeah?" Leo leans in and drops a soft kiss on his mouth. "Well, the first part of this was pretty awesome, so I guess I'll trust you."

"Gee, thanks." Cisco lets the laugh bubbling up in his chest escape. "C'mon, this way."

Walking through the silent, deserted mall is a strange experience. Not bad—definitely better than trying to make their way through people searching for post-Christmas bargains. Cisco mentally estimates the number of times he'd be stopped for an autograph if they did this during regular hours and—it's a lot. Paying for them to open up early had definitely been one of his better ideas.

Like this, walking hand in hand past the shuttered

shops and unmanned kiosks, they could be the only people alive. It's not as eerie a thought as it could be. If Cisco had to pick just one person to be left with on Earth—well, thankfully he doesn't have to choose, because there are a lot of people that he loves. But Leo has been on top of the list for almost ten years. That's not changing any time soon.

Leo seems content to walk in silence, too, a small smile playing on his lips. Every so often he'll look over and meet Cisco's eyes and the smile will widen. Even the slight clicking of Totoro's claws on the floor doesn't break the spell.

It's a perfect moment, and Cisco almost wishes it wouldn't ever end.

Of course, that's not an option. Almost as soon as he thinks it, they come into sight of the rink. Nadie is nowhere to be seen, but the ice is fresh and smooth and the nets are ready. Waiting for them.

Leo doesn't get it at first. Not until Cisco leads them to the nearest bench, where two gear bags and several sticks wait for them.

"Cisco—"

This had seemed like such a good idea when he came up with it, but suddenly Cisco's stomach sinks. What if it's too much? What if it makes Leo feel bad, or—

"We don't have to, if you don't want—" he's babbling, he knows he's babbling, but he can't stop. "I just thought—"

"Cisco!" Leo's hand cups his cheek, turning his head until their eyes meet. And that—Leo's eyes are shining again, his smile even wider than at the aquarium. "I want to. It's perfect."

All the air left Cisco's lungs in a rush. "You're sure? I don't want to—"

Leo shuts him up with a kiss, long and lingering, only

stopping when it threatens to become too much for a public space. "Cisco. No matter what else, being on the ice with you—it was always good. And having the chance to do that again is—" he shakes his head. "I never would have thought to ask for this, but it's perfect."

"Okay." Cisco isn't sure if he's talking to Leo than to himself, but he's glad the bench is there to support him while his legs remember how to work. "They said the dressing rooms are this way."

It's a little strange to be putting his gear on with only one other person in the room, not to mention a dog, but Cisco isn't about to complain. This isn't something he ever thought he'd get to have again, sneaking looks at Leo and finding him sneaking them right back. Walking toward the rink with Leo, with barely a pause to settle Totoro in at the bench.

Stepping onto the ice with Leo.

They just circle the rink at first, leaving their gloves, helmets, and Leo's goalie pads at the bench in favor of holding hands. But he can see the looks Leo keeps giving the net, so after a couple of laps, Cisco steers them back toward the bench.

"Think you've got what it takes?"

Leo smiles ruefully. "Well, one of us has been playing for the past seven years and the other one—hasn't. So, probably not?"

"It's like riding a bike." Cisco knelt down to start fastening the bottom of the pads to Leo's skates as Totoro watches curiously. "Besides, you won't have a whole team coming at you. It's just you and me, baby."

The smile bleeds into something softer, more genuine, with just a hint of teasing. "True. Now if it was Lightning coming at me—"

"Wow. Rude." Cisco moved to the other pad, securing

the bottom and shifting back to let Leo kneel on them so they can start fastening them. "I see how it is."

Leo's cocky, shit-eating grin is maybe the most beautiful thing Cisco's seen. "Just telling it like it is. You telegraph your moves, babe."

"I'll show you telegraphing." Cisco helps him on with the rest of his pads and hands him the jersey. It probably makes him a bad person, but he can't help the feeling of satisfaction when Leo pulls it on, seeing his name and number emblazoned across Leo's back.

"That doesn't make any sense, you know." Leo reached for his gloves. "Go on, get the pucks. I'll be out there in a minute.

Cisco loves hockey, okay? He's loved hockey since the first time he held a stick, loved it even when it was the reason he wasn't there for Leo. Some days it still seems unreal, waking up and realizing that he gets to do this thing he loves, that he gets paid to do it. Even bad days, bad games, aren't so bad, because he gets to play.

But it's been a long time since he felt this kind of pure, uncomplicated joy in it. Sharing the ice with Leo again, trying to fake him out enough to get a puck in the net, the answering grin he sees behind Leo's mask—

It might not be a perfect day, but it's damn close.

Their allotted hour goes by too quickly. Long before Cisco is ready, the mall starts to come alive around them, people getting the stores and kiosks ready to open, curious glances coming their way from time to time. And the rink doesn't open until eleven, they could probably keep going. It's not that Cisco can't afford it.

But as good as this is, he's selfish enough not to want to share it. So he follows Leo off the ice to the dressing room with Totoro shadowing them as always, holds his hand as Nadie leads them back through the service hallways to the parking garage, and does his best not to think about the past or the future. Just now, this moment. Leo glowing next to him, hair damp with sweat, happy and here and his.

It's perfect.

## 16

## LEO

"So." The woman sitting across from Leo—Teravia, with rainbow-colored braids and skin a few shades darker than Gen's—fixes him with an open, sympathetic look. "It's been a few years. What brings you to see me today?"

"Well—" Leo had thought he might have trouble talking about it, but he opens his mouth and the whole story spills out like it has a mind of its own, all the details he hadn't told her years ago. Meeting Cisco, dating. The draft, and his breakdown, and the seven years since then. Seeing Cisco again. The way that, even though things are good on the surface, he can't escape the feeling that Cisco is slipping through his fingers. Again.

When he finally runs out of words, Teravia nods slowly. "Have you seen anyone for therapy in the past few years? Since the last time you saw me, I mean."

Leo shakes his head, reaching down blindly to find Totoro next to him. "I didn't—I didn't feel like I needed it. Things were good. Life was good. I had my job and my dog, I was thinking about dating again..."

No matter how he searches her face, he can't find a hint of judgement in her smile. "It did seem a bit like we were going in circles back then. And now?"

"Now—" Leo pauses, swallows down the lump in the back of his throat. "Shit. I don't want to—he deserves better than me, you know? But he—somehow he still wants me?"

"What do you want, Leo?"

He picks up the little bottle of liquid and glitter on the end table next to him, turning it over and over in his hands, watching the swirling sparkles. "I want—I want him. I want to be with him. I fucked it up once. I don't want to be the reason I lose him again."

"That's a good start." When he risks a look at her, Teravia is smiling back, searching his eyes. "And it sounds like the two of you are working on that. Have you talked to him about these feelings?"

"No." Leo doesn't even have to think about the response. "He's—he's already walking on eggshells around me. Like I'm breakable. And I don't want to be, but sometimes I feel like it."

The glitter swirls in the jar as he turns it over again, bright sparkles catching the light from the window.

"Those feelings aren't going to go away instantly. For a little while, it may feel worse before it gets better."

Leo forces himself to meet her eyes. "But you think it can get better?"

"You've never been afraid to do the work." She picks up the notepad sitting next to her. "So yes, Leo, I think it can get better."

He lets out a breath. "Okay. Let's do it."

She nods. "I want to go back to something you said a minute ago..."

"Hey." Cisco pulls him in for a kiss, soft and lingering. For a moment, Leo forgets that he has to go to work, that Cisco has to go to practice, that anything exists outside of the two of them.

Unfortunately, they don't exist in their own private bubble, so eventually he has to pull away. "Gotta get to work, baby."

"Yeah." It should not be adorable to see a grown man pout, but somehow Cisco pulled it off. "Oh, want to get lunch? Practice is over by one."

"I—oh, I can't." Leo does his best not to cringe, or blush, but he's not sure he manages It's probably the guilt talking, but he thinks Totoro is giving him a judgmental look. "I have an appointment, sorry. Rain check?"

Cisco smiles, just a second too slow. "Sure. You know where to find me."

Leo can't resist leaning in for another kiss, something to get him through the day. "I sure do."

When he and Totoro finally get out the door to head to work, he's running five minutes late. At least weaving through traffic distracts him from the curl of worry in the pit of his stomach, the memory of Cisco's eyes not quite meeting his.

*Tomorrow,* he promises himself. *I'll tell him about therapy tomorrow.*

Leo slumps back against the couch, feeling like he's just been bag skated. His cheeks are wet, his sinuses clogged with tears, but lifting the tissue in his hand to deal with it seems like too much effort. Next to him, Totoro shifts to lay his head on Leo's thigh. "Shit."

"You're doing really well, Leo." Teravia sets the little machine she'd been using aside, taking his pieces from his slack grip. "This is hard work, but you're doing great."

As wrung out as he feels, Leo somehow manages to take her statement as fact. "Thanks."

She settles back in her chair, still watching him. "How are you feeling now? Physically."

He does a quick scan through his body, one hand resting on Totoro's head. "Tired, but...good, I think. I don't think I'm as tense, especially in my stomach."

"Good. Remember, this can stir up a lot of things, especially when you dream, but also just in day-to-day life. Text me if you need me before next session, okay?"

"I will."

She smiles. "We're almost out of time for today, but I want to give you a little homework."

If Leo could find the reserves, he thinks he might have actually whimpered out loud. But—this is his choice. This is what he needs to do, for Cisco, for him, for the two of them together. "Okay. Hit me."

"This is two parts, actually. First, the next time you have the opportunity to do something outside of your comfort zone, I want you to say yes. This is on the honor system; don't push yourself to an extent that's going to trigger a panic attack. But sometimes taking little risks can get us a big reward."

He swallows. "Okay."

Something in her eyes says she knows he's panicking a little right now, but she doesn't relent, doesn't give him an out. "Which brings us to part two. I want you to think back to a time when you did this in the past. Stepped outside of your comfort zone, took a risk, and it made your life better. We can talk about it next time, or not, but when you feel that fear, I want you to remind yourself that this can work."

Leo is suddenly grateful for how blotchy his face must be right now, because otherwise her sharp eyes would absolutely have detected his blush. "I will."

"Good." She comes to her feet, smiling when he follows suit. "I'll see you next week, then."

He has no idea what he says in response, or how he gets out of her building to his car. Maybe Totoro guides him as his feet carry him on autopilot, most of him lost in memory.

*LEO WINCED as the final buzzer sounded, the score frozen in hard, unforgiving lights. He knew, they all did, sometimes this was just the way it goes. You could do your best, leave it all on the ice, and still lose.*

*Like Captain Picard said, that was life.*

*But it was hard to remember that sometimes. When his fingers twitched, itching for his blocker and glove, every time Jacks missed a save. When his heart was in his throat as he watched from the bench, filled with the bone-deep certainty that if he was just on the ice, it would be different.*

*And that didn't even take into account how much it hurt, watching his team—his friends—slowly crumble under the weight of the loss. They all took it differently—some of them, like Cisco, turned inward, getting quieter and quieter, while others got louder, more aggressive, looking for a reason to throw a punch.*

*Even though he hadn't been on the ice for this one, Leo couldn't escape the guilt coursing through him as he followed* the rest of the team back to the room. His team had needed him, and he wasn't there.

The post-game coach speeches were blessedly short, even if the atmosphere in the room and the showers was still heavy as the team got showered and dressed. Leo only took the most cursory rinse; since he'd just sat on the bench in his gear, he wasn't anywhere close to as sweaty as he usually was post-game. Once his normal clothes were back on, he settled into his stall to wait for Cisco.

The longer he waited, the more worried he got. Cisco was moving fine, clearly not injured, but he was just as clearly not seeing the room around him. Leo's chest ached just looking at him. If he felt this much guilt after not even playing, what was Cisco feeling? Especially considering how he always took the weight of the world on his shoulders.

After an agonizing forever, Cisco pulled a hat down over his hair and shouldered his gear bag, looking surprised to see Leo still there in the nearly-deserted room. "Ready?"

Leo just nodded, not commenting on the rusty sound of Cisco's voice, a sure sign that tears weren't far behind. "Yeah, let's go."

They made their way back to their apartment without speaking, their breath clouding the cold winter air in front of them. Cisco still looked a little like he might burst into tears at any moment, but he didn't flinch away from Leo when their shoulders bumped, when Leo risked taking his hand, so it could be worse.

He waited, biding his time, until they were standing in their room. "What do you need, baby?"

Cisco shook his head, his eyes firmly fixed on the floor. After nearly a year together, Leo had enough experience to interpret this as "I don't think you'll want to do this" or "I'm embarrassed to ask you."

"*Baby.*" *He reached out, framed Cisco's face in his hands.* "*Look at me.*"

*Biting his lip, Cisco finally looked up, his eyes wide and wet, pleading.*

"*I love you.*" *Leo invested the words with as much weight as he could, all of his emotions laid bare.* "*Let me help. Please.*"

"*Fuck me.*" *The words sounded like they'd been ripped out of Cisco's throat.* "*Please, I just—I need to not think—*"

*Leo pulled him in for a kiss. He'd meant to keep it soft, gentle, but Cisco quickly turned it hot and desperate, his hands frantic and just this side of bruising as they dragged at Leo's clothes. Leo didn't mean to grab them as hard as he did, his hands circling Cisco's wrists and pulling them back.*

*He especially didn't expect the way Cisco went still at the touch. At the restraint.*

"*Cisco? Baby, are you—*" *Leo started to let go, only stopping at the whine Cisco lets out.*

"*Please.*" *His pupils were blown wide and dark when Leo managed to catch his eye.* "*Please, don't let go. I need—*"

*Leo waited, but Cisco couldn't seem to put more words together. He wasn't having a panic attack, or at least, it didn't look like any panic attack Leo had ever seen, or experienced. But something was happening here, something Leo wasn't expecting and wasn't sure how to navigate.*

"*Baby? I'm not going to let go, but I need you to talk to me, okay? Do you still want—*"

"*Yes, please.*" *Cisco looked up at him, half-pleading, half-trusting.* "*Please, I want you to.*"

*Despite his uncertainty, Leo's reaction to Cisco asking for sex was basically Pavlovian at this point, but he did his best to think, despite the blood draining to his cock. This was important. Cisco was important. Something told him that if he fucked this up, the consequences would be serious.*

*As always when he was uncertain, Leo fell back on repetition, confirming what he was already pretty sure of. "You want me to fuck you?"*

*Cisco nodded frantically. "Please, please."*

*A deep breath, doing his best to suppress the shiver sliding down his spine. "And you want me to hold your hands?"*

*It was almost like Cisco had forgotten, the way he flexed his arms in Leo's grip. Not pulling away, just like he wanted to feel Leo's grip against his skin. "Yeah, it—it feels good. It helps."*

*And that—Leo might not understand what's happening here, but he wasn't capable of denying Cisco something that would help him. Not now. "Okay. Okay, baby. We can do that. But I'm going to undress you first, okay? I want you to stand here and let me do that."*

*Cisco nodded, biting his lip but not otherwise protesting when Leo let go of his wrists and reached for the hem of his t-shirt. He was naked in a matter of minutes. Leo only hesitated for a few seconds before stripping out of his own clothes, too. If Cisco wanted him to hold on, better to have as few interruptions as possible.*

*"Good." He reached for Cisco's hands again. Standing like this, so close, it was impossible to miss Cisco's reaction to the words, the shiver that ran through his whole body, the way he melted into Leo's touch. "Okay, let's get you on the bed, baby."*

*Cisco went obediently where Leo nudged, climbing up onto the bed and waiting for Leo's instructions. He seemed like he'd happily stay there forever while Leo considered logistics, completely ignoring his cock, hard and leaking against his thigh.*

*"On your stomach, baby." The words were barely out before Cisco obeyed, dropping down to lie on his stomach. After a little maneuvering, Leo managed to get Cisco's wrists crossed at the small of his back, close enough together that he*

*could hold them with one hand and retrieve the lube with the other. "You're sure?"*

*Cisco blinked his eyes open, dreamy unfocused stare sharpening a little when he saw what Leo was holding. "Y-yeah."*

*"Okay."*

*They didn't speak after that, but the room was far from silent, full of the slick sound of Leo's fingers moving in Cisco, opening him up, the little whimpers and whines as Cisco tried to rock back, to get more, deeper, faster.*

*"Are your shoulders okay?" Leo knew he was stalling. Cisco probably would have been fine long ago, but there was something almost fragile about him right now, something that made Leo want to handle him more carefully.*

*"They're good." Cisco sounded like he'd been double-shifting, breathing in huge, gulping breaths. "Leo, please, I need you."*

*Leo swallowed. "Yeah, okay. I've got you, baby."*

*Sure enough, Cisco's body opened easily for him, letting him push home in one long, slick slide. It was so, so tempting to just let go, to selfishly chase his own pleasure. But this wasn't about him. This was for Cisco.*

*Wiping his messy hand on the sheets, Leo reached for Cisco, getting one wrist in each hand and pressing them to the bed next to his shoulders. He meant to ask if it was okay, really he did, but the movement shifted the angle of his cock, and Cisco's whole body shook under him, pressing back to meet him, to demand more.*

*Leo lost track of everything outside the bed, his focus narrowed to the two of them, to Cisco's body blanketed under his, Cisco's hands in his grip. From this angle it was more of a grind than a thrust as he moved inside Cisco, but from the little noises and movements Cisco made, it was as good for him as it was for Leo.*

*"So good." Leo gasped the words out, nuzzling at the back of Cisco's neck as best he could. "So good, baby, just perfect—"*

*He lost his words, his train of thought, as Cisco gasped and came under him, going impossibly tight around his cock. Between the physical sensations and the knowledge that Cisco had just come untouched, it took an embarrassingly short time before Leo came too.*

*Collapsing on top of Cisco was less a choice than a necessity, since Leo's arms refused to hold him any longer. He lay there for an endless, perfect number of breaths. In this moment, nothing was real except the two of them, skin on skin, as close as it was possible to be.*

*Eventually Leo recovered enough brain function to realize that it must be difficult at the very least for Cisco to breathe when they're like this. Pushing up took a couple of tries and got him a protesting noise from Cisco.*

*"I'm heavy. It can't be comfortable, me on top of you like that."*

*Cisco didn't respond in words, just got a hand free to grab at Leo's side, to try and pull him back down.*

*"Okay, okay, baby, let me try something."*

*After a few seconds of maneuvering, Leo finally managed to get them rolled onto their sides, which Cisco eventually accepted, once he'd pulled Leo's arm and leg over him.*

*At some point, Leo was going to have to get up, to find a washcloth and something to drink, to get them some food. Eventually, they would have to leave this bed.*

*But right now, he held Cisco and breathed.*

"YOU KNOW, you don't have to—"

Leo raises a hand, cutting Cisco off. "Yes, baby, I know

I don't have to. I knew that the first time you told me, and the second, and the third."

"Sorry." Cisco chewed on his bottom lip, staring out the windshield. "I just—I didn't think this was your kind of thing. And leaving Totoro—are you sure?"

It's the perfect opening to tell him about therapy, about Teravia and his homework, about saying yes. Leo opens his mouth, still not sure how to say it except to just blurt it out—

—and Cisco's phone rings, a familiar name popping up on the screen mounted in the dash of his Rover.

"Hold that thought, okay, baby?" Cisco presses a button on the steering wheel. "Hola, mami."

"Chico!" Yesenia Reyes sounded exactly the same as the last time Leo had spoken to her. He has to swallow, hard against the memories trying to well up. "Tienes—"

Cisco clears his throat. "Leo's here with me, Mami."

"Oh! Sorry, Leo. How are you, honey?"

Much to his surprise, Leo's voice actually comes out somewhat normal. "Don't worry about it, Mrs. Reyes. I'm fine. How are you?"

"Leo, please, I've told you, it's Yesenia."

"Mami, you know if he called you by your name you'd think he wasn't being respectful." Cisco rolled his eyes melodramatically in Leo's direction. "Now what do I need to do?"

"Have you booked your flight yet? I need to know if we're going to be having Easter lunch or dinner. Leo, you're coming for Easter, yes?"

Leo looks over at Cisco on reflex. Easter?

*Sorry,* Cisco mouths. "Mami, we're meeting the team and we just pulled up. I'll call you tomorrow with the flight, bien?"

Leo's pretty sure that isn't going to work and, from the

expression on his face, neither is Cisco. But his mother just says, "Oh, of course. You have to celebrate after a game like that. I'll talk to you tomorrow, Chico. You two have fun!"

"Te amo, mami."

Silence settles between them once the call ends, nothing but the sound of the wheels on the pavement and the traffic around them.

Finally, Leo can't take it any longer. "Easter?"

"Oh, uh." Cisco slows as they get closer to the club, looking for a parking space. "Mami wants you to come home with me. If you want to."

It shouldn't be so hard to get the words out, but it takes Leo several tries before he can speak. "Do you want me to?"

Cisco pulls into a spot and reaches for his hand. "Baby, I always want you with me. But I don't want to rush you. Or force you to deal with my family before you're ready. It's your call."

Leo takes a breath. It would be so easy to say no, that he's not ready.

*Say yes*, Teravia's voice suggests in his memory.

"What do you think the chances are that Paola will murder me?"

Cisco laughs, squeezing his hand. "I'll protect you. And if you bribe the kids, they'll help."

"Okay." Saying it is scary, but the light in Cisco's eyes almost makes him not care.

"Yeah?"

Leo smiles back. "Yeah. Now let's get in there before I change my mind and drag you home instead."

Cisco lifts his hand to his lips for a kiss before letting go and reaching for his seatbelt. "You can drag me home after."

Circling the car, Leo takes his hand again. "I'm holding you to that."

THE CLUB ISN'T as loud as Leo was expecting. Which isn't to say that it's quiet, not with the heavy bass line and the people filling the dance floor. But up in the VIP balcony, where the team has taken over, it's actually possible to talk without yelling into someone's ear.

Leo had forgotten what it was like, being surrounded by players. They're Cisco's team, not his, but still, it's good, familiar. The chirping Mikey and Tolly get, along with half-serious threats of fines, the As circulating to keep an eye on the rookies, the guys diagramming a play with shot glasses and salt shakers at the next table—it feels like team. Like home.

"So!" Cisco's d-partner, Trevor—no, Cisco calls him Angel—drops into the booth next to them. "You're Leo! Not gonna lie, dude, there was a serious pool on whether Cisco made you up."

Cisco rolls his eyes, shoving Angel with the arm he doesn't have wrapped around Leo's shoulders. "Stop it or I'm telling Coach to put me with Guns instead."

Angel theatrically mimes being stabbed through the heart. "Stop what, bro? Just want to meet your boy. Unless you're afraid he'll take one look at my handsome face and drop you like a bad habit."

Leo can't help laughing. Angel's cheerful irreverence is infectious. It's easy to see how he and Cisco balance each other out. "Sorry, dude, you're not my type."

"Just as well." Angel drains the last of his beer, smile firmly in place. "My girlfriend would make me have a serious relationship talk if we were going to add a third, and I'm too drunk for that."

"You definitely are." Cisco lifts a hand to wave down a pretty, statuesque brunette standing at the balcony entrance. "If you're nice to me, I won't tell her you said that."

"Yeah, but she's not here, so you don't scare me."

The brunette slides onto Angel's lap. "Who's not here?"

"Baby!" Angel's whole face lights up, staring up at her adoringly. "You came!"

"Told you I would." She wraps an arm around his shoulders to keep her balance, smiling down at him for a moment before turning the smile toward Leo. "Hi. I'm Breanna."

Her smile is also infectious, or maybe Leo is just that happy. Either way, he finds himself returning it, taking her offered hand. "Leo. I guess you're Angel's girlfriend."

"When he's lucky." She winks. "Nice to meet you, Leo. I've heard good things."

He does his best to keep the smile on his face, to squelch the curl of anxiety that tries to rise in his throat. Cisco's arm, warm and solid around him, helps. "I hope so."

"Trev says you make Cisco happy." She says it so simply, like that's the only thing that matters. Maybe it is.

"Let's dance!" Angel surges to his feet before they can say anything further. "Dance with me, babe."

Breanna laughs, but allows herself to be pulled toward the dance floor. "Later, boys."

"Do you want to dance?"

Leo considers it for a second, but the prospect of the dance floor crowd is enough to overshadow the thought of dancing with Cisco. "Not tonight. This is good."

"Yeah, it is." Cisco's hand squeezes his shoulder for a moment.

They sit in comfortable silence for a few moments. Having time like this, a chance to just be, together, is almost more intoxicating than the beer Leo's been nursing. For the first time since that moment in the penalty box—maybe for the first time ever—Leo has a vision of their future. Of evenings with the team, like this, or at home, with Totoro sprawled happily over both of them. Of sitting in the stands to cheer Cisco on, of bringing him to the office Christmas party, of visiting Cisco's family for holidays.

It's so close he can taste it, and he *wants*.

Before the emotions welling up in his throat can choke him, though, a handy interruption presents itself in the form of Seth, Mikey, and Tolly deciding to join them, all three sweaty and laughing from a stint on the dance floor and clearly on the far side of tipsy.

Leo can't help but smile. "Having fun, children?"

"I'm older than you are." Seth does his best to keep an aggrieved face, but it keeps slipping into a smile.

"Dude, that guy was super into you." Mikey glances back over his shoulder at the dance floor. "You should go get his number."

Seth just shakes his head, leaning back against the booth and wiping an arm across his forehead. "Nah, I'm not feeling it tonight."

Mikey opens his mouth, probably to persist, but closes it again when Tolly whispers something in his ear. And Leo knows that look, that mingled combination of love and incredibly urgent lust.

No one is surprised when Tolly stands again, pulling Mikey after him. "I think we're gonna head home."

They don't wait for a response, weaving their way

through the tables to the stairs without letting go of each other.

"They're cute." Seth reaches for a bottle of water that one of the captains had left on their table. "Reminds me of some other people I know."

Cisco snorts. "Were we that obvious?"

Seth rolls his eyes. "Sunshine, there was a serious pool going on who was going to catch you two fucking in the showers. Barney swore up and down he was gonna win it."

"That explains a lot." Leo does his best to pretend his face isn't on fire, but from the look on Seth's face, he isn't managing it. "Nobody won it, right?"

"Nah." Seth drains half of the water. "Anyway, it's good to see you two together again."

"Yeah." Cisco turns his head, lips brushing over Leo's temple. "It's pretty great."

That earns them another eye roll as Seth settles back to sip the rest of the water. "Even if you are still fucking gross. At least I won't be around to deal with it for much longer."

"They're sending you back down?" Cisco goes stiff in the seat next to him.

Seth shrugs. "They haven't said yet, but they only called me up in the first place because Mikey was out. Once he's cleared to play, pretty sure I'm gone. Honestly, this is more CHL games than I ever thought I'd get to play."

"You never know," Cisco insists. "You've been putting up decent numbers."

"It's okay." Seth smiles at them. "Easier if I'm ready for it. But it was fun playing with you again."

Cisco sighs, but allows the change of subject after Leo elbows him. "Yeah, man, it was good. And Calgary isn't that far. Come see us sometime, okay?"

"Yeah, if you really want." Seth looks at Leo for confirmation.

He nods, the bubble of warmth in his chest threatening to overwhelm him as he realizes that when Cisco said "us," he doesn't mean the team. He means the two of them. "Yeah. Come see us when you can, Seth."

Seth lifts the nearly-empty water bottle in a salute. "Okay."

## 17

## CISCO

"**R**eady to get back to your boy?"

Cisco startles, turning away from the plane window he'd been staring out of. "Huh?"

Angel chuckles. "Wow, dude, and I thought you were bad before the two of you got together. Can't even be gone for two games without missing him, huh?"

"Shut up." Cisco shoves at his shoulder half-heartedly.

"It's okay." Angel pats him gently on the head. "It's normal to miss him, especially when you're going to be gone for three whole days. This can be a confusing time for a boy, but I'm here if you have any questions—"

He cuts off with a yelp when Cisco wrestles him into a headlock. Despite Angel's best efforts, Cisco is able to ruthlessly exploit the element of surprise and keep him pinned.

"Sunshine?" Stewie's voice is light and amused as he comes walking up between the seats. "Do I want to know why you're trying to strangle your d-partner?"

"He was being a dick."

"I was just trying to distract him from missing his boy."

Despite still having Cisco's arm restraining him, Angel somehow manages to affect an innocent face."

Stewie rolls his eyes, looking over his shoulder. "Obi-wan?"

"Fine on Angel for being a dick, and Sunshine for trying to murder him." Obi-wan's resonant baritone sounds even more amused. "Now settle down, children, it's going to be a long flight."

Cisco lets go with a grumble, settling back in his seat and doing his best not to pout.

After a few moments of silence, Angel nudges him with an elbow. He stares out the window, ignoring it, but then it comes again, and again.

"Seriously, man. Are you okay?"

Cisco shrugs, still looking out the window. Even if he couldn't see Angel's reflection in the glass, he'd know he was still listening. "I—I should be."

Angel doesn't speak, just makes an encouraging noise.

"I should be great. I've got him back, you know? And things are good. He's going home with me for Easter."

"But?"

Cisco sighs. "I don't know. It's just a feeling. Like, sometimes he can't get together and it seems like he's just making an excuse. But then I see him, and it's good. I just —I feel like he's going to slip through my fingers again. Like I'm going to wake up one morning and he's just going to be gone. And there's not going to be anything I can do about it."

"Wow." Angel hums thoughtfully. "So, and I realize this is a radical suggestion, but have you considered, maybe, telling him how you feel?"

"Fuck you." Cisco rubs a hand over his face. "I just— what if that makes it worse? What if he gets super anxious about making me feel that way and that's the thing that drives him away?"

When Angel finally speaks again, his face and voice are so serious that Cisco nearly does a double-take. "Bro. You can't build a relationship—a life—if you're walking on eggshells. Especially not if you're convinced he's going to leave, like, all the time."

"I know." Cisco can hear the whine in his voice and he hates it. "I know. But—I just got him back."

"And I'd put money on him being in this." Angel squeezes the back of his neck. Gently, but enough to ward off the panic rising in Cisco's chest, tight and strangling. "But you won't *know that* if you don't use your words and *talk to him* like an adult."

Cisco sighs again. It feels like the breath takes all the air out of his lungs. "I know."

"So talk to him." Angel shakes him gently. "The longer you wait, the worse it'll get."

"Yeah." Cisco shakes his head. "When did you become the emotionally mature one?"

Angel winks, letting go and settling back into his seat. "I always have been. Boom, mind blown."

It feels good to roll his eyes at Angel's antics. To laugh. It doesn't entirely mitigate the knot of worry in the pit of his stomach, but it helps.

He won't be able to send it until they land, but he unlocks his phone and types out a text anyway. He needs to take the time to get this right.

***We need to talk*** is obviously right out. Even with everything that's been happening, he knows better. The last thing he wants is to make Leo worry, or feel anxious, or be afraid that Cisco wants to break up. And similarly, it's a dick move to dump it all out via text, to type ***I love you***

**and sometimes I'm so afraid that you're going to leave me again I can't breathe.**

Even if it wasn't, some superstitious part of Cisco would stop him. It's too much like the texts he sent back then, the ones that, for all he knows, are still floating in some digital void, unread and unanswered.

He types a half-dozen messages, then a full dozen, in the time before the plane touches down in Denver. In the end, he deletes them all. The three words he comes up with aren't the perfect, eloquent message he'd like to send, but they're going to have to work.

**I miss you.**

*"BABY, BREATHE." Cisco pulled Leo into his arms, rubbed circles on his back. "It's gonna be okay."*

*He knew, even as the words slipped out of his mouth, that it was a stupid thing to say. Even if he hadn't been there for the phone calls, the silent, shaking panic attacks after each one, he would have to have been blind and deaf not to see the change in Leo when he talked about his father. The way he'd been wound increasingly tight every day since he found out about this visit.*

*"I just don't know why he's coming." Leo looked just as bewildered as if it was the first time he'd said the words, not possibly the hundredth. "He's not an alumni, and he doesn't make donations to schools that aren't Ivies. And he doesn't care about hockey."*

*"It's family weekend?" Cisco knew his part in this conversation by now, could recite his lines in his sleep. He just wished that he could somehow break free, could steer it to another outcome.*

*Leo shook his head. "He's never cared before. And he's not* even coming for the weekend, he's 'too busy.' He's going to be here and gone before anyone else's parents show up. Probably for the best, anyway."

"It's gonna be okay." Cisco couldn't stop promising it, even if he won't be able to deliver. "I'll sic Mami on him, okay? He'll never know what hit him."

Before they could finish playing it out, a sleek, dark car pulled up to the curb in front of the house, clearly visible through the living room windows. The windows were tinted enough that they couldn't see inside, but after a moment a man in a suit stepped out of the driver's seat, closing his door and opening the next one.

Even if Leo hadn't shown him pictures, Cisco thought he would have known instinctively that the second man out of the car was Bradford Carrington. He looked like an executive from a movie, someone who sat at the head of a boardroom table and made hard decisions. His suit fit him perfectly, his shoes shone enough that the light flashing off them temporarily blinded Cisco for a second.

Most of all, he looked around like the entire neighborhood was something he'd like to scrape off his shoe. This was definitely the man who cut Leo to shreds without ever raising his voice.

Cisco half-expected Leo to dissolve in a panic, had several strategies prepared for that exact scenario. He didn't expect Leo to straighten and step out of his hold, his face smoothing into a calm, pleasant mask that was almost, almost good enough to fool Cisco. If he didn't look in his eyes.

"I need to ask you something." Leo spoke so quietly that Cisco could barely hear him, his eyes fixed out the window as his father started up the sidewalk.

"Anything."

Leo nodded slightly. "While he's here—please—don't touch me. I have—I have to keep it together."

*Cisco's heart cracked open. Forcing down the need to grab Leo and head out the back door, to just start driving and never come back, he nodded. "Whatever you need, baby."*

*"Thank you." Leo swallowed, a second before a firm knock sounded on the door. Smiling that tiny, terrible smile, he walked into the entry hall, reaching for the doorknob and swinging it open. "Father."*

*"Leonard." Mr. Carrington had a surprisingly pleasant voice. He should have sounded like Satan; the pain he inflicted on Leo should have left its mark in his voice. But it was just a smooth, rich baritone. A voice that said* you can trust me. *"Good to see you, son."*

*Leo stepped back, pulling the door open wider. "Please, come in."*

*Cisco forced his frozen feet to move, getting to the entry hall just as Mr. Carrington walked through the door. One look and it was immediately clear where Leo had learned that implacable mask. Except Mr. Carrington had clearly had years to perfect his, because the contempt from earlier was nowhere to be seen.*

*"You're looking well, son." He extended a hand for Leo to shake.*

*"You, too, sir." Leo shook firmly, maintaining eye contact. "Father, this is Francisco Reyes, one of my teammates."*

*Mr. Carrington turned to Cisco, offering him a hand. "Ah, yes. Defenseman, aren't you?"*

*"Yes, sir."*

*The next few hours were some of the most surreal of Cisco's life. If he didn't know better, he would have thought Mr. Carrington was a good, caring father. A little distant, maybe, not quite sure how to express himself or his feelings, but someone who genuinely loved Leo.*

*The hell of it was, maybe he was.*

*Somehow, Cisco couldn't decide what was worse. If the*

*father slowly driving Leo insane was doing it on purpose, or accidentally, because he cared.*

*He was still mentally wrangling with that question when Leo excused himself from the table to go to the bathroom.*

*Cisco had tried to politely demur when Mr. Carrington invited him to join them for dinner. He didn't want to leave Leo alone with his father, but he also didn't want to seem like a money-grubbing poor classmate, looking for a handout. Mr. Carrington had insisted, with equal politeness, and Leo had looked at him with pleading eyes out of that awful mask of an expression, so Cisco had conceded.*

*The restaurant was good, the kind of place where there were no prices on the menu, and the food was objectively delicious, but Cisco wasn't sure he'd really tasted any of it. And now Leo was gone, and Mr. Carrington was fixing him with an expression that he wasn't sure how to interpret.*

*"Francisco."*

*Despite himself, Cisco found himself sitting up straighter. Maybe the effect of his full name in those authoritative tones. "Yes, sir?"*

*Mr. Carrington sighed. "Let's speak frankly. I know that my son has become attached to you. I've overlooked it so far, because he was bound to make foolish choices at some point. Now, when it won't affect his future, is the best time for him to make this sort of mistake."*

*Biting back the instinctive retort, Cisco forced himself to remain silent, not to rise to the bait.*

*"However, that time is quickly coming to a close. My sources tell me that you're likely to pursue a professional hockey career, possibly within the next year or two. Leonard, as I'm sure you're aware, is meant for different things. I've indulged him in this sport, but when he graduates, he will enter medical school. He has the intelligence and the nerve to make an excellent doctor."*

*Mr. Carrington paused, as if expecting a response, then continues when Cisco remains silent. "But there's more to being a doctor than education. It's a political career, almost more so than actual politics if he wants to rise as far as he's able. Leonard will need someone who can support him in that. A spouse who can be at his side for the required social functions, who is able to always be there for him. And you, Francisco, are not prepared or suited to be that kind of partner to him."*

*Cisco forced his breathing to remain even. Mr. Carrington would pounce on any sign of weakness, he knew that as surely as he knows his own name. "Why are you telling me this, sir?"*

*"Leonard is too soft-hearted to see this clearly." Mr. Carrington sat back in his chair with a sigh, his face radiating fatherly concern. "He isn't capable of cutting off a relationship with you, not if he believes himself to be in love. If someone is going to end it, it will have to be you. And I'm prepared to make it worth your while."*

*"Is this the part where you offer me money to break up with him?"*

*Mr. Carrington shook his head. "Oh, no. If you remain uninjured for even a few years, you can expect to earn enough in your professional sports career that any monetary offer I can make would be meaningless. No, my boy, what I'm offering is nothing so basic as money. I serve on a charity board with the owner of the Boston Banshees. I understand that they're looking to increase the depth of their defensive line."*

*Cisco was dizzy, and he wasn't sure if it was because of the offer, or the rising anger, choking the words in his throat.*

*Before he could answer, though, Mr. Carrington raised a hand. "Leonard is on his way back. You don't need to answer me right away. Think about it. This is your future, both of you."*

*Cisco didn't say much for the rest of dinner, or in the car on the way back to the house, but he didn't think Leo noticed, too wrapped up in his own coping. Mr. Carrington dropped them off with a firm handshake for each of them and a reminder for Leo of some plans over the Christmas break.*

*Once they made it inside, Cisco was mostly too busy holding Leo together as he tried to shake apart to think about it. But once they were curled up together, touching everywhere they could, drifting off to sleep, the conversation came back, anger flooding through him again.*

*He held Leo just a little bit tighter, but it was a long time before he could fall asleep.*

WHEN ANGEL COMES into the locker room to find Cisco already half-dressed, he raises an eyebrow. "Someone's excited."

Cisco shrugs, taping his socks. "Didn't have anything else to do."

"Your boy didn't have time to meet up with you, huh?" Angel kicks off his shoes and reaches for his own socks. "You know, some people have things called jobs."

"I know." Cisco pulls his pants on. "I know."

Thankfully Angel subsides before the rest of the team notices, but he keeps shooting Cisco worried looks as they gear up.

When they skate out for warmups, Cisco's eyes go to the penalty box as if magnetically attracted. But instead of Leo's familiar figure, there's an older man, silver hair reflecting the blue lights of the arena.

Muscle memory carries him through the warmups. *There's a good reason,* he keeps telling himself. After all, he hasn't been able to check his phone for the last hour or two. Probably there's a text from Leo explaining why he isn't there. Probably they'll meet up after the game.

Somehow Cisco manages to put it out of his head, to find the focus required to do his job. He can't think about it. If he thinks about it, he'll curl up into a ball on the ice or the bench, he'll strip out of his gear and drive through the city to Leo's apartment.

So he doesn't think about it. He puts it away in a box in his head, and he plays hockey. And if he relishes the chance to drop his gloves when the Banshee's d-man accidentally-on-purpose gets tangled up with Tiger, pushing the net completely out of place, well.

It's part of the job.

They win, but he has no idea how. It's a blur of skating and not-skating, sitting in the locker room nodding as the coaches go over their strategy and picks apart their play, and going back out to do it again.

Finally they troop back to the locker room. Finally he can pull his phone out of his bag.

The lock screen is completely empty of notifications.

Cisco forces himself to breathe through the instinctive panic. Maybe Leo just forgot there was a game tonight, or fell asleep and missed it. Opening Whatsapp, he forces himself not to demand answers, to send a simple *missed u tonight. can I come over?*

Some of the nearest guys are starting to look at him strangely, and Angel looks like he's about two seconds from saying something comforting, something that Cisco absolutely can't deal with right now.

Turning away, he busies himself stripping out of his gear, dropping it wherever it lands. His phone is still stubbornly empty of new messages when he finishes, so he rushes into the shower.

After the most cursory rinse-off he can manage, he redresses hurriedly, dragging clothes on over still-damp skin. Grabbing his gear bag, he heads out the door, not making eye contact with anyone.

He makes his escape, and the phone still doesn't buzz with an incoming text or call.

Sheer force of will carries him to his Rover before he makes the call.

It doesn't even ring, just goes directly to voicemail. Fear and memories nearly choke the breath out of him, but he manages to speak by the time the beep sounds. "Hey, baby. Just wondering where you are. I missed you tonight. Call me?"

He has no idea how he gets to Leo's apartment. One minute he's turning the key, the next he's pulling into a visitor parking space, barely remembering to lock the doors. Making his way into the lobby, punching the pass-code with trembling fingers, wiling the elevator to Leo's apartment to go faster.

No one answers the door. No matter how hard he listens, he can't hear any signs of life, not Leo, not Totoro.

Eventually he forces himself to move before someone decides to call the cops. He makes his way back to the Rover, autopilot steering him back to his building.

He falls asleep with the phone in his hand, waiting.

**18**

---

**LEO**

"What else do we need to talk about?" Teravia watches him, her face patient. Like she can wait forever.

Leo twists a wooden toy between his hands, clicking it open and closed, open and closed. "I—"

She waits, as he gathers his thoughts, as he opens his mouth, closes it again. Opens it again.

"I need to talk to Cisco."

When nothing else seems to be forthcoming, she prompts. "About?"

His laugh burns coming out of his throat, making Totoro raise his head. "Everything? I haven't told him I'm back in therapy."

"Why not?" Her words are even, sincerely questioning, but he still flinches away from them.

"I don't know. It wouldn't bother him."

She cocks her head slightly to the side. "Why do you think you haven't told him?"

"Because—" Leo breathes in, breathes out. "He was there for the worst of it, you know? Everything but the actual breakdown. He knew exactly how fucked up I was. And he—he loved me anyway."

"You said *he knew.*" She settles herself in her seat a bit more. "You don't feel like he knows where your mental state is right now?"

"He shouldn't have to know." Leo stops, hearing the words he just said. "I mean—he was always there, calming me down after my panic attacks, taking care of me. He shouldn't—I shouldn't need him for that. I shouldn't have to lean on him for that."

Her open, sympathetic eyes pin him in place. "It's not wrong to need other people, Leo. It's not weak. Humans need other people. That's how we're wired."

Tears well up, choking him. "I shouldn't—"

When she sees that he's not going to say anything else, she says, "You can't depend on another person to be the foundation for your mental health, it's true. But Leo, that's not what we're talking about here. You absolutely deserve to have people in your life who support you when things are hard. And part of having a relationship with Cisco is letting him in, letting him see you."

"But—" He trails off. The two parts of his brain, the logic that knows she's right, and the emotions that scream she's wrong, grapple with each other, choking his words to nothing.

"I'm not saying it's easy. It's maybe the hardest thing to do. But you did it before. Do you remember it? That feeling, what it was like for him to see all of you and love you?"

Tears overflow from his eyes, even after he closes them, grabbing blindly for the tissue box on the table. "Yes."

"If you let him see where you are, will he use it against you?"

"No!" Leo doesn't even have to think about the answer.

"No, he—he wouldn't. He doesn't even hold a grudge for me ghosting him for seven years, even though he probably should."

She waits until he opens his eyes again to speak. "You said when you came to see me again that you wanted to make this work. Do you remember that?"

He nods.

"Then this is your next step. It doesn't have to be a huge thing. You can tell him that you're back in therapy but you're not ready to talk about everything yet. From what you've said, he'll respect that."

"Yeah." He may not be sure of much right now, but he's sure of that.

She smiles gently at him. "Then that's your homework. Between now and our next session, I need you to tell Cisco that you're seeing someone, that you're working on things. That's all."

The fear is still there, whirling in circles like the world's smallest tornado, but there's also relief. He has a goal, and directions, and a deadline. "Okay."

"Okay." Her smile somehow becomes even warmer. "You can do this, Leo."

He repeats it to himself as he leaves the office, like a mantra. *I can do this.*

Leo is so wrapped up in going through the list of candidates that he almost doesn't notice his cell phone vibrating against the desktop. He gives a moment's consideration to just ignoring it—he has enough time to finish before he needs to leave for the arena, but only barely. It's probably a telemarketer anyway.

When he sees his sister's name on the screen, though,

he scoops it up, absently noting that he needs to charge it, since he's down to barely twelve percent, and swiping to answer. Worry twists in his gut as he lifts the phone to his ear. They don't call without texting first. "Elaine?"

"It's Father."

He's not sure, but he thinks he loses time for a moment, his senses shutting down.

"Leo?"

"Sorry." The word falls automatically from numb lips. Elaine hasn't ever talked about their father to him, not since he asked her not to. She wouldn't, unless— "What —is he—"

When she speaks, he can hear it in her voice, even before she says the words. "It's cancer. He didn't see anyone until it was—it's bad. They said—they said maybe a week. He—he asked to see you. I told him I would tell you. Let you decide."

He can't speak for a moment, paralyzed by the words he's never really been able to forget. Even Totoro's warmth can't thaw the ice creeping through him. "He really—"

"He did, I swear." He halfway expects Elaine to be offended, but she just sounds sad. "I don't blame you if you don't want to. You don't owe him anything. But if you decide to come, there's a ticket in your name at the airport, and one for Totoro. The flight leaves in three hours. We can get you another one if you don't make it through customs in time, but—" she swallows.

"It's that bad?"

"They didn't tell him, but—they told me a week was being generous. Probably only a few days."

Leo can't imagine it. Can't picture it. Sudden untreatable illnesses happened to other people. Not to Bradford Carrington. He knows this train of thought is him stalling, his brain trying to protect him from making a decision. But he doesn't have that luxury.

Almost every fiber of his being is screaming at him not to go. But when he tries to picture the future, knowing that his father is dead, that he never got to say any of the things he needs to say—

"I'm coming. I have to go get Totoro's stuff, but my apartment is on the way to the airport, so I should make it."

"Call or text if you don't." The briskness in Elaine's voice doesn't hide the fact that she's going to burst into tears at any moment, but it covers it enough for them to pretend. "His assistant will book you on the next flight."

Leo bites back the instinctive protest. His father can afford it, and from the sound of things, he won't need the money for much longer. "Okay. I've gotta go. See you soon."

"Love you."

"I love you, too."

Grabbing his keys and Totoro's leash in trembling hands, he heads out the door, speaking over his shoulder to the receptionist as he goes. "I have to go. Family emergency. I'll text Gen and let her know when to expect me back."

Saadhav looks startled, but doesn't stop him, so that's something. "Hope everything is okay."

Leo doesn't have the time to tell him how very not okay everything is, but that's probably for the best.

The drive to his apartment is a traffic-clogged blur. He does his best, but somehow every light seems to be red and everyone seems determined to drive at least 20 km below the speed limit. By the time he's there, unlocking his door, he feels like he's going to shake out of his skin.

He manages to pull it together enough to scoop some

of Totoro's food into a baggie, to throw travel bowls and a couple of his favorite toys into a tote with the food. For a moment, he thinks about packing for himself, but there's no time. They have stores in Boston. He can buy what he needs, or send someone out for it. All he really needs is his passport.

What with everything, he almost manages to walk out the door without locking it behind him. Thankfully he remembers, and even more thankfully, Totoro is in working mode and is being the most well-behaved dog in the history of time, taking advantage of Leo stopping outside to relieve himself quickly and efficiently before climbing obediently into the car.

If he'd thought the drive home was a mess, the drive to the airport is nothing short of torturous. Minutes tick away and he seems to only be crawling along at a snail's pace.

But finally they're there. He pulls up to the valet parking at the departures gate—fuck the price, it doesn't matter. Totoro gets a few looks, but it's entirely possible those looks are for him, very nearly sprinting to the airline check-in desk.

The very professional agent prints his boarding passes and sends him toward security with a minimum of small talk. Leo does his best to appear calm as he and Totoro walk toward the checkpoint; the last thing he needs is to be randomly selected for an extra screening.

Maybe it works, or maybe they don't want the bad press of hassling someone with a service animal. Whatever the reason, he makes it through in the normal amount of hurry up and wait. And by some minor miracle, there's a free Customs kiosk, so that also goes as smoothly as can be expected.

Speedwalking down the terminal, Leo lets out a sigh of

relief when the gate came into sight. He doesn't fully relax, though, until he double-checks the screen and compared the flight number to his boarding pass.

His boarding group is one of the ones listed as boarding, so he joins the line, handing his passport and boarding passes to the attendant when his turn comes. Although she looks charmed by Totoro, she's thankfully educated enough not to try and interact with him, sending them on their way with a "Welcome aboard."

Leo doesn't realize until he checks the boarding passes for seat numbers that his tickets are for business class. It seems ridiculous, but maybe no other tickets were available? He can practically hear Elaine in his head, telling him that their father can afford it.

The plane attendants don't do more than blink at Totoro, who settles obediently to the floor in front of the window seat at Leo's command, looking curiously out the window. Leo sinks down into the aisle seat, letting out what feels like his first full breath since he'd answered Elaine's call.

Pulling his phone out of his pocket, he texts her quickly to say that he made it on the plane, then Gen to tell her that he had to leave.

*take as much time as you need,* she sends back instantly. *don't worry abt the game, i'll tell them to get somebody else.*

Leo's entire body jolts like he's been shocked. Somehow he'd forgotten about the game, about Cisco, in the mad rush to get to the plane on time. *thx,* he sends back, switching to his text thread with Cisco.

The phone flashes a one percent battery warning as he starts to type. *elaine called, father's dying. have to go to boston—*

His screen goes dark as his thumb reaches for the send button.

Well. Shit.

"Your credits will all transfer to BU." His father cut off another bite of chicken with precise, economical motions. "Minnesota agreed to drop your grades for that semester, so they won't hurt your GPA. You can finish your last year, take the MCAT, and be back on track before you know it."

Leo took a deep breath, trying to remember everything his therapist had told him. "It's good that my credits will transfer, but I'm not going to take the MCAT."

His father looked at him, the look that always made him feel like a specimen under a microscope. "Excuse me?"

It was an out, a chance to take it back and knuckle under. Just like he always did. But this wasn't always. Leo was still putting the pieces of himself back together, but it turned out thinking you were dying had a way of putting things into perspective.

"I said I'm not taking the MCAT." Leo forced his hands to be steady as he reached for his water glass. "I'm not going to medical school, so there's no reason for me to take it."

"You—" His father's anger had always run cold, so cold Leo felt like it would shatter him. Maybe that was because neither Leo or Elaine had ever defied him to this extent, because right now his eyes looked hot enough to burn. He got himself back under control fairly quickly, though. "I must have misheard."

Leo sipped, set the glass back down. "If you heard me say I'm not going to medical school, then you heard perfectly. I don't want to be a doctor. That kind of pressure wouldn't be good for me."

"We're going to find you a different therapist tomorrow." A

*muscle jumped in his father's jaw. "I knew that one was too soft."*

*"It's not about the therapist." Anxiety still roiled in his stomach, aching, but there was a dizzying freedom in this. Even if it seemed very much like the freedom of jumping off a cliff, destined to end in brokenness and pain. "I never wanted to be a doctor, Father. But you were determined, and the idea of failing, of disappointing you, was so terrifying that eventually I couldn't do it anymore."*

*His father's eyes narrowed. "Are you blaming me for your weakness?"*

*"No." Leo sighed. "No, that was my fault. I knew it was hurting me, and I kept going. But I can't go through that again. I won't."*

*"You're weak." The words weren't growled, or yelled. They were spoken, simply, as if irrefutable fact. "You always were. I thought eventually you'd manage to stand on your own two feet, to be a man. But that's never going to happen, is it?"*

*It hurt. It was probably always going to hurt. But it didn't break him, and Leo was proud of that.*

*"Not like you mean, no."*

*"Then you can get the fuck out. If this is how you repay me, if you're determined to throw your life away, I can't stop you, but I damn sure don't have to pay for it. Let's see how you do without my money."*

*Leo set his napkin on the table and got to his feet. "All right. Goodbye, Father."*

*His things were mostly still packed from the facility. It only took a few moments to gather the rest, to call a Lyft and make his way outside to wait. Pulling out his phone, he texted Elaine.* I hope you meant it, because I'm omw to yours.

of course i meant it. *The response was nearly immediate, as if she wasn't halfway through her first semester of med school.* just don't wake me up when im sleeping or ill end you.

deal

*He hesitated before locking the phone again, just like every other time. He wanted to text Cisco like it was a physical need, wanted to call him and hear his voice.*

*But what would he say?* sorry I ghosted you for almost six months, but want to support your parasite of a boyfriend when you don't even know if you're going to be playing in the CHL this year?

*Cisco was about to have to work harder than he'd ever worked before. Leo knew it was an excuse, even as he thought it. But confronting his father had used up whatever store of bravery he had left. As much as he wanted Cisco, so much his chest physically ached—he couldn't.*

*Maybe tomorrow.*

LEO'S BREATH starts to quicken as the Lyft turns into the familiar neighborhood. It's not that he likes hospitals, but he'd expected one. He knows how to brace himself for one.

The fact that his father is at home, even with round-the-clock medical care, drives home the severity of his illness in a way nothing else could. Despite Elaine's professional assessment, despite everything, some part of Leo keeps thinking it's a mistake.

Being at home, with hospice staff to keep him comfortable, says more clearly than words that it was true. Bradford Carrington is dying.

The car stops in front of the familiar townhouse long before he's ready. Leo gathers Totoro and his one inadequate bag, fumbling his phone out of his pocket before he remembers that it's dead. He'll have to remember to charge it so he can tip.

He stares at the door for a long, long moment. Despite everything, the grueling flight, the belief that he's made the right choice in coming here, for a minute he just wants to say fuck it. To turn around, walk until he can hail a cab, and then go the fuck home.

Totoro nudges in closer to him, a warm, reassuring presence. Before Leo can give in, the door opens and Elaine closes the distance between them at a run, pulling him into a hug.

Leo wraps his arms around her in return. They stand there like that for a moment before pulling back, both of their eyes bright with tears.

"You made it." She wipes at her eyes, taking his hand to lead him inside. "We weren't sure you would."

"How is he?" Leo's voice lowers without his conscious direction as they cross the threshold.

She shakes her head, lips pressed together. "They've given him meds for the pain, so he's not feeling it, but it's —he's close His kidneys have shut down. It's just a matter of time."

Leo swallows hard when they turn the corner into what used to be his father's study. The furniture has been rearranged to make room for a bed. For a minute, his brain refuses to believe the evidence of his eyes. The gaunt man in the bed isn't his father. There's been some kind of mistake.

But then he opens his eyes, and Leo can't lie to himself any longer.

"Leonard." The word is more breath than sound, accompanied by a rattling sound as his father struggles to breathe. "You came."

Swallowing, Leo crosses the room to stand beside the bed. "I came."

"Good." His father's hand shakes as he lifts it from the blankets, reaching for him. "Needed to say—sorry."

Hearing that word, the one that has never crossed his father's lips before, as far as Leo could remember, only adds to the surreal, detached feeling. Only the pressure of Totoro's body against his legs, steady and comforting, grounds him in the moment. He needs to say something, anything, but all he can do is echo. "Sorry?"

For a moment his father's eyes sharpen. For a moment, he almost looks something like his old self, if Leo just maintains eye contact. "Too many—things to count. I wasn't—a good father."

He barks a laugh when neither Leo or Elaine contradict him, a sharp, painful sound. "No lies for the dying man. Don't—blame you. Shouldn't have—well. Everything." He shakes his head. "Too late. Did it anyway, without me, didn't you. Made yourself—a good life."

"I did." Leo doesn't know why he's surprised. Of course his father would have kept track of him, even after officially washing his hands of him.

"Good." His father's breath rasps in his throat. "So. Sorry. Doesn't fix—shit I did. But I am."

Leo swallows back the words that tried to rise in his throat, the questions or recriminations. Rehashing everything that had happened won't change the past, and from what Elaine said, they don't have the time. "Thank you."

His father's eyes flutter shut.

For a minute, Leo thinks this is it, but then he sees the slight rise and fall of his father's chest, hears the rattle in his throat.

"He's been in and out." Elaine's voice is quiet as she takes his hand, squeezing gently. "That's the longest he's been lucid in the last couple of days, actually. Are you okay?"

Leo thinks about it. "I have no idea."

"Fair." They stand there in silence for a moment before she nudges him toward the chair by the bed. "How long can you stay?"

He sinks down into the chair, his hand going automatically to Totoro's neck, breathing a little easier at the familiar texture under his fingers. "I—I don't know. I didn't pack anything—"

"We can send his assistant out to get you things if you need them." She pulls another chair closer. "But if you need to go, you should go. You don't owe him more of your time."

Leo rubs at his face with his free hand. "I know, I just—"

She smiles sadly when he doesn't finish. "I know. It's your call. I'll back you up, whatever you decide."

Before Leo can say anything, Totoro comes to quivering attention under his hand, eyes and snout pointed at the bed.

It takes him a moment to realize that the rattling has stopped.

By the time his plane lands, Leo is nearly delirious with fatigue. He does his best to sleep on the flights, but every time he starts to drift off, he would hear the hideous, labored rattle of his father's breath, snapping him back awake. He even takes an Ativan when Totoro noses pointedly at the pocket where he kept one for emergencies. It makes him groggy, like he's sleepwalking through thickened air, but it doesn't let him sleep.

None of it helps.

He can't call a Lyft with his phone still dead—he hadn't thought to buy a new charger cord until he was already boarding the flight from Toronto to home—so he stumbles out of the airport to where taxis wait, despite the late hour. Or is it early? He remembers to let Totoro find a plant to do his business, then makes his way to the closest cab.

The driver looks skeptically at Totoro, but something about Leo manages to shortcut the usual suspicion about why a young, able-bodied man needs a service dog. At least the man doesn't think he's drunk, and if he suspects drugs, well, he's right, even if they are the legal kind.

Giving the driver his address, he leans his head back against the seat. It should only be about twenty minutes at this time of night. He's not going to be able to sleep, not until he's in his own bed, probably. But he can close his eyes, gritty and burning behind the lids.

He doesn't sleep, but he must achieve some kind of doze, because the next thing he knows, Totoro is nudging him insistently. He manages to fumble a credit card out of his wallet for the driver and get it back afterward, which should count as an accomplishment.

"Buddy, are you okay to get inside?"

It takes him a few seconds to realize the driver has spoken, which probably doesn't help. "No, I—Totoro's got me. Part of his training."

The driver gives him a skeptical glance, then gets out to open the door for him. Leo thinks he waits to drive away until they're inside, but he can't be sure if he just imagines it. He needs most of his focus just to get to his door, though, to get the key into the lock and turn it.

Tears well up in his eyes once they're inside, in his familiar, safe space. He doesn't try to stop them, just forces himself to refill Totoro's bowls before collapsing face-first on his bed, leaving the door open behind him for Totoro.

The next thing he knows, light is coming through the windows. Which is odd, because he can hear thunder. Or, no, his sleep-deprived brain realizes. Someone is pounding on the door.

After a couple of tries Leo remembers how to stand up, stumbling through the apartment to his front door. He barely gets it open before Cisco storms inside, angrier than Leo has ever seen him.

Leo knows that normally he would be quivering internally, unprepared to face that anger. But he's slept maybe five hours in the last twenty-four, still a little fogged over from the medication, and right now he's hollow, emptied out, with no more room for emotion.

"What the fuck?" Cisco doesn't get in his space, because even angry, he doesn't use his size to intimidate like that, but his hands clasp together so tight his knuckles look white. "What the fuck, Leo? You weren't at the game, you weren't here, you didn't answer any of my calls or texts, I thought—"

Leo knows what he thought, and he was wrong. He's not empty, because his heart is breaking for both of them. He doesn't mean to interrupt, but the words come out all the same, and Cisco stops to listen, because that's who he is.

"My father is dead."

## 19

## CISCO

As the hours go by without a text or a call, Cisco can't decide if he's sad or angry. Both emotions swirl through his body, fighting it out until he feels empty, helpless. Like that boy from seven years ago, with the shattered heart and the fake smile.

He sleeps fitfully, waking multiple times per hour to check his phone. By the time morning light starts glowing around the edges of his curtains, he can't stand the tossing and turning any longer. Standing under a hot shower doesn't do much to wake him up, but at least he feels cleaner.

He makes twice his usual amount of coffee, drinking it down without tasting it. His thoughts are still slower than usual—thank fuck he doesn't have a game tonight—but they're working. Not that he likes the conclusions he's reaching, at all.

Leo isn't at his apartment—well, he wasn't there last night, or at the game like he'd promised. For a moment, Cisco's brain conjures up a terrifying picture of Leo collapsed in his apartment, injured or sick, unable to call for help.

But logic banishes that almost as soon as it arises. If that had happened, Totoro would have barked until someone came to help, or maybe figured out a way out of the apartment to find someone. And the apartment had been completely silent.

Draining the last of his coffee, Cisco goes to find his coat and boots. He'll stop by the apartment one more time, and if Leo still isn't there, he'll go to his job. Part of him cringes at the thought, at how stalkery it feels. But if—he shudders, but forces himself to face the thought head-on— if Leo wants to end it, that's fine. Cisco has lived without him before, and if he has to, he can again.

He can't live with the possibility that Leo might be hurt somewhere. He needs to know.

The drive to Leo's apartment passes in a blur. Cisco is sure he follows the traffic rules, because he makes it in one piece and he doesn't remember any honking horns or shouted curses. But he honestly cannot remember a single moment between leaving his place and pulling into a parking space at Leo's building.

Making his way to Leo's door, he knocks maybe a little louder than is strictly necessary. It's as if now that he let himself think that maybe Leo was hurt or sick, the image was burned into his brain.

When Leo opens the door, all he feels at first is the warm, soothing wash of relief. Leo is here, he's alive, no visible injuries, nothing broken. Relief transmutes quickly to anger, though, when Cisco realizes the implications of Leo's perfectly healthy state.

He pushes his way inside, some part of him aware that it's entirely too early to be having this discussion in the hall. Once the door closes behind him, the words pour out, like water forcing its way through rock.

"What the fuck?" Cisco clasps his hands together; he'd never thought he was the kind of person to use violence off the ice, but the anger in his gut scares him with the urge to rip and claw, to make Leo feel the same pain he's been feeling. "What the fuck, Leo? You weren't at the game, you weren't here, you didn't answer my calls or texts. I thought—"

He doesn't want to say what he thought, to put words to the fear he's been living with every day since Leo came back into his life—maybe since he received that fateful text from Elaine. Thankfully, Leo stops him. Leo opens his mouth, eyes wide and dark and hurting in a way Cisco hasn't seen in years.

"My father is dead."

For a moment, Cisco can't process the words. What do they mean, what do they have to do with this conversation? And then the meaning sinks in and he can't help but reach for Leo, can't help but pull him close and try, like he'd tried so many times before, to put himself between Leo and the world.

Leo sways into him, losing his balance for a second. It's almost not noticeable, but it makes Cisco's heart clench in his chest, especially when he puts it together with the rumpled clothes, the dark circles under Leo's eyes, the way his hair always sticks up first thing in the morning.

"Here, baby." He guides them to the couch so they can sit down. It takes a bit of maneuvering to find a way that he can keep holding Leo, but neither of them wants to separate. Totoro hops up on Leo's other side, sandwiching him protectively between them. "Do you want to talk about it?"

Wetness blooms where Leo's face presses against his neck. "I—not really. But sometimes that means I should."

"When you're ready." Cisco rubs circles on his back with one hand. The anger that had been burning in him is small now, nearly meaningless in the face of Leo's pain, but not the nervous energy it had brought with it. He wants to run, to scream, to hit pucks at a net until he can't lift his arms. But right now, Leo needs him. "Whenever you're ready, baby."

They sit like that for a moment, before Leo turns his head enough to speak. "You should be yelling at me."

"No I shouldn't."

He pushes back enough to see Cisco's face, his eyes wet and red with mostly unshed tears. "Maybe not yelling. But you—you should say what you came here to say."

"Baby, your father just died." Cisco pauses. "I mean, I'm assuming—

Leo lifts a hand, stopping him mid-sentence. "I'm not saying you should be, like, calling me names or something. But if this—if we're going to make this work, you have to be able to talk to me when things are bothering you. You can't just keep the broken stuff inside. It'll cut you to pieces."

Cisco bites back the retort that wants to come out, breathes deeply through his nose. "I'm not gonna—is this really the time?"

"If not now, when?" Leo's face sets in determined lines Cisco knows all too well. "I shouldn't have interrupted you, before. It was a dick move. I should've let you talk, and not derailed things with my shit. I just—I wanted you to know that I didn't just leave."

"I needed to know that."

He smiles, a little sad. "But that made it about me, and my feelings. Again. I want this to work, Cisco. I want us to work. But if you treat me like I'm breakable, like I can't handle you having feelings, it's not going to."

Cisco has no idea how to respond to that, he realizes. But when he opens his mouth, the words just come out. "I just—I don't want to be like your dad. I don't want to use my feelings to make you feel small."

"Oh, Cisco." Leo leans in again, holding him close. "You won't."

"How can you be sure?"

Leo's lips curve into a smile against his neck. "I know, Cisco. I trust you, even when I don't trust myself. But I need you to talk to me, baby."

Part of Cisco's mind screams at him not to do it. But just like before, the words come pouring out. How he felt when he got Elaine's text, how he had to smile and act happy during the draft. How terrible the days afterward were, then the weeks, and the months. Moving to Alberta, getting everything he ever wanted.

How hollow and empty it felt, without Leo.

How he'd felt like Leo was pulling away, was keeping secrets, and then—

"And then I did it again." Leo sighs when he finally comes to a stop. "I'm surprised you didn't just wash your hands of me entirely."

Cisco sags back against the couch, feeling like a limp cloth, damp and wrung out. "I—I can't do that again, baby. I love you. I want to be with you. But I can't do the silence. Not again."

"Do you want me to start carrying a second phone?" For a second, Cisco actually considers it. Leo must sense it, because he moves back to where he can make eye contact again. "I'm serious, baby. If that's what you need to feel safe, I'll do it."

"Maybe just one of those backup batteries so you can

charge it." Cisco closes his eyes, lets himself lean into the touch of Leo's fingers carding through his hair. "Or—"

After he goes quiet for a moment, Leo nudges him. "Or?"

"Never mind."

The soothing hand stops. "Please tell me, baby."

"Or you and Totoro could move in with me." Cisco keeps his eyes closed. "And then if you have to go somewhere suddenly, you could leave a note."

When he gives into temptation, opening his eyes just a little, Leo is looking at him with a wondering expression.

"Unless it's too soon. It's probably too soon."

"Cisco." He can hear the smile in Leo's voice. "I've loved you for almost ten years. But how about we put a pin in that for a minute and I tell you why I've been turning down lunch dates for the past few weeks?"

Part of Cisco isn't sure he wants to know, but if Leo's smiling like that, it can't be bad. "Okay."

Leo's hand starts moving through his hair again. "I realized, on my birthday, that the thing I was the most afraid of was messing this up—messing us up again. I didn't want that. So I texted my therapist."

Cisco's breath leaves him, not in a rush, but a slow, steady exhale. As he listens to Leo's voice, as he breathes in again, he identifies the elusive feeling glowing through his body. Not just love; love he knows, love he recognizes. But more than that.

Hope.

✕

*"I can't believe the season's over."*

*Cisco nodded, careful not to dislodge Leo's head where it*

rested on his shoulder. "I know. It was a good season. Now we just have to make it through finals, and then summer."

Leo snorted. "You say that like you aren't staying here to do extra training and classes all summer."

"You have no room to talk, Mister It's Easier To Take A Full Load When There's No Hockey."

"Maybe we should just accept that we're both nerds."

Cisco laughed despite his nerves. He had no reason to be nervous, but he still was. "Maybe so. But, uh, speaking of us and the summer...I wanted to ask you a question."

"Yeah?"

There was only a little bit of anxiety in Leo's voice, which Cisco took as a win. "The house is going to be closed for repairs, and next year is probably my last year before the draft, so I was thinking maybe we could get an apartment?"

"Francisco Reyes." Leo tried to be solemn, but Cisco could hear the laughter lurking underneath. "Are you asking me to move in with you?"

"Yes." Cisco pressed a kiss into his hair. "I don't want to waste a minute that we could spend together."

Leo smiled softly at him. "You're such a romantic. But you're also kind of slow. I don't think I've been back to my dorm since February."

When Cisco stopped to think about it, he couldn't help but smile. He hadn't noticed at the time, but it was true that Leo's things had been making a slow migration into his room ever since they first started dating.

"Well then. Don't think of it as moving in together, since we already did that. Think of it as getting a place with thicker walls and a bigger bed."

"Mmmm." Leo tilted his head back, dragging his teeth lightly across Cisco's neck. "Maybe with a headboard I can tie you to?"

*Cisco swallowed hard but he still sounded a little wrecked when he answered. "Yeah, that—that'd be good.*

*"Let's find a place with very thick walls." Leo's hand slid slowly down Cisco's chest, teasing over his nipples and making him shiver before curling around his half-hard cock. "Some place I can take my time with you, where you can get as loud as you want."*

*"Please." Cisco didn't know if he was agreeing with Leo or begging. It didn't seem to matter, though.*

*Either way, Leo surged up to capture his mouth, all the while jerking him slowly, torturously, back to fully hard. "We're not there yet, baby. If you want another round, you're gonna have to be quiet. Can you do that? Can you be good for me?"*

*Cisco let go, lets himself start to slip into that headspace where all he had to worry about is doing what Leo tells him. Being good. He can do that, it's safe.*

*Leo had him.*

*"Yes."*

*"Yes what?" Leo nipped at his ear, but the sting was faraway, barely noticeable.*

*Cisco whined when Leo's hand leaves his cock. "Yes, I can be good."*

*"I know you can." Leo's voice was a caress, like the audible manifestation of the way he touched Cisco, reverent and possessive. "Roll over for me, baby. Show me how good you can be."*

*Cisco's last coherent thought before everything became a mixture of heat and sensation was how lucky he was, to have Leo in his life, every day. For the rest of his life, maybe, because he is a romantic, and that should feel scary, but it didn't.*

*It just felt right.*

WHEN LEO YAWNS TWICE in the same sentence, Cisco pushes them up from the couch, still holding him tightly. "You need to sleep, baby."

"But—"

He presses a kiss to Leo's forehead. "What time did you get in?"

"I dunno. Three, maybe? Four?"

"It's barely eight. Sleep. I'll be here when you wake up, and we can talk more."

Leo sighs. "I guess. Sleep with me?"

Cisco kisses him softly. "Anytime."

They do have to separate eventually. Cisco undresses Leo, tucking him into bed, and reaches back to pull his own t-shirt off just as Totoro whines from the doorway.

Leo sits up. "He needs to go out. I'll—"

"You'll lie back down and let me take him out." Cisco stares him down until he settles back down onto the pillows. "I'll be right back. Promise."

Any argument Leo might have made is interrupted by the jaw-cracking yawn that takes over his whole face. Cisco takes advantage of the opening, slipping back out to the living room to find his coat and Totoro's leash.

Grabbing the spare key from the hook by the door, he takes them both out into the freezing air. Thankfully Totoro isn't any more inclined to linger than he is, and they're back in the apartment in record time.

Double-checking that the door is locked, Cisco hangs the key back up and makes his way to the bedroom as fast as he can without actually running. Totoro goes to his bed without complaint, licking at Cisco's fingers before laying his head down. Despite the speed with which Totoro took care of business, Leo is already asleep, snoring softly.

Cisco stands and looks at him for a moment, letting himself breathe, letting himself believe. This is real. Leo is here, not disappeared for another seven years, or forever. Leo wants to be with him. They're going to make this work.

Suddenly the weight of his sleepless night catches up with him. Taking off his clothes and slipping into bed uses up the last of his energy.

He only stays awake long enough to register Leo wrapping around him before he slips into sleep.

## 20

# LEO

When Leo wakes up again, afternoon light glows red-gold through the window. Cisco's chest rises and falls under his hand, and when he looks up, Cisco glances away from his phone to smile down at him.

"Hey."

Leo can't help smiling back, warmth blooming in his chest. "Hey. What time is it?"

"A little after two." Cisco rubs a hand over his back, familiar soothing circles. "Feel better?"

"Yeah." Leo leans into his touch, then nearly jumps out of his skin. "Wait, don't you have practice? Why are you still here?"

Cisco shakes his head, urging him back down. "It's fine, baby. My boyfriend's father died, they completely understand."

Leo swallows. It's not that he had forgotten, exactly, what had happened in Boston. He'd just pushed it to the back of his mind, focused on what he and Cisco need. But with the words, it comes pouring back.

"Are you okay?"

He has to stop and think about that. Is he? He's sad, yes, but— "I think so? You know we weren't exactly close."

"Yeah, but still." Cisco presses a kiss to his temple. "It's your father."

"I lost him a long time ago." Leo tastes the truth in the words as he says them, no matter how bitter they are. "When I told him I wasn't going to med school, he told me not to come back until I was done wasting my life. That was the last time I talked to him, until last night."

Cisco nods. "I'm glad you got that chance."

"Yeah. I'm sad, but—" He shrugs. "I did my mourning a long time ago."

"Okay." Cisco rolls over to face him. "Want me to make us some breakfast for lunch?"

Leo opens his mouth to say yes, but then he remembers something from the morning. Or thinks he does. "Maybe in a minute. Did you actually ask me to move in with you?"

Cisco's cheekbones flush pink. "Um. Yeah?"

"Did you mean it?"

"Baby." Cisco curls a hand around the back of Leo's neck. "If it wouldn't have scared you off, I would have asked you after that first dinner. I've been stopping myself from asking for weeks. But if you need more time, I totally understand."

Leo laughs. "We've had seven years apart. I think that was enough time, don't you?"

Cisco drags him in, answering with his kiss instead of words. There's a wondering, reverent feel to his kiss, like he doesn't quite believe that they're here, doing this. Together.

"Can I take a slightly longer rain check on that dinner?" Leo asks when they break apart. He's not quite sure when his hand ended up on the small of Cisco's back, but he's definitely willing to take advantage of the location.

"Sure." Cisco cuts off with a gasp when Leo slides that hand down, squeezing his ass gently. "Did you have something else in mind?"

Leo kisses him first this time, deep and dirty and hungry, pressing their bodies together and starting a slow, filthy grind. "Well, we did have a fight. So I think we deserve make-up sex. Or maybe we're-going-to-move-in-together sex."

Cisco sucks in his breath when Leo ghosts a fingertip over his hole. "Whatever you want, baby."

Leo rolls them over until Cisco is on his back, leaving him sprawled over Cisco's naked body like a blanket. "You might want to take that back if you plan to leave this bed anytime soon."

"Why would I want to leave?" Cisco looks up at him, love shining out of his eyes. "You're here."

Swallowing back the tears prickling at his eyes, Leo leans down to kiss him again, as long as he can before the insistent drumbeat of blood in his cock recalls him to what they were doing.

Fortunately the lube isn't hard to find, still in the bedside drawer where it got tossed last time. Leo slicks up his hand quickly, letting the bottle fall somewhere on the bed while he reaches between them.

"Remember the first time?" Inhaling sharply at the sensation, he gets their cocks liked up, wraps his hand around both of them. "The party?"

"Yeah." Cisco sighs out the word, rolling his hips a little to fuck up into the circle of Leo's hand. "I seriously thought I was going to embarrass myself and come in like, thirty seconds."

Leo laughs. Somehow he'd forgotten what it was like,

laughing during sex. "Me too. I was so nervous. I wanted you so much."

"Always." Cisco's eyes flutter shut, every muscle in his neck and shoulders tense. "Always want you. Please, baby."

"You're so good." It's not fair, but Leo can't resist, loves the way Cisco shudders at the word. "I'll fuck you after your game tomorrow, if you can be good and stay out of the box. Can you do that for me, baby? Can you be good?"

Cisco moans. "Yes, yes, I can be good, please, baby, please—"

"What do you want, Cisco?" Leo is right on the edge himself, but he can wait long enough for this. Long enough to see Cisco come apart under him, wrecked and perfect and *his*.

"Please, let me come, please—"

Leo waits for one stroke, too, gauges the tension in Cisco's muscles, the wetness dripping off his cock. "Come for me, love."

He barely has enough time to enjoy watching Cisco come before he tips over the edge himself, adding to the mess on Cisco's stomach and chest. With supreme effort, he manages to roll to the side instead of collapsing down into the puddle of semen and lube, but he keeps a hand on Cisco's chest, unwilling to be separated.

"Fuck." Cisco groans the word out, shivering all over. "That—fuck, baby."

"Too much?" Leo kisses his bicep lightly, tries to remember how to breathe.

Cisco opens his eyes, grinning lazily, his heart hammering solidly against Leo's palm. "Only if you don't fuck me tomorrow."

Leo can't resist the urge to kiss him, to feel that smile against his lips, to taste the happiness glowing off Cisco like sunshine. "You know what you have to do, then."

"Mmm." Cisco slides an arm around his shoulder, pulling him close. "Shower, then food?"

"Whatever you want."

Neither of them moves for a moment, though, and then Cisco goes stiff next to him. "Wait. Was Totoro—"

They both look over at Totoro's bed at the same time, finding it empty. Leo wants to laugh at Cisco for the way he nearly collapses with relief, but manages to use the energy to slide out of bed instead. "Come on, baby."

Cisco groans, but lets Leo pull him to his feet. "Next time, we're closing the bedroom door."

*LEO BLINKED HIS EYES OPEN. When did he close them? He had no idea, but it had felt nice for them to be closed. Had he overslept and missed a class?*

*He couldn't worry too much about it, though. Not when everything was warm and floaty and good. He had a vague sense that there was something he should be worried about, maybe the slight ache in his mouth that seemed like it belonged to someone else. But the floating was nice. He'd think about it later.*

*"How are you feeling?"*

*He turned his head to see where the voice came from. A strange strangled noise filled the room and he realized a few seconds later that it came from him. But the hottest guy he'd ever seen was sitting next to him, asking how he felt, so he thought he could be forgiven for being surprised.*

*Suddenly he realized he didn't answer the question. "Um. Fine, I think? Kind of floaty."*

*"They definitely gave you the good stuff." Hot Guy reached out and took his hand!*

*Leo's soul made a creditable attempt to leave his body and* ascend to a higher plane of existence. Or at least he thought that's what the feeling in his stomach was.

Hot Guy laughed. "A higher plane of existence, huh?"

"Oh shit." Leo clapped his free hand over his mouth. "I said that out loud?"

"It's okay." Hot Guy squeezed his hand gently. "I'm just glad you're not hurting. They'll come check on you in a little while to make sure you're doing okay before they let you go home."

Leo nodded. He wasn't thinking too clearly, but this definitely looked like a doctor's office. It made sense that someone would come to check on him. But it was nice that Hot Guy was here in the meantime.

His mind was moving more slowly than usual, so it took him a couple of minutes to realize the implications. If a nurse or doctor was coming to check on him soon, he'd need to act fast if he wanted a chance to see Hot Guy after he left.

He definitely wanted that.

"Hey." That seemed like a reasonable way to start, right?

Hot Guy kept smiling at him, so it must not have been too bad. "Hey."

Shit, what should he say now? After a couple of seconds, Leo decided that straightforward was the way to go. Mostly because he couldn't think of anything else. "Would you want to get coffee or something sometime?"

He almost couldn't bring himself to look, to see the reaction, but when he peeked, Hot Guy was smiling at him. Like maybe he thought Leo was cute. "Are you asking me out?"

It must have been the medication, but Leo didn't feel nervous anymore. Just excited. "Yeah, I am." Thankfully he managed to stop talking before he started saying how hot Hot Guy was. Which— "Um. What's your name?"

Hot Guy looked like he wanted to laugh, but not in a bad way. Not like he was laughing at Leo, not meanly. "I'm Cisco."

"Cisco." The name seemed kind of familiar, but Leo couldn't quite put his finger on where he'd heard it before. "I'm Leo."

"Nice to meet you, Leo." Cisco took his hand when he held it out, shaking it firmly. "And yes. I'd love to go out with you. We should probably wait until after you're recovered, though."

The smile felt a little twingy around the sore spots in his mouth, but Leo didn't care. "That makes sense. It's a date, though?"

"It's a date."

Leo's eyes were heavy again, so he let them close. Cisco held onto his hand the whole time.

WHEN LEO WOKE UP, his mouth was Sahara-dry, throbbing in the space where his wisdom teeth used to be. He groaned before he even opened his eyes. "Ow."

"Welcome back, sleeping beauty." Cisco sounded far too cheerful, so it must not be too early. "I have meds, but you have to drink this smoothie with them."

Leo grumbled his way up to sitting, rubbing at his eyes. "Thanks for not making me eat something."

"The surgeon said you probably wouldn't want to chew for a few days." Cisco had a large pill in one hand and a glass in the other, complete with a straw. "Here you go."

Swallowing the pill was a bit of an ordeal, but it went down okay with a little of the smoothie. After a couple of swallows, he could think past the cool, refreshing liquid feel of the smoothie and recognize the flavor. "I thought we were out of almond butter?"

Cisco shrugged. "I sent Seth to the store for more. Figured you wouldn't be up to chewing right away."

"You're so good to me." Leo managed a couple more swal-

*lows before a memory forced itself into his awareness. "Did—Did I hit on you when I was coming out of anesthesia?"*

*"You did." Cisco's grin was entirely too smug, but under the circumstances Leo didn't think he could blame him. "It was adorable."*

*The only good thing about the pain in his jaw was that Leo couldn't hold on to embarrassment for long. "Oh my God."*

*"I mean, I said yes." Cisco leaned in and kissed him gently on the forehead. "I always will."*

*Maybe the medication was finally kicking in, maybe the smoothie was soothing his stomach, but suddenly, Leo didn't feel so bad.*

*Of course, Cisco had to ruin it. "I got video."*

*The medication really must have kicked in, because hitting him with a pillow didn't hurt at all.*

LEO IS CURLED up with Cisco on the couch, bickering happily about dinner plans since there isn't a game tonight—takeout or delivery preferred—when Cisco's phone vibrates against the surface of the end table.

He glances absently at the screen and stops mid-sentence, the smile sliding off his face.

"What?" Anxiety makes itself known in Leo's stomach, of course, but mostly he just feels tired. Haven't they been through enough already?

"It's Seth."

Leo sucks in a breath. "He's being sent down?"

Cisco shakes his head. "They traded him, to the Thunderbirds."

"To Dallas?"

"Yeah." Cisco taps at his screen. "I have to call him."

Leo reaches for his own phone. "When does he have to leave? Do we have time for dinner?"

"I'll ask." Cisco lifts Leo's hand to his lips, brushing a kiss across his knuckles. "Hey, man, I just heard."

Even as close as he and Cisco are sitting, Leo can't make out the words, just the determined cheerfulness in Seth's voice.

"When do they want you down there?" Cisco pauses, listening to whatever Seth has to say. "Yeah? Okay, so we're taking you out to dinner. No, you don't get a choice. I'll text you the restaurant and the time."

Seth says something else, a little sad but a little fond at the same time.

"Yeah, me too. See you in a bit." Cisco ends the call, lets his body slump back against the couch. "He doesn't leave until tomorrow. You find a place with a private room we can get tonight and I'll text the team."

Leo squeezes his hand and hits the button to dial the first restaurant. "Hello, is your private room free tonight? And how many people does it fit?"

The person on the other end gives him the answers that he needs, so he shoots Cisco a thumbs-up while he finishes the process of reserving the space, double-checking that they won't give him shit about Totoro. As soon as he hangs up, he sends Cisco a text with the address and time to be forwarded on to the team's group text.

"Come on." Cisco pulls him to his feet as soon as the message goes out. "We'd better get dressed if we're going to make it in time."

Leo follows him willingly into the bedroom. "Are you gonna be okay?"

Smiling, Cisco pulls him into a hug. "Yeah. It would be great if he could've stayed, but that's not how the game works. And the Thunderbirds defense sucks ass, so they'll probably keep him up for most of the season, if not all of it. It'll be good for him. Better than here, really."

"But you'll miss him." Leo finishes, squeezing Cisco one last time before letting go and turning to his dresser. "I will, too."

Cisco just nods, dressing in silence.

Loading Totoro into the back seat, they drive to the restaurant without much conversation, arriving just moments before Seth walks in the front door. The hostess ushers them back to the private room, assuring them that she'll bring the rest of their party back as soon as they arrive.

Cisco wastes no time hugging him. "How are you doing? Getting everything lined up?"

Seth shrugs. "I think so? They don't have a captain right now, but they want me to room with one of their As, so at least I don't have to live out of a hotel for the rest of the season."

"That's good." Leo hesitates for a second before reaching for his own hug, but Seth leans into it willingly. "We're gonna miss you, though. Texas is a little further away than Calgary."

"Just a smidge." Seth smiles, happiness and uncertainty mingled in his eyes. "But you could still come visit. And it's not like I don't know anybody down there."

Cisco nods. "Oh yeah, doesn't Will live in Dallas?"

"When he's not going on fancy author book tours and shit." Seth shakes his head, smiling at the memory of his college d-partner. "Still can't believe it."

"Maybe we can come visit this summer." Leo looks up at Cisco. "It's not that far from where your mom lives, right?"

"Yeah," Cisco said. "Let us know when and we'll be there."

Seth's smile widens into something more genuine-looking. "I'm gonna hold you to that."

They don't have time for any more conversation before the rest of the team starts to stream in, passing Seth from person to person and group to group.

"You know Dallas in summer is going to be hot as hell, right?" Cisco pulls him toward a table as Suzie, Obi-Wan, and Stewie start trying to get everyone to sit down so they can give the long-suffering waitstaff their orders.

Leo shrugs. "It'll be worth it."

From the smile on Cisco's face, he definitely agrees.

"You have to go." Leo knows it's true, but he doesn't let go.

"Yeah." Cisco makes no effort to move away from the wall he's leaning against, tilting his head to steal another kiss.

Leo falls into the kiss for a moment before forcing himself to pull back. "Your team will never forgive me if I get you scratched."

"Yeah, yeah." Cisco presses a kiss under his jaw.

Taking a breath, Leo forces himself to step back. "Come on, baby. How am I gonna keep my promise if you don't play tonight?"

Cisco shrugs lazily. "I mean, if I don't play, I won't end up in the box."

"That is not the point." Leo straighten's Cisco's tie, then his own. "Go on. Do your job. I'll be here after."

"Promise?" Cisco manages a light tone, but his eyes tell a different story as he catches Leo's hand in his.

Lifting their hands to his lips, Leo brushes a kiss over Cisco's knuckles. Hopefully it won't take that long, but he plans to spend the rest of his life making sure Cisco believes he'll come back. "Promise. And my phone is at a hundred percent."

"Okay." Cisco sighs, pushing off the wall. "One more kiss? For luck?"

"If you win, you're gonna make me do this every game, aren't you?"

Cisco grins. "You know me so well, baby."

Bracing one hand on Cisco's shoulders, Leo uses the other to pull Cisco's head down. He means to keep the kiss soft, quick, but Cisco's lips part under his, inviting him in, and Leo is always going to want to take that invitation.

A sharp whistle startles them apart. When Leo looks back over his shoulder, Chiagoziem, one of the As, is grinning back at him, teeth white against his dark brown skin. "That's a fine, Reyes."

Cisco kisses Leo lightly before letting go. "Worth it."

"Get your ass in the room, Sunshine." Still smiling, Chiagoziem walks around the corner without waiting for a reply. Totoro whuffs softly, as if in punctuation.

"I have to go."

Leo can't help smiling at Cisco's reluctance. "I know, baby. Go, before you get fined again."

Cisco starts walking, slowly, like he's waiting for something else.

"Cisco?"

He turns around. Waiting.

For a second, Leo thinks about brushing it off, but he squares his shoulders and takes the leap. "I'm probably going to ask you to marry me someday."

Anyone looking at Cisco's face in that moment would understand completely how he got his nickname. "Yeah?" He clears his throat, eyes shining. "I'm probably going to say yes."

Leo's face hurts from smiling as Cisco disappears around the corner. He doesn't have much time to stand here and bask in this feeling, but he gives himself a moment to savor it, to be thankful for every step, every moment, that brought him to this place, this choice, this leap of faith.

This time, he doesn't have to jump alone.

# EPILOGUE

Leo's knee starts moving as soon as the Lyft pulls away from the airport, jittering up and down just like it had on the way to catch their plane. And at the gate, waiting for their flight. And on the plane, and their connecting flights, all the way until they landed in Tulsa.

Totoro whines softly, nudging his nose under Leo's hand as Cisco reaches out, resting his hand gently on Leo's leg.

"Sorry." Leo's hands clench in Totoro's fur.

"Nothing to apologize for, baby." Cisco squeezes gently, then switches hands so he can hold Leo's, too. "I know telling you not to be nervous isn't going to help."

Leo shakes his head, another jerky motion so unlike him. "Not even a little bit."

"Yeah. But I'm here with you, and so is Totoro. We've got you, okay?"

A deep breath, and Leo nods. "Tell me again?"

"It's just going to be Mom, Paola, Chris, the twins, and us. And Totoro. Small family lunch. You don't even have to say anything. Just eat your body weight in torrejas and pupusas and Mami will be thrilled."

"I thought you said pupusas weren't usually an Easter food?"

Sometimes it takes Cisco's breath away, realizing that this is real. That he has Leo, that Leo has been with him long enough to remember things like that. "Nah, but Mami always makes my favorites when I come home. So there's going to be pupusas and pasteles and carne guisada and more food than we could eat even if there were twenty of us. She's gonna send leftovers home with us. We might need an extra suitcase."

Leo laughs, like he thinks Cisco is joking. That's okay. He'll learn soon enough.

It's been awhile and some of the buildings have changed, but Cisco recognizes the area outside the car windows. "Another five minutes, or so, baby."

"Okay." Leo inhales slowly and deliberately, exhales the same way. "Okay."

The Lyft turns off Memorial onto 91st, then into a residential neighborhood. It's probably shallow, but every time Cisco comes to visit, he feels the same swell of pride at the knowledge that he was able to buy his mami a house in this neighborhood. Not as big a house as he'd wanted to, but still. Big enough that they could have fit his tiny childhood home in there at least twice. Maybe three times.

Leo's knee starts moving under his hand again, so he squeezes gently. "We've got you."

Before Leo can answer, they turn into the driveway, pulling up behind what must be Paola's car. "Okay." Leo takes another deliberate breath and reaches for the door handle. "Okay."

Cisco unbuckles his seatbelt and follows him out that

door so he doesn't have to let go of his hand. "It's gonna be good, baby. Promise."

Retrieving their bags, they walk hand in hand up the sidewalk to the front door, Totoro trotting sedately along beside them. Leo's grip tightens as Cisco reaches for the door handle, but he follows when Cisco leads the way into the house filled with the mingled scents that tell him he's home.

"Tio! Tio!" Paola's twins come skidding around the corner and nearly take him out at the knees. "What did you bring us?"

"Sophia! Gabriel!" Paola follows in their wake. "Stop it!"

Cisco sets their bags down and squats down to their level so he can whisper. "I'll show you later."

"Stop teaching my children bad habits, baboso." Paola turns her children around. "I know you heard Abuela tell you to go wash your hand before we eat. Go. Wash. Sing Happy Birthday two times. Tio will still be here when you're done."

The two of them trudge off toward the nearest bathroom, looking back over their shoulders every couple of steps.

Standing up, Cisco pulls Paola into a one-armed hug, still holding Leo's hand with the other. "I see you survived plague season."

"No, actually I died. My ghost is haunting your ass." She brushes bangs back out of her eyes, avoiding Cisco's meaningful stare, and offers her hand to Leo. "Good to see you again, Leo."

"You too." His other hand has a death grip on Cisco's but he manages to smile as he shakes her hand.

Paola must take the threats Cisco had made in their last phone call seriously. Or, more likely, she can see that

Leo's scared to death and about two minutes from hyper-ventilating, because she turns and leads them toward the kitchen. "Come on, Mami's just about got everything ready."

The kitchen is larger and fancier than the one Cisco grew up with, but the smells are the same, the food covering every available surface is the same. And the woman turning from the stove to greet them, aside from a couple of extra lines around her eyes, is much the same, too.

She pulls them both in for a hug with each arm, holding on for a long, long minute. "You made it! The food is almost ready. Take off your coats and you can help take things to the table."

They turn to obey, but she catches Leo's hand, standing on tiptoes to press a kiss to his cheek. "Welcome home, mijo. It's good to have you back."

Leo's eyes shine as he looks back at her. Or at least, Cisco thinks they do. His own vision is a little blurry.

Leo's smile might actually be the most beautiful thing Cisco's ever seen. Their eyes meet, and Leo squeezes his hand before letting go, absolute truth ringing in his words.

"There's nowhere I'd rather be."

# ACKNOWLEDGMENTS

This book was a struggle to write, more so than any I've written so far. Between Leo's anxiety being so similar to mine, my depression and anxiety hitting all-time lows, and other factors, I really didn't think I was ever going to manage to finish it.

But I did. Because I have amazing people in my corner. I hope I don't forget anyone, but if I do, please know that it's my sieve of a brain that's the problem, not you. You're amazing.

To the OMGCP Nano and Hockey He🏒🏒 Discords, for being my first sounding boards as I grew this idea into something that could be a book and gleefully suggesting dozens of moments that made it into the final version. You know what you did, and I love you for it.

To all the readers of the first three books who waited so patiently, far past when I originally expected to be done, and were so understanding with the delays. I hope it's worth the wait.

To the Patreon supporters, who didn't gave up the faith

even when all I had to offer were delays and apologies, who read and commented along and wanted to know more.

To Michaela Grey, for reading my partial draft and reassuring me that it was something worth finishing, for letting me brainstorm and bounce ideas off you and helping polish the draft into what it is.

To Nix, for reading the almost-final draft at a truly amazing speed and reminding me of how much more important Totoro needed to be.

To Paloma, for helping me with Cisco's relationship with his mother when I doubted myself every step of the way.

To the self-publishing Discord, for always being there when I needed to whine and vent, especially when the book grew two extra, not-outlined chapters, for celebrating with me when I reached each milestone. For being there.

As with every book in the series, to Dana, thank you for letting me take your initial concepts and run with them; none of this would have happened without you.

Always and forever, to Alex and Brittany, for celebrating with me when things went well, for letting me whine when things went badly, for giving me space when I needed it and getting me out of my own head when I needed that. I love you.

# ABOUT THE AUTHOR

Ariel Bishop is an American romance and erotica author who feels strongly that all love triangles are best resolved through healthy polyamory. She lives in the Ozarks with her partners, their children and two bunnies that rejoice in the names Reginald von Pancakes and Snickers.

More information about her books can be found at her website or by signing up for her mailing list, and you can chat with her directly in her Facebook Group. You can also find her on Tumblr, Twitter, and Facebook. For sneak previews of upcoming books in the Tripping series and other rewards, you can support her on Patreon.

Keep reading for a list of her other works and a sneak peek at book 5 in the Tripping series, *Blue Line,* as well as the companion spinoff novel, *Fictitious.*

# BOOKS BY ARIEL BISHOP

**Tripping Series**

Soft Hands

Three-Man Advantage

Holding

Two Minutes

# BLUE LINE

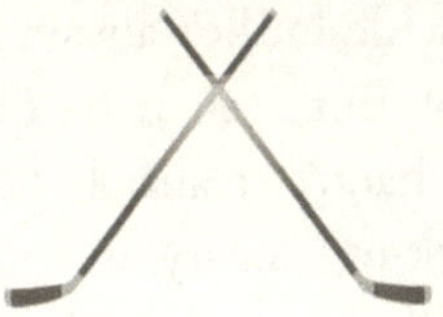

The call comes on an off day, at least.

To be honest, Seth has been waiting for this for awhile now. He's been having a blast with the Abs, playing actual CHL games. But he was only called up in the first place because Mikey got injured, because Tolly needed a new D-partner.

Ever since Mikey came back, Seth has been expecting the call. The *Thanks for what you've given us, but—*. The *you're a good player, son, but the salary cap—*. The *you're playing strong out there, I'm sure we'll see you up here in no time.*

When the call comes, though, it isn't the one he's expecting.

"Say that again?"

His agent sounds simultaneously harried and amused, which is pretty par for the course with Devi; he's never heard her sound any different. "They traded you to the Thunderbirds, kid. Pack your bags."

Seth has no idea what he says for the rest of the conversation. The words must make sense, because Devi doesn't call him on not paying attention. Of course, he is paying attention. He could repeat back her side of the conversation verbatim.

He's just also processing.

When the call ends, he sits there, staring around at the short-term rental the team had found him. He'd never bothered to really settle in; he's always known his presence here was temporary. But even if he didn't personalize his surroundings, he hadn't realized how much he was expecting to go back to Calgary, to still have the option of spending time in Edmonton sometimes, until that option was gone.

Before he could stew too long, the phone rings again. He's surprised to see Cisco's name on the screen, then surprised at himself for being surprised. Of course someone would have told Cisco, and of course Cisco would call him.

"Hey, man, I just heard." Cisco doesn't bother trying to sound overly cheerful. Seth appreciates that.

"Yeah, well, that makes two of us."

Something rustles in the background of the call, maybe Cisco, maybe Leo. "When do they want you down there?"

"They're actually on a roadie right now, so I'm supposed to fly out tomorrow and meet them in Boise."

"Yeah? Okay, so we're taking you out to dinner."

Seth finds himself grinning. "Do I get a choice?"

"No, you don't get a choice. I'll text you the restaurant and the time."

"They should give you one of the As, if you're gonna boss people around for free." Seth can't keep the fondness out of his voice. "I'm gonna miss you, Sunshine."

There's a smile in Cisco's voice when he says, "Yeah, me too. See you in a bit."

The call ends, but an answering smile stretches Seth's

face as he gets up to look for clothes. No matter where Cisco has in mind, he probably should be wearing something nicer than a UMinn t-shirt long past its prime and a pair of sweatpants he hasn't washed in at least a week. Maybe two.

Instead of getting a text directly from Cisco, it comes in through the team group text. Seth shakes his head, but he can't deny the warm feeling in his chest at the number of replies, at how many members of the team are dropping plans and rearranging schedules to come say goodbye.

Once he's dressed, he has a few minutes before he needs to leave for the restaurant, so he pulls up video from the Thunderbirds' last game. One minute in, he can't control the wince at what he's seeing. Like, he knows the Abs have one of the strongest d-corps in the league, but watching the Thunderbirds d-men completely fail, over and over again, to do their job, is just painful.

He get so caught up that he loses track of time, enough that he has to rush a little to not be late to his own goodbye dinner. But even as he's weaving through traffic, he's feeling a little more settled, a little better about the whole thing.

Maybe they actually need him.

# FICTITIOUS

It takes a few rings for the buzzing of his phone against the desk to penetrate Will's concentration. He frowns down at the phone screen, planning to decline whatever telemarketer has his number this week.

But it's not a random unknown number. It's Eva, his agent, who only calls when she feels like she has to, because she knows his thoughts on phone calls. Reluctantly, he swipes to answer, lifting the phone to his ear.

"Yes?"

"So nice to hear your pleasant voice, too. I'm fine, thank you, and you?"

Will rolls his eyes. "Sorry, you caught me in the middle of that revision you asked for."

"So it's all my fault, is what you're saying." The laughter in her voice removes any guilt he might feel. "Well, I've got good news, although you might not think so."

"Oh, God." Will's mind starts racing, trying to figure out what she might be talking about. "Let me sit down."

This time she laughs out loud. "You're already sitting down, asshole, if you were working on revisions."

"Is that any way to talk to your favorite client?"

"You're only my favorite as long as you keep pulling in the big bucks, Jimenez. Speaking of, I was talking to Cindy and she said everything is going smoothly, and they should hit the release date with no problems. And—"

He groans when she lets the pause stretch out. "Do you torture your other clients like this? Spit it out."

"Only my favorites. Anyway, Cindy had me talk to Marketing and they're paying for a book tour!"

Will sits in silence while he digests that information.

"Come on, Will, say something."

He shakes himself out of his reverie. "How many cities?"

"Twelve, over two weeks. But there is a downside."

Will snorts. "A bigger downside than going to twelve cities in fourteen days while I'm trying to finish a major revision?"

"The tour doesn't start for another couple of weeks, so you've got some time to work on those revisions," Eva says. "But yes, something other than that. Tours are expensive, so they're sending two of you."

*Jesus.* "So to recap, I'm going to have to leave home and travel to twelve cities in fourteen days, while trying to finish a major revision, *and* I'll have to make nice with a stranger. Why did I get into this business again?"

"You tell me, buddy." Eva laughs at him and he tries to remember why he likes the fact that she doesn't take any of his shit.

"Is it at least somebody I know?" Will is trying to find a silver lining here, he really is. They'll both be writers, right? Maybe this other person will be happy to work in near-silence in whatever free time they have.

And maybe pigs will fly.

"I don't think so, but I don't know your life." Eva

sounds entirely too cheerful. "He writes gay erotic romance under the name Jake Grant. Bought any of those lately?"

It was times like this that Will wished he had a camera he could stare into like a character on *The Office.* "The publisher is sending an erotic romance author on tour with me? How does that make any fucking sense?"

Eva laughs. Of course. "They said his latest is a historical, set in the Old West. Hell of a coincidence, huh?"

Will seriously contemplated banging his head gently against the desk until he woke up from this nightmare. "Yup. Lucky me."

"I'll send the tour details to your email as soon as I get them," Eva said. "I just wanted to give you the good news so you had time to get it out of your system before the tour starts."

"Get what out of my system?"

It's Eva's turn to snort. "That stick up your ass."

"I do not—"

"Buddy, if it was any bigger I'd be able to see it all the way here in New York. Seriously, give this guy a chance. You might be surprised."

Will sighs. "Fine, I'll try."

"Good, then you can have cookies and milk after school if you make a new friend."

"We should start Skyping for these so you can actually see me flipping you off."

She laughs. "It's the thought that counts. Anyway, I'm going to get back to my other clients, but do yourself a favor and check out Jake Grant's Instagram. You can thank me later."

Before Will can react, the call ends. He sets the phone back down on the desk with another sigh. Eva does love to get the last word, but he hired her specifically because she doesn't take any shit, and she doesn't dance around things like his first agent.

Sometimes it's hard to remember that, though.

He really does mean to go back to his revisions, but somehow he finds himself searching "Jake Grant Instagram" instead. Just for a minute, to assuage his curiosity, then he'll get back to work.

The page loads and all the moisture disappears from Will's mouth.

Jake Grant or whatever his name is—hadn't Eva said it was a pen name?—knows his audience. His account appears to be equally divided between shirtless selfies and pictures of cats. The main exceptions were pictures of him shirtless while cuddling cats.

All of which was ignoring the fact that he might be the most attractive man Will had seen in his life, with dark hair and eyes and the kind of muscle definition that would make a supermodel weep. It was almost insulting. Will was way too old to be this damn thirsty.

And he clearly wasn't the only one suffering from an excess of thirst. When he accidentally clicked on one of the pictures, the comments were—well. No one has offered Will that many sexual favors since back when he played college hockey. Maybe not even then.

Closing the tab, he returns to the chapter that keeps stubbornly refusing to be revised. If he only has a couple of weeks before the tour starts, he needs to make the most of it. They don't pay him to lust after pretty men, no matter how strong the temptation might be.

www.ingramcontent.com/pod-product-compliance
Lightning Source LLC
Chambersburg PA
CBHW050337190726
48284CB00007BB/2044